W9-ABZ-469

On Margate Sands

BY THE SAME AUTHOR

On Margate Sands

Bernard Kops

Secker & Warburg
London

First published in England 1978 by
Martin Secker & Warburg Limited
54 Poland Street, London W1V 3DF

Copyright © 1978 by Bernard Kops
SBN: 436 23650 8

PR
6061
.06
.05

Printed in Great Britain by
Cox & Wyman Ltd, London, Fakenham and Reading

For Erica

02880

Acknowledgements

The author wishes to acknowledge the help of the Arts Council, whose financial award helped him write this book.

The author and publishers would like to thank the following for permission to reproduce copyright material: Famous Chappell for 'Dolores' from the Paramount film *Las Vegas Nights*, music by Louis Alter, lyrics by Frank Loesser, © 1941 Paramount Music Corporation; B. Feldman & Co. Ltd for 'The White Cliffs of Dover' (Burton/Kent) © 1941, and 'Goodnight' (Friml/Hooker) © 1925; the Peter Maurice Music Co. Ltd for 'Red Sails in the Sunset' (Kennedy/Williams) © 1935; Bosworth & Co. Ltd for 'The Happy Wanderer' (Möller/Ridge) © 1954; Faber and Faber Ltd for three lines from 'The Waste Land' and for two lines from 'The Love Song of J. Alfred Prufrock', both from *Collected Poems 1900–1962* by T. S. Eliot.

'On Margate Sands.
I can connect
Nothing with nothing.'

T. S. Eliot

'. . . The first half of the 1950s saw major developments in drug treatment, in particular with the drug group known as the Phenothiazines. The particular significance of these drugs lay in the fact that they enabled doctors to control the disturbed behaviour of the psychotic patient. As a result not only was the need for locked doors greatly reduced, but it was also possible for doctors and nurses to develop contact with patients who had hitherto been almost entirely cut off from the real world around them. These drugs did not cure illness, but they did enable symptoms to be controlled and relieved and hence made it possible to prevent or at least reduce to a considerable extent the social and personal deterioration accompanying prolonged psychotic illness. These developments led to what has been called the "open-door" policy. The function of the hospital was seen increasingly as being for treatment and rehabilitation rather than cure and control. The discovery of the Phenothiazines and more recently the long acting derivatives was important, but one should not underestimate the significance of other developments . . . changes in staff attitudes, the introduction of non-physical approaches to treatment, the development of Social Security and other forms of support outside hospital . . .'

BETTER SERVICES FOR THE MENTALLY ILL. A White Paper presented to Parliament by the Secretary of State for the Social Services by command of Her Majesty, October 1975.

Winter

I

There were only three sorts of people in the world, the pre-mad, the mad and the post-mad. Brian was post-mad and very proud of his new status. He walked across the sand through the drizzle, purposefully, as if going in a certain direction, and the deserted beach did not depress him, even though he was consciously killing time.

He stopped for a moment taking in the sea, enjoying this domain of his new freedom; and he closed his eyes, inhaled deeply, sucking in all the fresh winter ozone that Margate could manufacture. Then he continued his journey.

No longer was he going to be hunched up into himself. No longer would he slouch through the world. He was free for the first time in his life. And all the sediment of depression had been drained out of him and washed away.

Nevertheless, he refrained from cartwheels. It would be inappropriate. This was a public place, even if there was no public about.

'Madgate.' The shouted word was gobbled up by the gulping wind. There was the sea and here was Margate. 'The last resort.' He laughed, and he was sure that he had not killed his mother.

He was sure at last. There was not one lingering doubt left in the attic of his mind, nor upon the dark staircases, nor within the basement, nor within the whirlpool, nor the sludge beneath the basement of his mind.

He was absolutely, positively sure at last that he had not butchered his mother.

If anyone was watching him now, they would think that he was walking towards a definite objective, but nobody was watching him. His mother was dead and God did not look down upon him, or Margate. And if God wasn't there then neither was the devil, and that was the real reason why he had chosen Margate. It had been one of several possibilities. He had opted for a place devoid of Jehovah and his smiling reflections. He could manage on his own. Brian Singleton was in command of Brian Singleton; at last.

And not only had he not killed his mother all those years ago, he had not been in any way responsible for her death, even though he had been mad for as long as he could remember. But all that was years ago and belonged to the past. He would not need to dwell there anymore.

The singing wind and the shrieking gulls accompanied the song of joy within his head; the joy of just being alive and free and stepping like this away from the past, and into the present.

Her face came to him on that beach, he could conjure her up without remorse, without overwhelming sadness. Clear days made him feel less safe, nothing then could stop you being sucked into the vacuum of the universe.

But his mother was there now, having forgiven him for everything he had not done. The great overhanging mass of cloud was her body, hovering, protecting him. The gulls were vortexing down through her gaping mouth and up into her nostrils where the blue of eternity showed through.

There was smoke on the beach. Far away on the other side, closer to the water; somewhere to head for. 'Where there's smoke there's fire.' It attracted him; fire meant life, and life is what he needed, a new life, life as it is lived.

'Where there's life there's . . .' the cliché was left unfinished. After the shore maybe he would go to the public library and devour a thousand books before lunch. He was hungry for books. He drew all his strength from books. He was a vampire for books; he needed the blood of books, the words and the pulp of books. Books sustained him; good books and bad books.

Or maybe he would go to the library tomorrow. Brian Singleton had all the time in the world. He certainly intended to live until the following week. He was sure that he would not kill himself before Saturday. If he could last until then, he could last until the day he died. No, he was not as mad as all that anymore. He was not mad anymore.

He shouted back at the wind, 'Mother, I'm not mad anymore. I've been discharged.' She liked that. Then he thought about his sister.

He had this sister living in Southampton. Maybe he would go

4

and find her soon, maybe tomorrow. He would get permission.
Or maybe next week. He would certainly write to her. He would
certainly telephone her. Maybe now, after this sea, he would try
to trace her and talk to her. No, he was not entirely alone. There
were other people far worse off than himself. But he had not met
them yet, that was all.

There were other creatures on the beach, far in the distance. He
could just make them out. Creatures that had to be human beings
like himself. Objects with toes and fingers coming out of hands
and a head sprouting out of a thing called the neck, and therefore they were bound to be human. He walked towards them,
where they were huddled round the distant smoke.

Joy surged within him. He was as warm as toast; he was
immune, he was not mad anymore. He had been declared sane.
This was the day of his coronation. He had been crowned human.

He was not mad and he was not angry anymore. He had been
discharged from Clayton that very morning; discharged from
'THAT PLACE'. That's what the local villagers called it. But
what did that matter now? He was free of that place forever; that
institution tucked away in a tidy corner of Essex, where the lost
were deprived of the right to take their own lives.

He had been in Clayton twenty-six years. Almost three decades.
He had been locked away there twenty-six whole, endless, empty
years. He had lost twenty-six years. Approximately nine thousand
and five hundred days. That was two hundred and twenty-eight
thousand hours; thirteen million and six hundred and eighty
thousand minutes; seven hundred million eight hundred thousand
seconds to be precise. Almost! Brian was no mathematician. He
merely added another day's total to the already existing score. A
score he knew too well. But he had found himself a new beginning;
a new childhood starting from here. He was being born today. It
was Easter Sunday, he had risen, he was walking on the water,
he was leaving footprints in the sand.

He was forty-six years old, and he'd been away for twenty-six
years and now he had a chance to start again. He had served his
apprenticeship into sanity. He had paid his debt and his life was
not yet over. There were years yet, quite a few years in this open
world; years to explore, years to enjoy.

Yes, he could definitely see them, he could definitely make
out the figures on the sand. He would go and talk to them. He

would make contact; he would, he was human and as sane as anyone!

He would not keep himself to himself anymore.

His pace quickened. He was almost upon them. They did not turn round. He was there; he was standing above them.

'Hello,' Brian said, mastering a cheerful human voice. 'Hello.'

The two male faces turned and looked up at him. One was old and smiling, the other was young and vacant. The older face smiled too much, far too much for comfort. It was the smile-mask of aggression. The white eyelashes of the man made Brian uneasy. human beings on Margate beach, warming themselves before a There was egg yolk stuck to the stubble on his chin and he was crouched on his haunches. He wore a fur hat on his head. A hat that lived and died long before these latter days.

'Hello.' The old man spoke at last, but there was more question-mark than exclamation in the word; and he never stopped smiling. But the younger face was not at all sly or aggressive. On the contrary, the boy was in another place; his mind was simply not there. Brian had come face to face with this sort before.

Brian was sure they were not cannibals, they were merely two bonfire on a perishing day. And only now did Brian become aware of the intense cold. His teeth were chattering, but he did not mind, he was warm inside and nothing touched him.

He remembered seeing a television film once. A native in the New Guinea forest was also crouched on his haunches; he looked up at the camera, smiling, as his teeth continued tearing at the human offal.

'Cold.'

'Yer, cuts right through yer.' The smiling face was a cockney and Brian was pleased. The dialect gave him geography, human-ity; he was not from the forests of New Guinea.

The young man with the vacant face lost interest and started blowing on the fire, and stabbed it with a stick. Brian became rooted there, unable to move away, but he was no longer afraid; he had to get used to people, to other persons, to normal humans, this was good practice. He would be all right, he would survive. Nobody would use him as badly as he had used himself. But all that was in the past; he had turned his back on all his madness and anger and bitterness, and he was facing the future. He was going to meet the world at least half-way. It would not be easy

6

Due to a printer's error, a line has been transposed on page 6. Line 11 should appear after line 20.

but at least he would try to embrace each coming moment, and each moment would have to be relished rather than feared. He would make the attempt. It was up to him and no one else. He might even learn to love himself. His tentative days were over.

'Mind if I warm my hands?'

'Help yourself,' the man replied, and Brian edged in closer and opened his palms to the little licking flames.

'It's fresh today.'

Continents were explored and won by small-talk. Columbus landed on the uncharted shore and said to the first Indian who approached, 'It's fresh today.' Brian was in a new world.

'Yer, good for yer though.' The old man's smile subsided a little, and Brian felt less afraid. He breathed deeply, relishing the tingling, vibrant air. The days of his madness were well and truly dead. He knew that now. No longer would he have to fear that he would be compelled to carry desires and thoughts over into action. He could think horrible thoughts; imagine disgusting and horrendous deeds, but that was all there was to it. There the deed died. There in the cesspool of the brain, far from this living-room of action.

Thoughts did not need to be translated into reality. You could do anything in the mind; you could rip open your stomach and eat your intestines in your mind; you could stab out your eyes with meat skewers; you could kill every child upon the earth in your mind; you could kill yourself in your mind. It was better doing it there than doing it in the world. Your terrible thoughts had no power over you. You ruled over them. You were the king; the ruler, the emperor over your deeds and dreams. You could banish your darkest thoughts if they ever dared to show their face. It was entirely up to you. No longer was he doomed; he had mastered himself at last.

'You look happy. Hey, Buzz, look, someone's happy.'

Buzz did not look.

Brian decided that from now he would try to smile all the time. It would help him survive. It would help to make people like him. After all, he needed to make contacts, to develop relationships. It was possible that he would not be able to trace his sister for quite a few weeks; therefore he would have to settle in here first. He would try to keep himself clean and he would smile and the faces in return would smile upon him. And here was the proof. He was

7

definitely making human contact here on this empty beach, in Margate, in the year of our crucified God 1978.

'It's nice at the seaside.'

'Is it?' The old man's teeth were black and crumbling. Brian looked away for a moment, drinking in the dirty dishwater ocean. There it was, waiting; it could afford to be patient. It had waited a long time, and soon it would pour right in, God would pull the chain and everyone, everything would go down with the shit. The sea could afford to bide its time and be magnanimous.

Brian was proud of his thoughts; of the words he knew. The images, the stories from Greek myth; his recollection of the paintings of the mighty; his knowledge of dates, episodes, happenings, events from history; places; movements of symphonies; general knowledge; names of footballers, politicians, boxing champions, film stars. Heads of State. Books; books. He'd got it all from books. Book after book he had climbed. Book after book he had put behind him. Book upon book. Brick upon brick. He had escaped, he had lived in books. He had travelled deep into the past and far into the future, and sideways into geography, and downwards into history, and upwards into literature. And this afternoon he would find the public library and start to find himself; his new self.

His outcast years could now work for him. He could turn his desperate experiences to his own advantage; books had been his food, his anti-bodies. He was immune from anything that anyone could do to him. He was ready for the world, for there were books here in Margate to sustain him.

'Ain't seen you before.' The old man was curious. Brian didn't mind; curiosity was the clockwork for human relationships.

'No.' Brian decided not to give himself, not all at once. And certainly not to a stranger, and that included everyone that he had met so far since the day he fell into this world.

'Where you from?' The old man continued the inquisition.

Brian shrugged. 'Nowhere in particular. Do you mind if I stay here for a while?'

'Help yourself, flames is free.' This time the boy named Buzz replied. These were the first words he had uttered. The accent was north country, the voice was gentle and honest, but the boy had not looked at him. He just sat poking the flames with the charred piece of wood; sending occasional sparks into the air.

Brian crouched and stretched his open palms towards the heat, and did not mind dirtying his raincoat upon the sand. To converse with people and make human relationships was more important than anything.

Soon he would go to Hazelhurst House and have his lunch. He would return to his new place of refuge, where he had dumped his bags earlier, and he would get to know all of them, and the kind lady who was in charge of the place. And her husband.

'Why are you on the beach?' Now it was his turn to ask questions.

'Why are you?' The old fox replied.

Brian pretended not to hear as a cascade of sparks flew upwards.

'Look, Larry! Sparks! Sparks!' The boy Buzz looked with wonder at his fountain.

So, now he knew the old man's name. But that really didn't tell him anything. Why, for instance, did he need to smile all the time?

2

'You after-care?'

'After what?' Brian did not understand the question. He stared back blankly, shaking his head without determination.

'You know, you know what I mean.' The old man persisted. 'Have you been dumped here? Are you after-care, my old son?' Then Larry nodded. 'Course you are. Can always tell an after-care. You just arrived? They just let you out?' Larry and the boy laughed together now, sharing the joke.

'After-care? After-care?' A metallic taste came to his tongue, and the roof of his mouth. The steel clamp around his head was being wound, tighter and tighter. He tried with all his might to not clench his eyes and teeth, not jump up and down and scream. He was in the world where one had to act like a man, and not a child. He would not scoot away; he would continue to face the face. He closed his eyes to calm himself, thought of The Three Stooges; and it worked, as it had always done of late. The storm passed.

'Yeah, it's obvious you've just arrived. Always tell people who've just arrived.'

And now Brian knew that the man had sensed his anguish. 'Don't fret, we're all in the same boat.' He spat. 'Least we were, the boat's gone down. Welcome to Margate, God's gift to suffering insanity.'

'I arrived on the 11.33, from Victoria.' Brian was much better now. He felt his new self, as he travelled on the train.

It was his first train-ride for almost forty years. He was not with his mother and his father, for they had been dead for donkey's years, and donkey's years were dead. He was on a train that was shooting through the outer outskirts of London. A cemetery danced by. The yawning sky stretched its arms and the gates of Clayton were closed behind him. He was a voyager, a nomad, a mad nomad, an abominable nomad. He had been released. He was free. He was unmad.

'Croydon, I am unmad.' He sang inside his head. 'Croydon, I am come amongst you. Leper has changed his spots. I am Lazarus come from the dead. I am come from mad land.' The pishy orange squash sloshed in the paper cup in the refreshment car as the train grew speed. He drew a boat, tracing his finger through the spilled liquid. Then he unpeeled cellophane and munched into his cheese sandwich, and with his wet fingers picked up and ate every single crumb. Today he was being born, and there to prove it was the world outside; and nobody was with him, watching, guarding. Today he was being ejected, rejected. He was afraid. He was happy.

He was smiling across at the little girl who was with her mother, on a journey, visiting an aunt maybe, or her grandmother. The child was happy; no fears clouded her face.

It was winter. God was pissing on the world and the sky had closed down. He was going to the seaside and he was on his own, because he belonged to no one except, of course, his sister. But she was busy, following her own star somewhere in Southampton. He could not blame her; he could forgive her for not having been in contact for all those twenty-six Clayton years. He would not stand in judgement, he had hated her during the blackest days, but ever since he had returned to near normal all that had changed. He understood, she had to be where her profession demanded. He loved her; he wished her well. He would contact her soon, Southampton wasn't far. It wasn't on the other side of the world.

But, apart from her, there was no one. Nobody would help him. No one would arrive to eradicate his monstrous thoughts and he was glad. He could only help himself.

The train shot through England, hurtling down into Kent; cutting through sleeping fields; chopping down hissing trees; slicing through screaming houses; chasing howling cataracts of alleyways, swallowing waterfalls of high-rise flats, fuelling itself; sucking in, feeding upon the people floating through the world.

The train was cutting through everything. Cutting the cords of his previous existence. They had thrown him away. They had taken one look at the newborn monster. 'Hey, look, another twisted one, chuck him into the furnace.' And they did. And they took up his afterbirth, called it Brian Singleton, and they nurtured it and locked it away from the world. A specimen. A prototype to future man. A natural mutation. A forerunner for all coming generations.

He had always been separated from the world until now. Others participated, others loved and hated, and were involved with each other. Others had intercourse and belonged, but he could not aspire to being ordinary. He had never been able to get through the glass; could not pay his entrance fee. He stooped towards his reflection.

'Who is that young man?' It was amazing, astonishing. This placenta, this mass of viscera was Brian Singleton, smiling: the one who had this morning been released from Clayton Psychiatric Hospital, after twenty-six years of incarceration. The institutionalised suddenly de-institutionalised; the inhumanised humanised. The mad suddenly made sane.

How was he not an old man? How was he not ugly and horrid? His thoughts were dark and twisted, he had seen so much, experienced so much, suffered so much, and there he was in the mirror of the train window, apparently untouched by it all. The face of a boy, the face of inexperience, someone who had not lived. Why did the horror not show upon his face?

He touched himself, smoothed the skin across his cheek. There were no lines there, none under the eyes. It was the face of a baby. All the lines were inside. In there he was as criss-crossed as the junctions of hell. Inside, he was as old as the world, and out here he had the face of a child. He had been everywhere, been hurt by everything, and yet he had been nowhere. And there he was, going to Margate.

His life until now had been a corridor, a Clayton corridor, a place to pace. He had made no journeys, except into books. There he did his climbing and his conquering. There he had done his loving, his deeds of incredible valour. He had lost himself in books and found himself in books. He had entered the halls of Valhalla, climbed the primitive frescoes, played with tempera clowns, worn the golden crowns, tumbled down Giotto hills, ridden bareback upon the huge snorting horses of Ucello.

He had entered the maze of fiction gladly, and stayed there. But that had not been life.

This was life. This for the first time was life and there was no escaping it. 'Is there life after birth?' Now he would know, for Singleton, shaken out of books, banished from madness, from sickening sanctuary, was normal, was flesh and blood hurtling towards Margate. In the winter of endlessness nineteen seventy-eight, he had no choice, he was being born all over again. He had been commanded to make human contacts, and be a good boy and try to survive.

He snarled. He growled at him. He cocked a snook at the face in the glass; smiled, giggled. The child giggled back. The little girl going for a train-ride with her mummy giggled across at him. He poked out his tongue and the mother jerked the child's hand, returned her to her own solemnity. Brian dismissed the child, returned to the men huddled around the fire on the empty beach.

'I love the seaside. Pity there are no donkeys in winter.'

'What about us?' The old man laughed and coughed and spat. 'What's your name?'

'I'm Brian. Brian Singleton. My sister's a famous actress.'

'I'm Larry, he's Buzz.'

'How-do-you-do.' It was all strangely formal suddenly. The little man stood up; he and Brian shook hands.

The claw was damp. Larry was a crab, and Brian was comforted. People became less dangerous when you could place them. He could deal with crabs. Brian held on to the limp claw for a little while longer than politeness dictated. 'How-do-you-do, how-do-you-do.'

They used to do that in the madhouse, years and years ago, after an argument. They were encouraged to make up by a benign guardian. Little children in a circle smiling, clasping hands, swinging them up and down. 'Shake hands! Shake hands and never do it again – if you do you'll get the cane. Punch and Judy got the cane. Shake hands – shake hands—' He could still hear the child chorus.

'Which looney bin were you in, then?'

'Clayton, near Romford in Essex.' He did not get indignant. Clayton was not a looney bin. Not any more. It had been when he was first taken there as a child of twenty. But things were changed now. New drugs had changed the shape of things. Madness had been abolished. Only the disturbed remained. He had changed. He had emerged. He was a walking chemical miracle.

He had been rescued from his inner oblivion. He took his pills religiously, holy mass and communion. It was his way of re-entering the human race, of taking his place, of becoming a member of the human family. 'Clayton is a psychiatric hospital. And it's very modern and up to date.'

'Call a spade a spade.'

Brian wondered if the two men could be winos. But there were no empty bottles strewn about, no smell of methylated spirits hovering on the air. 'It's obvious you're from the looney bin. Right? Don't worry, mate, we're all from the looney bin.' The old man's words were music. So that was it. Who else would be crazy enough to be standing on the beach on such a bitterly cold morning? Brian felt warm; relaxed. He was amongst his comrades; creatures of his own kind.

'It's nice that they send us to the seaside. It's nice of them to send us here.' He still found it hard to believe his luck. They easily could have dumped him in an ugly or featureless place, like Watford, or Harpenden.

'Nice of them be buggered. It's sheer economics, my old son. It's statistics. It boils down to this; it costs the National Health eighty-six quid a week to keep us in the looney bin, it costs them twenty-six quid a week to keep us here in Margate.' Larry thought he knew it all; but his facts were only one small part of the truth.

Things had changed dramatically because of the new drugs. 'Phenothiazine.' Brian spoke the magic word, but to no avail. Larry was none the wiser. The true facts of life did not seem to concern the little man. But Brian knew that it was only recently that the doors had been unlocked, and all the wild creatures allowed out to live amongst the rest of the human race. The new drugs had made his own emergence possible; and here he was; living proof. They had thrown him a lifeline and brought him out of the dark water. They had resuscitated him, and here he was, in his shoes and socks, not slobbering any longer, knowing his own name, alive at the seaside. And he would contact his sister and she would be proud of him, glad to see that he had risen above himself, and he would prove that his love for her had never died. And he would not be angry with her. All his hatred was in the past. How could he blame her for rejecting him? Who could love a blob of unfeeling dreamless jelly? And Phenothiazines had brought about this change; this resurrection.

Larry was still going on: 'Yeah, can always tell an after-care, can't I, Buzz?' Buzz did not bother to confirm or deny and Larry continued, 'Yeah, it's the way we talk. Our bad-fitting clothes, our expression. I can always tell us a mile off. Saw it as soon as you stepped on the beach, didn't I, Buzz?'

'The way I walk? How do I walk?'

'Yeah, the way you floated over, like someone walking on the moon.'

Brian knew what Larry was talking about, he knew the walk. The gormless glide. The sleeping street-walker. It was true that those wonder drugs took away your madness, but at the same time they marked you out; there was a screen between you and the rest of the human race. You were suspended in no-man's-land; floating slowly, the pain and laughter of the world was just made bearable. This then was the only alternative; either an uncaring day-to-day existence; or total chaos. Madness or numbness. He had opted for the latter, even though he really had had no choice. So here he was in Margate, with no more than one basic expression to wear upon his face. He would probably never be able to manage much more than a glazed stare from the back of his eyes.

Yes, Brian knew exactly what Larry meant. He had watched his fellow in-mates of Clayton in the village and on their day trips to Romford. The way they ambled, the way they were managed, shepherded by the nice dogs of authority. And he was no different; at least on the outside.

But it was time to change the subject, to rid the mind of all thoughts of madness, and to concentrate upon the world. Even zombies had to survive on their journey to the grave.

'Why have you lit a fire?'

' 'Cos it's cold, me old son. 'Cos my blood's turning to water.' Larry rubbed his claws together, then held them near the flames. 'Truth is, Buzz here likes to light fires. You could even call it his hobby. And beaches is safer than most places, ain't that so, Buzz?'

But Buzz was too far away to reply, his eyes held captive by the flames, his mind lurking through some dark continent.

'That's an unusual name, Buzz.' Brian said. The fire cracked and spat, if it wasn't fed soon it would die the death.

'Buzz! Buzz!' Buzz said. 'Buzz! Buzz!'

'I named him Buzz, 'cos he reckons fire gives him a buzz. It sort of seemed the ideal name for him. It stuck.' God the Father stroked the head of His Son, whose kingdom was not of this world.

'Set light to my father once. While he was asleep.' The boy suddenly became lucid and Brian was startled; but then he was always being jolted out of preconceptions. Buzz had seemed the sort of person who didn't have two words to rub together.

'Why, did you hate your father that much?'

'No, loved him. That was the problem.'

Buzz furiously stabbed the fire with his wooden dagger. Sparks flew upwards. He stabbed and stabbed and it snarled back at him. A dog slowly retreating, baring its fangs. The eyes of the boy were full of wonder.

Brian remembered a photograph in a library book. It was of a young man, on his knees, kissing the hand of the Pope. There was adoration and wonder in his eyes. Buzz stabbed and stabbed the fire.

Brian stood. He was cold and rigid. He had no neck; it had disappeared into his body. His plasticine head had been stuck straight down on to his plasticine shoulder. 'I also loved my dad, I loved him, I loved him, I loved him.' Brian turned around slowly, as if talking to all the points of the compass. 'I loved him, I loved him.' He was facing the others again, but they were not interested. He was just talking to himself but that didn't matter. He did not need to impress his sanity upon his new companions. They were nothing to write home about. 'Home.' He laughed cynically. This was home now. There was no other place for him. Margate was the last resort. If he could not make his life work here, if he could not wind himself up and spring into action, it was all over. Brian Singleton was kaput. Plasticine man to be rendered down again.

The seagulls twisted around and around, ravenous as usual, screeching. He hated seagulls. If he was lucky and closed his eyes and prayed, they might do him a favour and swoop right down and finish the job once and for all. If only they would dive and smash open his skull. He would be released from the intolerable pain of the world.

He held his head. He went down on to his knees. He was a child again and the others were laughing at him. He was the boy on the beach. He was seven years old. He was neatly dressed. He was in short trousers. The years were falling from his face, laughter from his lips. He was a child and he didn't care that all the other children on the beach were laughing. He was laughing. This playground went on and on, for as far as the mind could see.

The seagulls were flying above him. They were white, beautiful and free. They were the most beautiful birds in all the world. They were seaside birds and he was at the seaside. And there in the distance through the haze, were his mother and father. He waved at them, they wavered back but they could not see what he was really doing.

3

There was a child on a wide, wide beach. It was Brian. The beach stretched high into heaven. Sky, sea and shore were one and he was running and jumping. He was leaping over himself.

His father and mother had kept their promise, for here he was at the seaside. This was better than a birthday cake, because his father was even smiling and being nice to him today. Anyway, no children would have come to a party, to share his birthday cake. They had brought him on a train, the first proper train-ride in his life.

It was a misty day, yet the sun was out. The beach was crowded but he was alone. He wanted to play with the other children, but his mother was sitting upright in her deck-chair, not lying back with her eyes closed, not like all the other ladies. She was sitting forward with her hand forward, as if ready to grab him from the far distance, and her eyes were ever so sad.

He loved his mother. And he also loved his father. He loved his father because it was right to love both parents, and it was wrong to have favourites. But he loved his mother, loved his mother, loved his mother.

His father was not really cruel. It was his temper that made him angry, that caused him to smash things. He could not really be blamed for going red in the face, and biting his tongue and jumping up and down; and then when he went into a moaning crouch on the floor, you could not really blame him. You could only feel sad for such an unhappy frightened animal.

But today was different. The train was full with children, faces pressed against windows, pointing their fingers at cows, as excited as himself. As lucky.

Today they were even letting him get dirty. Father was asleep, newspaper over face, and Brian splashed where the sea had left its water behind. His mother was watching, watching him from all that far away, where all the adult people sat, but she was not calling him.

He was seven years old. He was Brian Singleton, not playing ball with the other children, not running towards the far away sea. If you went into that sea you would be covered over because you could not walk upon the surface because it was not even glass. It was water, the same stuff you washed with. He knew that much.

They kept him clean and tidy in Harrow-on-the-Hill. He was as clean and as tidy as the house. As bright as a new pin. You could eat off the floor. And he did not hide his shit behind the radiator anymore or under the oilcloth. He hated the house, he was afraid because it watched his every move. It was too clean. He was afraid of what he would do there. It was a holiday just to be away from there: 'Thirty-eight Laburnum Crescent, Harrow-on-the-Hill, Middlesex. And my name is Brian Singleton.' He knew the words by heart, just in case he got lost. 'And I am almost seven years old.' He feared one day his father would take him to Epping Forest, and lay him down, and chop off his head. That would be one way of not wetting the bed again. But his father did not hit him anymore for doing that. There had been a battle on the stairs. His father and mother screamed and shouted. On and on they went until they nearly fell all the way down. He hit her hard; again and again, and she scratched his face all down, and he got her round the throat. But then he came to his senses, begged forgiveness, made her promise not to call the police. Things became quieter after that and Brian was glad. He didn't want the police to come. They might take him away.

'He should be put away. He's not normal, not normal, not normal.' His father moaned into his hands as he slumped into the armchair.

'He's not normal, not normal, not normal.' Now the seagulls cried with father's voice, but the children on the beach were kind and they were not pointing at him. They were not calling him names. They were not children from Harrow-on-the-Hill. They did not stick their fingers up their noses, poke out their tongues, pull out their ears. Today was his birthday, and his father had even smiled on the train, and not once did he raise his hand or his voice.

Brian was seven years old. Brian would always be seven years old. He was a fool, but he was no fool. He knew something was wrong inside his head. He knew he was not like other children.

That's why they tried to keep him away from the others, as much as possible. He didn't blame them.

They seemed to think that he didn't know about himself. They talked in front of him, as if he had no mind at all. As if he wasn't there. He was there, even if he wasn't all there. The filter of his brainbox didn't function. That was all. The bogeymen came climbing out and he could not get them back inside.

But Brian knew about a lot of things. He knew that aeroplanes could fly through the sky, like birds. He knew that trains took you places, away from mothball rooms. He knew that every other child in the world went to school. He knew that his mother and father loved him and would love him forever. 'All the time that he was seven, and even after up in heaven.'

There was a swimming-pool on the beach, a deep dish on the shore, a dish with stone walls. And when the sea ran away, it left part of itself behind. Children were splashing and here Brian stood watching them. It was the happiest day of his life. The stone wall was lovely. It had a furry feel. Green hair grew upon it. He stroked and stroked, and jumped up and down; as he laughed, as he splashed. He knew that his mother was still watching him, watching over him, happy to see him happier. She would never let him be taken away. She would not stand for it. He was safe here, so he waved his joy and she smiled in return, telling him she loved him forever.

And his hand, feeling through the green hair, found something. A creature, crouching away, pretending not to be there. He gently pulled it out, inspected his treasure.

It was a crab. It was a sideways creature and it was beautiful. It was looking at him; pretending to be dead, but his bubbles gave him away. Brian stroked him as he crouched in the palm of his hand. It was almost as big as the palm of his hand. Then Brian looked for his parents. His father was talking now. His mouth was going up and down, up and down, up and down. His father was also talking with his hands; hitting one open hand with the finger of another. His father was now putting on his socks and his shoes.

'Brian! Brian! Come on! We're going now,' Father called.

The voice of God boomed across the water. 'Let there be dark.' And there was darkness upon the surface of the water, and there was no light anymore. And there was dark forever. And ever and ever. And God, in his better judgement, changed his mind, went back to sleep and the sun went out. And God did himself a favour, for man was never created.

Brian mused on the winter shore as Buzz poked the fire, and the little birthday-boy cried when his father called him. The day darkened, the ocean changed its mood, became angry.

Looking back at that child Brian was miles away; miles and years and years away; almost forty years away, watching that mad child; himself.

'I want a donkey-ride, a donkey-ride, a donkey-ride.' The furious child kicked the sand. He clutched the crab within his fist and cried with rage because he had to go from here. 'Want a donkey-ride, want a donkey-ride.' His day was almost over. 'Now the day is over night is drawing nigh, shadows of the evening steal across the sky.' In hospital they sang that hymn every evening in the child ward. And that nurse, she made him eat his sick, she forced it with a giant spoon back down his throat. But that was even farther back, even before his seventh birthday on the beach. Oh, the sadness of those nights at Highwood, and all the children sobbing in the dark. He was forced to swallow his sick over and over again, until he learned to keep it down. He had been left there all alone, with the crying kids and the strict nurse and God, who had turned his back upon him. God who caused the thunder and gave instructions to the nurses.

And Brian watched himself, with night drawing nigh upon that beach and in the mauve thickening he could see this line of donkeys being led through the mist. Each donkey with a happy child upon its back. All his life he wanted a donkey-ride. And he sobbed and sobbed, now with a definite object to hook his sorrow upon. 'I want a donkey-ride, I want a donkey-ride.'

His father was coming towards him, and the donkeys were being led away. One by one they were swallowed up by the enveloping black purple night. Night had come so suddenly.

'Come on, did you hear me? We're going home.' God the Father, Father the God, was drawing nigh; was pulling him away. Father was trying to be kind, trying to soften his words for the dawdling holiday crowds. Not for them the darkness, for they and their children were bathed in shafts of special family light. Not for them this curse of madness; of having a mad child thrust upon them; not for them a soft child, oozing out stinking fruit of their loins. For them just the bright day outside this black hole; for them the sand-castles, and the snow fruit, and Punch and Judy and the running into the sea, and the donkey-ride. For them everything. A day at the seaside.

'Come on, we're going home.'

'Donkey-ride! Donkey-ride!'

'Waste of money, we're going home.'

'Donkey-ride! DONKEY-RIDE!'

'You're the donkey. Ride yourself!' He laughed.

Brian did not want him dead. He scooted round the other side of the swimming-pool and hid there. Brian standing by the dying fire crouched beside himself, enjoyed the victory of the child, who opened his hands to release the crab.

The crab could not believe its luck, but it did not even attempt to dart away. A prisoner, let loose out of the dark, is for a moment afraid of his freedom, fearful that it may not continue. That crab had made an accommodation in the child's palm, had learned to accept its fate, but now, suddenly, it could dare to hope. It scuttled sideways, with the futile optimism of all creatures upon this planet and child Brian jumped up and down with delight. 'A crab, a crab.' His hands flapped before him, then he stooped towards the sand and picked up a piece of jagged shell.

Buzz stabbed the fire again and again.

Brian stabbed at the crab. He stabbed out the eyes with his piece of shell. He jumped up and down, and stabbed and stabbed.

It was forty years ago and it could have been on this precise beach where he murdered that crab. But it did happen and it was not a dream. There was the approaching father, and there the small smiling child, with the smashed crab in his hand. And now the child held the mutilated remains towards the horrified father.

'Look,' the child said. 'A crab.'

'What have you done, you horrible little monster?' the father hissed, his eyes narrowed.

Buzz prodded the dying fire, but it had spent all its sparks. It had happened all those years ago. One small murderous incident somehow tipped the balance. That day had become the dark landmark in the foggy marshland of his life. He could not get that smashed creature out of his mind. Nothing could erase it. He paid the penalty, paid the price. Paid for that action a million times over. But maybe now, at last, everything was changed. He had been dry-cleaned. He was dry and clean. He had outgrown his incontinence.

'Monster! Monster!' The cry of his father, still reverberating along the shore.

'He can come alive again. It can come alive again. You said God can make things come alive again.'

Christians were liars. They had brought so much pain and suffering to this world.

'Roll on Good Friday.' Brian rubbed his hands, Buzz chuckled and Larry laughed.

The child threw the crab into a small pool of water. Its innards oozed out. Death was as easy as that. There was to be no resurrection of crabs; this was to prove no crab Lazarus. Crab would not rise again.

The child huddled into himself as the man, his father, punched the little head. Blow after blow after blow rained down upon the crying, crouching child.

Every time the fist thudded into flesh the man screamed a word. The word that he had heard so many times; so long ago. The word that had been knocked into him; until he became the word.

'Monster, monster, monster, monster.' The father grabbed the screaming child, pulled him across the beach.

'Want a donkey-ride, want a donkey-ride, want a donkey-ride.' Brian sobbed as he was dragged out of childhood, out of paradise. That child's face covered the entire beach. The agony of the child, was the child. That agony became the man. The man who was here now.

But the past was dead, and his father was dead. The old man was as dead as the smashed crab. His essence had oozed out. He was a broken shell and he could not hurt the child or the man any longer.

'Why are you crying?' Larry, stretching, preparing to move away from the dead fire, had noticed the tears falling down his face.

'I'm not. The salt air always affects me like this.' Brian stretched and yawned. Larry smiled and nodded, and Buzz groaned as the old man pulled him away from the dead ashes of the fire.

4

They walked along the shore, Larry beside him, and Buzz dawdling behind. It was strangely relaxing to kill time like this, wandering with his new-found comrades; brothers from the world of institutions.

He could afford these sorts of friendships. They were superficial, necessary. They would not be all that interested in his terrible past, nor would they stand in judgement; indeed, they had accepted him already.

Therefore he felt entirely free, allowing his mind to roam over the past, as he wandered.

After he killed the crab, his father dragged him crying from the beach. And they took him home and locked him in his room. It was about then that everything started to slip away. He was running up a down-staircase; he was lost in the cupboard, he could not get out of himself.

About that time, maybe a month or a year, or a few days, war was declared and father had to go away. 'What is war? War is in my head. How can it be declared?' She said to the woman next door that he was not so mad. And then one day she cried all through the night, and he slept in the same room, close to her. 'Father has gone down, down to God—' she cried, and he sang a song to her and stroked her hair.

His father was no more. He was down under the water. A torpedo had hit him, so his boat went bang which caused him to swallow the sea and therefore he was unable to breathe air into his lungs, so he choked on water; and he died dead.

Brian was not happy that he was happy. He was ashamed when she told him, and cried for her. But he turned his back to smile, although he stopped himself opening the window and shouting with all his might down the quiet street, 'Hip, hip hooray. My dad got drowned in the war today.' But he sang with inner joy all that day, and for weeks and weeks until he got used to it. And she looked after him until she died, when he was twenty years old, when they dragged him from the house. The first time he had been in the front garden for seven or eight whole years.

But what were years? How long was long? 'Want to hear a poem?' Larry nodded. Buzz shrugged. He didn't mind telling them. He was proud. They wouldn't imagine it was about himself. They would think it was a poem that came from a book.

'First I was born, and cried and cried. Then I was seven and my father died. Then I was twenty and put inside. Now I'm over forty and I've been let outside.' He tapped the book in his pocket to put them off the track. He had given them too much of himself. He quickly retreated back into his thoughts.

His mother had died and that was that. They took him away and life became a living hell. Everything started to melt together. The day, the night, winter, summer. Years, faces, voices, hands, water, ceiling.

A man with a white collar came to his bedside when he was sailing on the spitting, kicking sea. 'Believe in me and I shall give you eternal life.' Brian remembered that he pissed upon the priest, and came back to earth.

'I love beaches.'

'Yeah, we spend a lot of time here. Nothing much else to do.' Larry replied.

Buzz was now an aeroplane, zooming around with his arms stretched wide. 'Buzzzzzzzzzzzz.' He was dive-bombing. Brian envied Buzz. Buzz was a happy mad.

'They used to bring me here before everything went wrong, or somewhere like here. I seem to remember this beach. Have you ever had a donkey-ride?'

Larry shook his head. 'Nope. I was never a child.'

'I was always a child. My dad was right I suppose. I was the donkey. My whole life's been a donkey-ride.'

'Got 'ny snout?'

'Snout?' Brian didn't understand.

'Fags! Smoke!'

Brian shook his head. 'No. Sorry.'

'Worth a try. Come on.' Larry nodded towards the promenade. There was no one about – just a few cars passing and a few dogs, sniffing and pissing around each other.

'Come on, Buzz.' Larry left the beach and Brian followed. 'Come on, Buzz.'

But Buzz didn't want to know; he was still being an aeroplane. Everyone had the right to be an aeroplane when they wanted.

Two dogs got stuck together end to end, and both were trying to get away, pulling in opposite directions. The male seemed pathetic, whining instead of barking. Larry kicked him and he yelped, and Larry laughed as they all scuttled off; the fucking couple still glued together.

Larry stooped, picked up a dog-end, tore off the end, lit it, and sat down. He drew the smoke deep into his lungs and sighed contentedly. Brian took the weight off his feet and sat on the wooden bench. Buzz was still buzzing down below.

His sister came to mind. Recently he had been thinking about her a lot, he wondered why she did not come to the beach for his seventh-birthday treat. Was she not a child when he was a child? Had something gone wrong with her brain as well? Come to think of it she was hardly there throughout his childhood. Certainly she had already left Harrow-on-the-Hill when his father went down at the beginning of the war. Because he and his mother had been alone until the day she died, and they dragged him away. She certainly was real. There was no doubt that she existed. Although there were times during the early Clayton years that he imagined that she was a figment, a desire, she certainly existed and she was certainly ten years older than him. 'Of course, that's it.'

Jeanette had left home as soon as she legally could do so. A talented, gifted artist needed freedom to breathe and grow. He could not blame her for deserting him. Every human being had the perfect right to follow their own star. And she had been his star. His morning and his evening star. The one person he could dream about, hope for. The one person untouched by the horrible Singleton curse.

'How long were you in that place?'

Brian pretended to be far away but Larry persisted. 'How long were you in the nuthouse?'

Buzz came up from the beach and joined them. 'Give us a drag.' The smiling boy took the dirty wet fag from the old man's mouth, sucked upon it, then returned it into the same place. Then he wandered off again and with his arms wide he tiptoed along the edge of the kerb, one foot in front of the other.

'What are you doing?' Larry seemed concerned.

'I'm in a circus.'

Larry shook his head, turned his attention back to Brian. 'So how long were you in the looney bin?'

Brian decided to be matter of fact. 'I was committed to Clayton Psychiatric Hospital in nineteen fifty-three. I was twenty years old at the time. I left there this morning.'

'Where have they put you?'

'Put me!'

'Yeah, where you staying?'

Brian searched his pockets for the address, finally he pulled out a scrap of paper. 'Hazelhurst House Hotel. I dropped my bags there, just before I came here.'

Buzz laughed. Brian's words had tickled him.

'Hey! That's where we live. Did you hear that, Buzz? Brian's staying at our place.' The old man seemed really delighted. 'We could do with a new face.'

'I haven't got a new face. Only an old one that looks young.' But Brian was glad.

'You'll probably be put in our room. There's room for one more.'

'There ain't.'

'There's always room for one more. Anyway, old Stinkey Simon died of galloping gangrene last week. There's his place. Cor, he stank to high heaven; you'd never believe a human body would smell so bad. Come on, Buzz, time we were pushing off.'

Buzz immediately scooted away, shouting over his shoulder, 'Come on, Larry, catch me, catch me.'

Larry ignored the boy. 'Some days he's worse than others. Don't worry, let's go. He'll come after us.'

They crossed the wide pavement and Brian could see the two dogs again. They were standing outside a tobacconist's still stuck together, looking rather pathetic and forlorn. Their companions had deserted them.

Even so, these dirty dogs were more fortunate than him. He had never had his end in, never got stuck.

It nearly happened once in Clayton. A girl patient, Harriet, stopped him one morning in the quadrangle. She said she had fallen madly in love with him, took him inside, and by a staircase she pushed his hand up under her skirt. 'Rub me, rub me. Lick it!

Lick it!' He went down on his knees, eyes closed as if in prayer, and gladly did as she commanded. She had nothing on under there. He would have gone mad, but he was already, so he continued being himself. A mad dog licking, licking, and trying to pull her down. Her irises disappearing upward into her brain and only the white showing.

But then she sedately came back to earth. 'Excuse me, I must go upstairs for a moment. Wait for me. Don't go away.' And so she went and he waited. He waited all that day and the next. All that week, all that month, he waited by the staircase. All day long, whenever he could dodge away from whatever else he was supposed to be doing. Then, one day, she appeared again, she walked down the staircase towards him. This was it. This was when he would get it, in and up her, and join the rest of the human race. Harriet would be his salvation. He smiled, held out his hand, eager, throbbing, hungry for her cut, for her hell hole. But she walked right past him, didn't even see him. And that was that; they never spoke again. So much for sudden love, so much for passion. A rub and a lick and a finger inside. That was his total life experience. These fucking dogs had brought the whole sickening experience back to him. He shook his head, dismissed Harriet. It wasn't nice. It wasn't love.

Buzz zoomed around and around; faster and faster, deep in galactic dog-fight.

'Hope he's not like this all the time?'

'No, funny thing is he seems to behave normal when there are locals about. He's really got the mental age of a four year old.'

Brian was beginning to feel peckish. Soon he would make tracks for Hazelhurst House, for lunch, with or without his new companions.

Brian stopped walking for a moment, and felt his face. Something he had not done for a long while. Of course, it was still there; of course, he was still alive. Buzz was making him uncomfortable.

Sometimes he was made of rubber, and he would clutch his arms, his shoulders, and he would pat himself. Otherwise he would certainly be sucked down into a drain. He prayed that it would not happen now, not when everything seemed to be going right at last.

'You all right?' The old man seemed genuinely concerned. 'Buzz! Shut up! Stop that bloody war-dance.'

Buzz came to a halt and Brian felt much better. He nodded and they continued walking.

'Funny, I never really had anything to live for, yet I've never really wanted to die.'

But Larry wasn't listening. 'Yeah, that's all Buzz lives for. Lighting fires. His whole life revolves around fire.'

Brian had seen them all. He had known the gentle arsonists. And the soft-spoken ones were usually the most dangerous. 'Yes, beware the smiling face. Takes all sorts to make a mad world.'

'What?'

'Nothing.' Brian replied. 'Just talking to myself.'

'Buzz'll do anything for me. He trusts me. Most people do.'

Brian nodded. 'Yes, you've got a trusting sort of face.'

'I let him start at least one small fire every day and that seems to satisfy him. He's never let me down yet, as far as indiscriminate fires is concerned. Psychology.' He tapped his temple, and winked. 'So you were in the bin for twenty-seven years!'

'Twenty-six!' Brian snapped. He hated exaggeration.

The danger had passed. He would not flop down on the floor. He would not punch the brick wall with all his might so that he would smash his bones and lacerate all the flesh. He would be able to reach the end of this particular street and come to no real harm. Today was the test. If he could only survive today, everything else would be plain sailing.

'Why did they keep you so long in that place?'

Brian shrugged. He would not tell the man a thing, for he was not to be trusted. But then, nobody was. He could not even trust himself. He certainly would not tell another living soul about the meat-skewers and the five-inch nails that he tried to stab into his own eyes, nor all those other terrible things. Here he could start again. The slate was wiped clean. Nobody here needed to know about all his stupidities. 'I used to do silly things to myself – in the past, you see.' He laughed; shrugged it off.

Larry nodded sagely. 'I'm more anti the world, if you know what I mean, instead of anti myself.'

'Yes. You're a psychopath.'

'Am I?' Larry seemed delighted, proud.

29

'Yoohoo, yoohoo! Catch me! Catch me!' Buzz zigzagged around, expecting them to give chase.

'He's more like me. Psychotic. Whereas you seem more normal, just neurotic.'

'What's the difference?' The old man said.

Brian remembered the exact definition. He had read it somewhere. He was glad to pontificate. 'The neurotic and the psychotic both came to a bridge, over a chasm. On the other side of the bridge there is a forest. The neurotic is afraid to cross that bridge, afraid to enter that forest, but he doesn't know why he is afraid. The psychotic, however, is afraid to cross that bridge, afraid to enter that forest, because he is afraid of the little green men who are waiting for him in that forest. That is a classical definition.' He folded his arms, satisfied.

Larry pulled the book out of Brian's pocket. 'What's this? The collected poems of Edgar Allen Poe!'

Brian snatched the book away. He did not want the claws of the crab touching his book. 'I did a lot of reading there. I read anything and everything. It passed the time.' Brian put the book safely into his inside pocket.

'You and me will get on well, 'cos I've read every book what's been writ in the world.'

'I don't believe you. You're a liar.'

And then Larry laughed and Brian joined in. It was only a joke.

'Come on, where's that bloody boy? Buzz! Come on, Buzz, we're going, we're going now.'

Buzz came, looking very dejected.

'Don't worry, we'll light another fire tomorrow.'

The boy's eyes brightened immediately, and he went quietly with the others.

5

Men were working high up in the air, making a new building, and there were now people in the streets. Cars speeding along the front; housewives entering and leaving shops.

He walked along with the others, happy to be just another passer-by, but then he noticed himself in the shop windows. That figure was Brian Singleton. The articulate proud person inside his head did not correspond with that floating oaf reflected on the glass.

He was sitting on a train with his parents and he was crying. Now he would never have a donkey-ride. The other people in the carriage pretended not to notice.

'We're going home, there's a good boy. We're going home,' she cooed, kissed his hair, over and over again, automatically.

'We must do something. We must get help,' Father said. They were all in their own worlds. The other people quietly left the carriage, and the three of them were alone now.

Brian cried louder and louder as he noticed the flying cows and sheep. She kissed his head. 'He'll be all right, he'll grow out of it.' She stroked and kissed his head. The train arrived at its destination and here he was in Margate. He stopped looking at his reflection and turned his attention to this new world, to streets full of people coming and going. Normal people. The pre-mad.

And then at once he noticed the other kind, people like himself. They stood out a mile. The after-cares; they loitered or floated in small groups, with their ill-fitting clothes and their ill-fitting expressions. These were his brethren.

They showed no concern whatsoever on their faces. Neither did they hurry from here to there. They were creatures from another place; spaced-out moonwalkers.

Inside a supermarket some ordinary people were rushing around, filling up their wire trollies.

'Take me, for instance, I find it convenient to have a screw loose.' Larry was going on. 'It lets you off the hook. Now take society as a whole; it's their crisis, mate. It's their inflation.'

A police car slowly cruised past them. The young, clean pink faces inside stared out, perused, lost interest. Then they sped away into the distance. Larry waved. 'See, they leave us alone. They know we're harmless. They've got their work cut out dealing with the sane ones. The muggers! The drunks! The bored housewives! Deprived old-age pensioners! They're the ones to watch for.' Larry grimaced into a shop window, and Brian realised that the old man was trying to focus on a clock.

'An hour till grub. Who fancies a cuppa?'

'Me, me.' Buzz came down to earth immediately.

Larry gave the boy a friendly cuff. 'He's not as dopey as all that, is he? Fancy a cup of tea?'

'Don't mind if I do,' Brian replied.

'Come on. There's our café over there.'

Brian saw the place and knew at once that this was the hive, a haunt for the haunted. Buzz dashed over and conversed with the few people dawdling outside the door of the place. It was obvious that he was familiar with them.

Brian was glad that there were other places to go, apart from the beach, the library and Hazelhurst House. Maybe they played chess in there. It would all help him survive at least until the spring. He didn't really mind being amongst the mad, didn't really mind the mad. Some of his best friends were mad. Madness was a club and you never really resigned from it.

'Come on, Brian. Your turn to buy the toast.'

'My turn? But, but, I only just arrived.'

'Exactly, first time you pay. We take it in turns.'

Brian didn't mind, he had plenty of money. Those few coins saved every week, by depriving himself of sweets and cancer tubes, had accumulated to an absolute fortune. One hundred and forty-three pence to be precise. It would be more than enough for toast and tea all round.

They crossed the road, and he was about to enter when some-body screamed.

'Yoo hoo, yoo hoo!' A fat smiling woman waved her arms frantically. Her titties beneath her sweater were over-ripe and ready to drop off. Those titties came closer and closer towards him, until they took up his whole field of vision. Margate was blotted out.

'Oh gawd, look who it ain't.'

'Dolores! Look, Larry, it's Dolores.'

'Hello.' A long-drawn-out greeting in the Mae West style; hand on hip, eyes looking downward, slight smile. An air of friendly disdain. A hint of sophisticated naughtiness.

Brian broke the spell of Dolores, of the titties, and noticed the young girl accompanying her. A quiet, pale-faced child, who did not smile and had no breasts at all. She was as flat as a pancake, in every respect. He would not have been surprised if her name was Anorexia.

'Hello, Dolores. Hello, Michelle.' Larry greeted the two females.

Dolores despatched an air kiss towards the old man, but Michelle did not respond in any way.

Dolores approached slowly, looked Brian up and down, especially down. 'Who are you? Someone new? I like someone new!'

She reeked of scent and he wondered what she was like between the legs. Was she wet or dry? He tried to dismiss his dirty thoughts, but she stood too close, looked at him in a certain way, that caused the prick to throb and swell. It was a glance of recognition. She knew that he was a man inside his trousers; that he was a sexual creature, that his prick was more than just a pissing machine. He closed his eyes and breathed her in, relishing the cocktail of perfume and sweat, and he swayed a little, to pretend that this was his own special kink, his peculiar brand of madness. He wanted to put her off the track, to not let her know that he wanted her, he wanted to push her down and suck and fuck her, to get stuck into her, stuck into her. He could not allow her to know this, otherwise she would have power over him.

'I'm Brian.'

'And I'm—' She slowed down her words for maximum effect. Perhaps she had been an actress. Perhaps she had heard of his sister. '—Dolores. Fly me, try me!' Her movements were so theatrical that she reminded him of a female impersonator. She was not a real person. She was a series of poses, an amalgam of caricatures, gleaned no doubt from ads. on the idiot box, cheap magazines and heyday Hollywood.

She was oblivious now to anything and anyone except Brian. As she stroked his lapels, she wriggled sexily and started to sing : 'How would you like to be with your Dolores? I – Yi – Yi – Dolores – not Marie, or Emily – or Doris – But I – Yi – Yi Dolores. I don't care if you are Brian or Boris –I – Yi – Yi – Dolores—' Her song petered out. 'Hey, Larry, did you ever see Carmen Miranda? She used to dance with all that fruit on her head. Pineapples and things.' But before Larry could reply, Dolores suddenly lost interest and dropped the sex goddess act, as quickly as she had adopted it. 'What are you lot doing?'

Brian warmed to her. He had been accepted, just like that.

'We're having a cup of tea and a bit of toast. Brian's treating us all, seeing he's just arrived.'

'Yes. You might call it my introductory offer!' Brian entered the spirit of the moment.

'Oooer, I like it. I like offers. I like introductions. I like anything being introduced!'

The smell of Dolores was enveloping him; a great billowing cloud of poisonous desire.

The girl Michelle said nothing, she just smiled with wide-eyed innocence as she looked from face to face. But, just before they were about to enter the café, her expression changed. Brian looked towards the cause of her sudden anxiousness. A group of teenagers were walking towards them.

Larry snarled, as if uttering a curse. 'Yobboes.'

There were two boys and two girls. The boys were distinctly unappetising but the girls were decidedly sexy. Brian could not take his eyes off them. Dolores smiled. 'You're frustrated, are you? I've got a quick cure for that!' She poked her finger into his ribs and Brian laughed, but Larry did not share the joke.

'Come on, come on.' He was alarmed and eager to enter the café; and Brian was willing to oblige, but a huge hand grabbed his shoulder.

'You were looking at my bird.'

'Oh yes. She's very nice.'

'Well take your rotting, shitting eyes off my bird, or you'll get done.'

'I always admire beauty. A thing of beauty is a joy forever.'

Everyone laughed. The yobboes with great gusto, but his own new friends in the doorway did so with much less conviction.

'You nutter! You idiot!' The face raged. 'Whole town's chocker with 'em. He needs a good going over.'

Brian noticed that the girls were chewing gum rather fast; their mouths chomping away at an incredible rate.

'Go on, Spud, give it to him.'

Spud did not need any prompting from his mates. The acne face loomed above him, the fat fingers taking on a life of their own, playing a crazy symphony on the air, flexing to gouge him. And then they struck. They poked and they pummelled. He didn't feel anything. The hurt would come later.

'I'll kill you. You bastards. I'll burn you. Burn you,' Buzz screamed.

Brian observed all this as if it were happening to someone else, in some other place. Buzz was intervening on his behalf. That was very nice of him, but unnecessary. But Buzz was crazed, red in the face and spitting. 'I'll burn you, you bastards. I'll burn you.' Buzz hammered his fists against the greasy leather jacket but the yob still smiled. A rhinoceros watching a fly assailing his hide. But then his expression changed.

'Right, get him!' And they all started to pound and kick the crying, cringing boy who lay on the pavement.

'Larry! Larry!' Buzz screamed.

Larry cowered and seemed unable to move out of the doorway. Michelle silently cried and Dolores watched and shook her head. Brian stood by a brick wall. His fists were irresistibly attracted towards brick walls. Brick walls were magnets. Brick walls were crying out to be pounded. The faces coagulated. The sky and street ran together. A smudged water-colour. The pavement was made of rubber, the house made of parchment. He could no longer cope.

He was twenty years. And there was his house. This was Harrow-on-the-Hill, and he was Jack who fell down and broke his head. But there was no Jill, no vinegar and brown paper; just these two policemen standing outside his house. And he was standing between them. An indiarubber boy with his brain all drained away.

Not a soul was in sight. The birds sang. It was remarkable that the neighbours had not assembled to see him being taken away. But then, neighbours were discreet in Harrow-on-the-Hill. Even

35

if you looked carefully you could not see their faces peering through the net curtains.

There was no doubt that he was being taken away. He knew the score.

'Come on, son.' The voice, from the man in the uniform, was kind. The hand touching him was remarkably gentle. And there was the car waiting. He was going for a ride in a car. He was going for a ride in a police car. They were going to take him away.

His mother's words had come true. 'Not while I'm alive.' She said again and again, and she was no longer alive, and he was being taken away because his mother was dead, was blue black meat. Someone had got in touch.

The woman next door was there. Yes, she was talking to the policeman. He was nodding. He understood, and despite his height and the thickness of his face, he was just as kind as this other man who was leading him so slowly to the car.

Somebody screamed. 'Mother! Mother! Let me in! Let me in!' Someone was waking up Harrow-on-the-Hill. It had to be Brian. It had to be himself, because there he was, running towards the house, to the door that had just been closed. But they soon came after him and he did not wish to anger them or hurt their feelings, so he behaved exactly the way twenty-year-old persons were expected to behave, and he restrained himself, closed down his brain to a certain extent, went limp enough to be slowly guided away, but not so limp that they would have to carry him.

'My mother's in there. I want to be with my mother.' Brian was whispering. 'Poor Brian.' But Brian was going to be a good boy, Brian wasn't really going to let him down.

'Come on, son, you'll be all right.' Gently they led him towards the kerb, towards the motor car. 'We're going for a ride.'

He smiled up at them. Anyway he did not wish to remain in Harrow-on-the-Hill, not now that she was no longer there. Now that she was gone nothing would shield him from the cruel eyes of the whispering people. No one would pull him close.

So now he was going away from those people and he was happy. He was going away from Harrow-on-the-Hill. He had gone away already, long ago. He was merely following himself.

One policeman released him as he opened the door. 'Nice ride. Have you been in a motor car before?'

Why did they think he was stupid just because he was mad?

Why did they talk to him like a child? He was even more than seven. He was thirteen years longer than seven; but he wanted to be nice to them, wanted to play the game.

He would act the seven year old, because he did not wish them to expect anything of him. It would be better this way. When he was three he couldn't remember how he was. He wanted to return to those days that he could not remember.

'I hate you, God, for now that I am alive I must die.' This had often been quoted back to him as the first whole sentence he had put together. It had been his mother's way of compensating, of showing him that he wasn't really touched; rather he had been touched by something different. By genius perhaps, a slight difference in the head. An imbalance. He was rather unusual rather than less than normal.

He continued smiling for the big policeman. 'Went for a car-ride once. It was nice.' He pitched his voice high. He was allowing the child trapped within to escape and assassinate all his subsequent years beyond seven.

But as the one policeman released his arm, he smashed it against the brick wall at the gate. He pounded it and pounded it. Again and again and again. All the warm red blood spurted upwards. It was so red, he was proud of the redness. And nobody looked out of the windows in Harrow-on-the-Hill, and he said to the policeman, 'Hurt myself.' And they smiled back, helped him into the car, and he never looked back when they drove away and took him far away.

His fist was not lacerated now. He was not a child. He was not seven. He was not even twenty. He was forty-seven soon and he was no longer mad.

He was facing two chewing girl things, and two leering louts, their faces full of blackheads, were coming closer towards him.

He could no longer stand back and pretend to be a child. He was in the world and he had no choice. The confrontation was here, and this time nobody would come to whisk him away.

6

Brian charged into them. He was Don Quixote and the Windmill, all in one. The yobs forgot all about Buzz and now turned to deal with him. 'You fucking nut.'

'You shitting idiot.'

'Put the boot in, Crapper! Kill the fucker!'

'Run, Buzz, run.' But the boy did not seem to hear his call. He just stood there, watching, but then Brian couldn't see him anymore; he went down to the ground, under a forest of thudding fists. He knew they were hitting him very hard, but he could feel nothing.

As in a padded dream, he rolled over and over and there was no sound. He smiled all the time so as not to give them any satisfaction.

'Larry, Larry.' He could hear Buzz calling the old man, but it was all over; when he could see again he saw Larry still cowering in his doorway.

Brian could taste the blood and he felt proud. He would see himself flat on the tarmac and licking his lips.

And then the yobs yelled and ran off, laughing, shouting, uttering lusty cries; dark heroes of Valhalla. And Larry came and tiptoed along the street, making sure that they had already turned the corner before he began to shout. 'Bastards! Come back here, you bastards, and I'll brain yer.' He brandished wild fists at the empty street. Then he returned to Brian. 'Did you hear me give 'em what for, Brian? They won't come back here in a hurry.'

Brian sat up and then he stood. Today was his real birth, his baptism of fire. First he had been released from the tomb, now he was lying in the world, covered with blood.

'Did you see me run after them, Dolores?'

'Lucky for you, you didn't catch them!' Dolores smiled back at the old man, and that smile said it all.

Larry hopped around, turned to another. 'Did you see, Buzz? Did you see what I did?' The boy snarled at the man and the man almost went for the boy. But the boy laughed and turned away, and they all turned their attention to Brian.

Dolores took out a tissue and dabbed his lip. 'Why are you smiling? You're a funny guy.'

'I won! I won!' Brian was victorious. 'I won! I won!' They didn't seem to understand that he had scored a victory. Michelle bit her lip, expecting something terrible to happen any moment.

'You won! You?' Larry ridiculed, but Brian didn't even bother to reply. He looked at his fist. It was the first time he had managed to turn it outward, to smash others rather than himself. Compulsions could be conquered. This was the good news. 'I hit someone! I hit them! I won! I won!'

Dolores dabbed his face with a fresh Kleenex, the other one was in the gutter, saturated with blood. His flag of bravery.

'Let's get back to Hazelhurst,' she said.

So, these ladies also belonged to the same hotel. It was obvious that the younger one was not entirely right in the head. The older one, however, Hot Slot Dolores, was a different kettle of fish. She seemed full of health and confidence and appeared perfectly able to cope with herself in the world.

But appearances were deceptive; otherwise his own exterior would have been beautiful, suave, poised and urbane. Cool; intellectual; indifferent.

She helped him to his feet.

'I'm all right.'

Buzz stared admiringly. 'You hit them hard, I saw. They ran away.'

'Yus, none of us ever usually fights back.' Then Larry added, ' 'Cept me.' And Dolores snorted. The old man put his hand on the boy's shoulder, but Buzz moved away, moved closer to his new friend.

'Tell you what we'll do after lunch, Buzz, we'll search for a waste site that we've never found before. And we'll light a really whopping fire. Just for the two of us. Okay?'

Buzz didn't respond and Brian felt sorry for the old man. And he felt pleased. Compassion was a sophisticated emotion. He had never been able to indulge in such extremes, until now.

'Are we 'aving tea and toast?'

Michelle nodded several times; looked like a mechanical puppet, as Dolores whispered, 'Go on then, inside.' She opened the door of the café, and Buzz and Larry entered. Michelle followed, and Dolores closed the door. Brian was outside and the three people within smiled out at them, as if enjoying a private joke. Dolores stood in his way, her arms outstretched. 'Not you, Brian. Not yet.'

'I don't understand.' But deep down part of him understood. Cock stirred, crowed.

'I like you, Brian.' She was very close and he was shivering. Things were happening too fast. 'I'm hungry.' He said.

'So am I,' Rita Hayworth purred, her eyes almost closed. 'I'm very proud of you,' she said.

'Thanks.' Inside the café many faces were now at the window, watching; excited faces, deformed by being pressed too close to the glass. An audience of horrendous gargoyles, anticipating his moment of truth.

Slowly, slowly he was being forced against a wall.

'It's really nice to see a new face. I'm so glad you came, Brian.'

He hoped she would be nice and kind to him. He wanted so much to open out towards someone, to have a true friend.

'Thank you very much for wiping my face.' He felt exposed and foolish with the others watching, but he didn't want to hurt her feelings.

'Don't mention it. You were very brave, Brian. And I think you deserve a little reward.'

Dolores was very kind. Maybe she was going to give him a trinket box or a pair of cuff-links. She came closer and closer towards him – or maybe she had a box of Maltesers for him. He loved Maltesers. He never had a whole box for himself. He was tingling with the heat or the cold. But he didn't want the others to see. 'Can we go around the corner?'

She nodded confidently. Dolores was a truly pleasant individual and he was sure that they would find much in common; even though she probably did not share his deep attachment to literature. At least, not yet. The fact that she was a female made no difference. Dolores could become a true comrade indeed. She took his arm and slowly pulled him away. And now they were alone.

It seemed like old Margate, empty houses, empty shops,

boarded-up streets. Demolition in progress, but no demolishers. In fact, not a soul was in sight.

Dolores smiled as she gently pulled him into the doorway of an old Off Licence. It had obviously been closed for years. Corrugated iron had intended to protect it from the interlopers, but this had been ripped away and there was evidence of dossers within; hundreds of discarded bottles and the thick smell of piss.

However, there were no humans in sight, just a cat crouching back against a wall.

'In here?' She pulled him towards the interior. 'Home sweet shithouse.' But he went with her, his cheeks burning and his temples throbbing. His mind was racing, was crashing.

'What you going to give me?' His veins would swell and burst. She had brought him here to die. She took his hand, and slowly moved it towards her. Then something dawned.

'Oh, I see. You ain't ever done it before, have you?'

'Done what?' Now there could be no more doubt; he knew what she was getting at. There was no way out; he didn't want to strangle her, there and then or even ever. He liked her.

'Bet you ain't even had a little feel. We'll soon remedy that.' She took his hand. 'I'll put it somewhere nice.' And slowly she pushed it down her neck. He thought his penis would burst out and take wing.

But he did not want this, not now. Not here and now, and not like this.

'Brian, your time has come,' she softly cooed. He seemed to have no choice. He was under her command and she pushed his other hand downward under her coat over her belly. 'Go on, don't be shy, you'll like it.' And then she started to hum her Dolores song again. 'Go on, stroke it, stroke it. Have you ever touched one before? Go on, it's dying for you to stroke it.'

He shook his head. Backwards and forwards, backwards and forwards. Brian the pendulum. No life of his own, he had spent nearly a year just doing that, looking out of a window. Backwards and forwards, to and fro, day in day out. He had no will of his own. She had brought him here. His arm was limp and she placed his hand between her legs. And he touched it through her skirt.

The band around his head was being pulled tighter and tighter. Mother clouds hung above the town, spitting down upon him. He was outside now, under the threatening sky. The seagulls admonished. 'Brian, be a good boy. Brian, don't lose your self-respect. Your mother's watching you.'

They had come out together in the same close position, one hand down her neck and the other being pushed up and up her legs, her thighs. It was too beautiful, too terrible. He had to have it, he had no choice, he couldn't take it, didn't want it, couldn't bear it any longer.

'I must go, I must go to Hazelhurst. Thank you very much. I must go now to Hazelhurst – because a fire was in my head.' Brian Butler Yeats managed to get away and he ran down the street.

He looked back fearful that she might be crying. And he was angry because she was almost bent double with laughter.

He had left the world of black and white. This was not Clayton, where you were loved or hated within seconds by the same person. This was no longer childhood, no longer hide and seek. This was the world with all its shades of grey and off-white. Nothing was tangible anymore. He had sucked the reassuring milk of mother Clayton for twenty-six years.

But those days were gone forever. He would have to get used to the world because there was no turning back. The institution had protected and deadened him. Now he was alone, exposed, terrified and excited.

He ran back to where he had left the others. They came out of the café to greet him, but he did not stop. Over his shoulder he saw that Dolores had followed and she was talking to them. Brian hoped that she would be kind about him. If they were still laughing at him in the afternoon, he would kill himself. He would walk into the dirty sea before teatime. He would join his mother and his father in heaven.

As he ran he looked at the sky. 'Mother, I'm still a virgin,' he shouted. He had not let her down.

He smelt his fingers. They smelled of Dolores. 'Stink finger.' He laughed, remembering the income tax inspector in Clayton who one day, whilst picnicking at Runnymede, used the knife on his wife instead of the cucumber. At Clayton he would enter the dining-room, holding a finger to the nostrils of the other inmates. 'Have you met Vanessa? And have you met Clarissa? And have you met Clitorissa? And by the way, have you met Gonnerissa?

And Syphilissa?' Each finger had probed and belonged exclusively to a certain vagina, or so he claimed.

Brian had come through. It was almost noon. He had left Clayton that same morning and he had survived so far. It was possible he could reach the end of the day, and even survive tomorrow and the day after. And if he could reach the end of the week, he could even possibly die of old age, in his bed. It all depended on them. He prayed that they would not ridicule him when he saw them again.

He ran through the wet quiet backstreets until he arrived. Hazelhurst House Hotel was nicely situated. It was not even a fart away from the Parade.

Its screaming yellow exterior greeted him with a smile, so he bounded up the steps, eager to enter and get acquainted, to settle in and have lunch, and phone his sister early in the afternoon.

7

The dining-room was crammed and Brian surveyed the faces of the other residents, poking breakfast into themselves. The night had passed in a flash. He had put his head upon the pillow one moment and lifted it the next morning.

'When do we get medication?'

'After breakfast,' Dolores replied.

The sea air had knocked him for six and he still had cotton wool stuffed into his head.

He wondered if one day soon he could stop taking the little pills that had changed his life. They had served their purpose, had steered him gently through these last fifteen or so years. They had made his day bearable, his years tolerable; but he had become dependent upon this automatic pilot, and now he wanted to take over the controls. He was almost ready; perhaps this morning he would talk to Mrs Killick, the kind lady who owned this small hotel. She had a kind of serenity. The kind he had only seen in his mother's eyes.

If he could only stop the habit, and shake the sawdust from his head, he could possibly become a fully paid up member of the in-human race. He needed, needed to be as uncaring and as any normal man in the street. He needed to stifle his inner life, obliterate his inner self; he needed to live on the outside.

The mad and the post-mad had one thing in common: their table manners were disgusting; they made a terrible noise when they ate. It was sickening to look around and see them tackling their breakfasts, having such a filthy relationship with their eggs or cornflakes. Meals should have been a divine time, a landmark in a featureless day; something to look backward upon. Meals broke up the numbness, the boredom. He had been looking forward to Margate, thinking it would be different here. And here he was with this disgusting mess. This porridge of people.

This was Margate; on the coast of Kent. Holiday seaside resort.

People dreamed about this place. People spent their whole year's savings to have two meagre weeks in this place, and here he was a guest, the whole year round, paid for by Her Majesty's Government. A resident of Hazelhurst House Hotel. It was silly getting depressed. It would be better after breakfast, there was the library and the After-Residents' Club and Dolores. And Dolores. Her leg was gently brushing against his leg under the table.

She smiled. He smiled back across his cup, through the steam of hot tea. Outside the sun bathed in a watery sky; bare black branches proved its present impotence. He was in Margate. Across the way was France and along the coast was Dover. Place of history, of myth. In his head he could hear Vera Lynn singing to an audience of soldiers. 'There'll be blue birds over the white cliffs of Dover—' And then she sang another, and this time all the soldiers joined in. But now they were too far in the distance for him to distinguish the words.

They stopped. The laughter of Buzz interrupted the splendid sound. Buzz had finished his egg and had turned the shell upside down in the egg-cup. 'Haven't eaten my egg yet, Michelle. I'm not going to.'

'Eat it! Eat it! You must.' Her eyes were full of pain. Brian could not bear to look at them.

Then Buzz banged the shell with his spoon and the shape disintegrated and Michelle's eyes came alight, and she laughed and laughed. Buzz lost interest and zoomed back into his universe.

Brian was sitting with his new friends and he felt extremely hopeful. Dolores had been kind, and she did not make a fool of him in front of the others. Nobody had laughed at him and all his tears the previous day had been for nothing. Dolores could prove to be a good friend indeed.

Larry was eating toast as if the end of the world was about to be declared; his eyes were darting all over the place as he munched and munched. A rat fearful that the rest of the pack might pounce and snatch his sustenance.

Brian's eyes roamed around. It was just like being in the dining-room in Clayton. These faces covered the whole spectrum of disturbed humanity, from the vacant autistic at one end to the grinning mongols at the other. No magic wand had been waved. Margate was hardly different from the madhouse. This after-care place was halfway-house, a no-man's-land between world within and world without. He had left one place, gone for a ride on a train to another place, this place, and here were all the people he had always known. The ones he had left behind. The over-sexed cow opposite. The lost little boy. The gone girl. The sly old man beside him. The filthy one. The old woman trying to look like a blonde bombshell. The fat man fearful of a speck of dirt. And all around the pathetic ones; those who were not aware that they were not aware. Those who needed their noses wiped, and the crumbs brushed off their mouths. There were just a few people inhabiting this earth, all others were merely duplicates of a few basic types.

Brian noticed that there were a few residents, shuffling around, working slowly; sweeping floors, clearing tables and washing up in the kitchen. They were as emotional as stick insects. None of them were suffering; everyone was enclosed within themselves.

But he was not depressed, for he was merely passing through. Margate was a corridor between two worlds. It was as good a place as any for marking time.

Mrs Joan Killick stood in the doorway surveying her flock, then she smiled at him. There was a special kindness, a softness flowing from her. She dressed more flashily than his mother, but then his mother had lived in a different age. His mother had been a pre-plastic person, but now the world had changed.

Joan Killick looked smart and clean. He had noted this the moment he had walked into the place, the moment she had greeted him. 'Hello, Brian. Yes, I thought it was you.' He liked her friendly north-country accent, and the many gold bangles she wore on her arm. He liked the way they clinked together. Her hair was all bronzed and he was glad she was not dowdy. Mrs Killick was obviously a modern and sympathetic human being. Nobody would undertake the task of looking after thirty to forty post-mad, unless they were mad themselves, or a dedicated humanitarian.

She wrinkled her nose, gave him a special smile. He waved back at her in return. And then Brian noticed Mr Killick in the background. He was in the kitchen. A place strictly out of bounds, apparently, unless you were working there. A small notice on the wall in bold red lettering made this apparent, in no uncertain terms.

Mr Killick's hair was too black; as if it had been smeared with shoe polish. He seemed at least twenty years older than his wife. And he was not a happy person. When Mrs Killick spoke, he quietly nodded, as if to confirm everything she said. He was a neckless, hunched man. Someone with all his giblets sucked out of him.

'What's he like?' Brian whispered. 'Is he as nice as her?'

'Nice as her?' Larry's hand went quickly to his mouth, to stifle ridiculous laughter.

'Mr Killick is a pathetic dogsbody,' Dolores said. Her hand under the table slowly stroked his knee, and then crawled up and down his leg.. The crab had come back to haunt and taunt him.

Brian moved his mind away and noticed that Mr Killick was now hunched up into himself, as if he were in pain or fixing contact lenses.

'Is he all right?' But no one replied; they sniggered instead. And Brian realised what was happening. Mr Killick was holding a bottle of whisky and pouring it out and knocking back glass after glass. He was certainly going it, so early in the morning.

It was 8.30 a.m. and the sun was still attached to the eastern corner of the sky. So, Mr Killick gargled whisky for breakfast. By the look of Mr Killick the water of life had become the water of death. The ways of the pre-mad were strange indeed. Unless, of course, Mr Killick belonged to the brethren.

But no, there was definitely a pre-mad glint in his eyes. Mr Killick had not yet gone through the fire. But he was approaching it.

'Whisky! He likes the whisky!' Larry nudged.

Buzz nodded. 'Yeah. Firewater!'

Brian felt close to the proprietor. Anyone who had to switch off reality so early in the morning could not be all bad. And Brian felt compassion. Mr Killick would not die of old age.

'Yus, anytime is opening time for old Johnny Killick.'

Dolores pushed her chair back and opened her legs wide. 'Anytime is opening time for Dolores. Come and get me during cornflakes.'

But Brian was too busy watching Mrs Killick hissing at her husband as she pulled the glass from his hand. It was obvious who ruled in this house. Brian did not resent women having a dominant role. Maybe they would rule with mercy when they took over the world. Anyway, they could not do a worse job than their predecessors.

'Dolores, sit properly and be a good girl,' Mrs Killick snapped as she returned to her fold. 'I'm not telling you again.'

'Yes, Mrs Killick,' Dolores sang back, but then she quietly mocked under her breath. 'Yes, Mrs Killick. Certainly, Mrs Killick. Mrs Fucking Killing. She'll get hers, the cow! The public benefucter!'

Brian was amazed at the outburst. 'Why are you so cross? Mrs Killick's very nice.'

'Nice like a cobra.'

Brian dismissed her vehement response. Dolores obviously had a personal axe to grind. But he would not change his mind. There was no doubt whatsoever that Mrs Killick was a decent and honourable human being. He would not be influenced by the emotional reactions of others. He would think for himself. Today, and until the rest of his life. 'She was nice to me yesterday. She was very kind.'

'Yeah, the kind who'd slit your throat to pinch your fag.' Now Larry chimed in.

Brian would not be swayed by mass attitudes. He would judge for himself. He pointed around the room, drawing their attention to the spanking clean interior. 'At least she runs this place well.' He breathed in the refreshing aroma of polish.

'She runs it! We run it,' Dolores spluttered angrily, then everything went quiet again. Buzz, in his far-off pulp universe, rocked with private laughter.

Michelle was attempting to knit. He watched her purling and plaining, casting on a line of twenty to thirty stitches and then losing them, and starting all over again; like Buzz, she was totally absorbed and terribly happy. He knew these people well, they lived with earthquakes and volcanos in their head. Irrational hatreds and incredible loves punctuated their lives. He envied them for they were the fortunate ones. He, on the other hand, had been cursed with self-awareness.

Dolores was smiling once more and again her hand fell upon his knee. It was just his pathetic luck to become the prime target of a sexual maniac.

But then she saw his pain and relented. 'Take no notice of me, Brian, it's only my jokes.'

48

She was a pathetic creature and he felt a great wave of compassion for her. He would be kind for she was not in control of herself.

He smiled and she became very quiet and sat there demurely beautiful, with a tremendous aura of sadness; someone seen in the background of a Lautrec, staring into space, full of emptiness.

And now his mind wandered off and concentrated on other things. Breakfast was the meal of hope. Cornflakes lined his pathway into the future. All time was one, but night intervened, separated yesterday from today; helped you to believe that things could be different. Cornflakes crunched away the dread drip of mortality. The universe paled into significance, with a soft-boiled egg. Breakfast was a new beginning.

'After my dad died my mother looked after me and I looked after her. I used to make her breakfast every morning,' he said.

Michelle was locked in her own world; Larry was winning a fortune on the coming day's dogs. He was marking his newspaper, placing his dream bets. And Buzz was deep in his monster universe.

Brian felt the need to tell Dolores all about his mother, so that she should know that she was not alone. There were creatures lost in this universe, desperate for contact, for human warmth.

Tears came into his eyes. He was not ashamed of them and did not try to force them back. His eyes were drowning; the dining-room was awash. 'I took my mother breakfast every day. Until one day.' Brian entered the room of the past, his mother's room. Her bedroom. He was seven; he was a child, and in the flickering of an eye his years flashed past. And he was twenty and had swallowed himself. And she was dead on the bed. His mother. And her eyes were open.

8

'It's you and me alone, Brian. No one's taking you from me, not while I'm alive,' his mother said, her eyes were closed and her mouth was not moving. She was dead, and she would not rise again.

Brian did not go to pieces, because it was happening to somebody else. He was twenty years old, and it would not do to jump up and down and scream.

'It's you and me alone, Brian. No one's taking you from me while I'm alive.' The sound hovered in the air around her bed. She droned on and on, and it was easy to know that she was dead. He did not curse her, or God, because it was too late for everything.

And he did not mind the sweet smell when he placed the breakfast tray before her.

He entered the room again and again. There were hundreds of Brians. The Brian of continuous slow-motion photography, opening hundreds of doors, slightly out of synchronisation, his image stretching to infinity. He brought her breakfast in bed for as long as he could remember because it was the one thing he could do for her.

He would wake up in the morning, sometimes even before the chattering birds, and he would line up his armies on the lino, and have all his battles over and done with, even before proper light. The Aztecs would cascade down the mountains; the Red Indians would leap five million miles; the cowboys would be hurled over by the giant rubber boulders and they would all be dead, so he would make her breakfast. Always the same breakfast. The cornflakes, the toast, the cup of tea. She trusted him at the gas stove.

It was all done in rotation. Last Wednesday's breakfast tray was removed, and all the other trays moved along one space and today's breakfast tray placed before her. The whole bed was covered with trays. She had not eaten breakfast for at least a week; maybe a few days more, maybe a few days less. But he did not think that she had been dead all that time. He was certain that he had seen her eyes move the previous Friday, even though the eyelids had been closed. But she had not changed her position, and every day the sweet smell of her grew in volume. That sweet smell had a life of its own.

Maybe in the afternoon he would open the window and watch it rolling along the road. And he would chuckle as it enveloped Harrow-on-the-Hill. That smell would roll down the hill like an invisible rubber boulder, knocking down all the cowboys on their way to business, obliterating the Aztecs with their bowlers, crushing the redskins under their black parachute umbrellas.

She was as dead as Harrow-on-the-Hill, as dead as his father under the sea, as dead as his father up in heaven. And soon they would come to take him away; he knew that much.

He sat there watching himself. Brian quiet and composed amongst such disorder. Towels, clothes and rubbish were strewn all over the floor. Shit was sticking to the uneaten toast, milk bottles full of golden piss were on the mantlepiece and the window ledge.

Brian Singleton was not inside his head; not inhabiting his body. There was a child sitting beside the rotting woman. Brian Singleton had been seven years old for thirteen years now.

A cup was still clutched in her hand. He had put it there to keep her company. He touched her hand, and it was cold; so now he had proof that she was dead. Nobody could tell him otherwise. They would come with soft words to coax him away, but he would not believe them.

He pushed back her eyelid and winked at her. She taught him how to wink but she was no longer there. She was being unreasonable. How could she do this to him? How could she die when he owned her so much? He loathed her. He would never forgive her. He smeared some jam upon the triangle of toast that he pulled from her crooked fingers and he munched it all up in the corner. And all the while he watched all her odours gathered into one huge ball of stench, ready to roll down Harrow-on-the-Hill.

He would never talk to her again. He laughed and went towards her and he shook her. She was a rag doll, lolling backwards and forwards, a toy left behind by his sister. It was all used up. He shook her and disturbed all her juices. He fell against her crying and there he stayed. He loved the smell of mushrooms when he entered the dark forest.

'Brian, Brian.' It could not be his mother calling. And he was right. It was a kind lady touching him. 'You all right, Brian?' It was Dolores, his mother of the moment. She was kind. He could trust her. She was the one person here that he could love. He studied faces and the movement of hands and for twenty-six years he had remained almost silent; his hobby had been watching, recording and waiting. His sole occupation had been breathing. But he could place people.

'Are you all right, Brian?'

He nodded. 'Miles away.'

'Eat your breakfast, there's a good boy.'

Michelle concentrated upon her knitting with all the intensity of someone creating an atom bomb, yet she still had not managed to achieve a second line of stitches. Her nose was running and she was humming 'Somewhere over the Rainbow', that immortal song of mortal Miss Garland.

Buzz returned from deepest space, swooped back down to earth breakfast. 'Want some toast. Want some toast.' It was all gone. Now it was time for Larry the Fox to jump to the aid of the party. 'I'll get you some more, Buzz!'

The young boy looked up and sneered. 'Don't want none. Changed my mind.'

This was the playground. The rehearsal that never came to an end, and these were the children, playing; acting. Play-acting.

'We don't grow up, we cover up,' Brian said.

'You're ever so clever, Brian. What does it mean?'

He wasn't quite sure and did not know how to answer her. 'Just a thought.' He shrugged.

Breakfast had now passed its zenith and there was growing activity in the kitchen. The clatter of plates was building to a climax. Brian's attention turned to the shuffling people who were clearing the tables.

'Our turn next week, Brian. We're on the list for next week. You and me.' Buzz was excited at the prospect.

It dawned on Brian. 'Oh, I see. All these helpers, they're not volunteers?' Things were fitting together. Everyone took it in turn. 'I see. We get paid for helping. It will be nice to earn some money.'

Larry sniggered and Dolores hooted. 'Money, out of Mrs Killick? More easy to get blood out of a stone.'

Brian was not concerned. They had their own reasons for hating those in authority. It was ever thus. But he would not join the derisive chorus. 'I like it here. I feel lucky.' Brian switched to something else. 'Does Mrs Killick employ any staff at all?'

To his surprise, Michelle shook her head; so, she was not a total zombie after all. He was glad. He was very glad.

'Don't they even have a nurse here?'

'No.' Larry replied. 'Not even a nurse.'

'I'll nurse you, Brian, if you care to step upstairs!' Dolores rolled her eyes.

'Who dishes out the medication, then?'

'Mr Pickled Killick.'

Brian felt slightly perturbed. Outside the window his mother's lips sailed across the clear blue sky. Fear always brought a cloud of pain and there was always this tightening of the band around his head. And two thin needles of flame behind the eyes.

'You'll get your happy pills, don't you fret.' Dolores touched him, because she could see into his mind.

One day he would be able to hide his hurt from the world and become just like anyone else.

'Anyway, even if we don't get paid, even if we do all have to take our turn to work, it doesn't matter; it's good for us. I like it here. I feel lucky.'

Larry's eyes went upwards to the ceiling calling upon his God to witness the ridiculous remark.

'You don't understand,' Brian continued. 'Miss Reeves at the hospital explained; it's to help us to get back to normal. It's for our own rehabilitation.'

'We'll be rehabilitated soon enough. In our coffin!'

'Work is therapeutic.'

'He knows long words. He's clever.' Buzz was proud of his new, worldly hero.

'Yes,' Michelle said.

'He reads books. Poetry!' Larry pulled the book out of Brian's pocket. 'He's suffering from thinker's doom. You wanna take it easy, mate.'

Brian retained his smile, snatched the book back before the old man could open it, and concentrated on trying to understand the people who owned this roof over all their heads. 'It must be hard for Mrs K. being married to a drunkard like that.'

'She's a cow. She's—' Dolores sought, but could not find a word bad enough to express her loathing. Just beneath the quiet surface feelings were obviously running high in Hazelhurst House. But he was determined not to be caught up in any engulfing hatred. It was far too early to point the finger.

'I'll wait before I judge.'

'All right then, baby blue eyes, where's your supplementary allowance?' Larry's words did not make sense.

Brian got up, manoeuvred through the tables and chairs, and went to the window. In the distance, at the end of the road, he could see the shore and the sea. A ship slid across its creased surface. On that ship were men; working seamen, like his father once was. A little boat bobbing between nowhere and nowhere in the universe. Brian once again recalled his father's last moments. How long did he hold his breath, before he took his last swig of water? Did his lungs burst? Did his eyes pop out? Where was his timeless skeleton now? Did the fins of deep sharks now disturb the sand around his gaping skull, under the Indian Ocean?

'Your pension book.' Larry had followed him to the window but Brian could not connect, at this moment he was remembering other words. Words of the poet who had also come here to convalesce from a breakdown. 'On Margate Sands, I can connect nothing with nothing.'

Brian could make out the figure of a man upon the beach. He walked and then stooped, then walked again. A suicide? A gas-fitter killing time between jobs? Lazarus walking out of the waves? The ancient mariner? His father? An after-care resident like himself? The wandering Jew? No, it was none of those. It was obviously Hitler, ninety-five years old, disguised as a beachcomber. That was damned clever. Who would dream of looking for him, here in Margate?

Hitler wandered out of his vision, across the windowpane, through the bricks. Brian put his poetry book back into his pocket. There was no future in poetry. He had to live in this world. Poetry would get him nowhere, but he would not burn his books just to give pleasure to his new-found young blond friend. He looked across at Buzz, then remembered Larry had asked him a question

54

long before he had wandered away in his thoughts. 'What did you say, Larry?'

'I asked about your pension book. Where is it?'

Now he could connect. He returned to the others. 'Mrs Killick took it.'

'Exactly! Like she took hers! And his! And hers! And all theirs! Like she took mine. She's breaking the law she is – that money is ours, by rights.' He took out a filthy wad of papers, spread them over the table, selected one of them and started to prove his point.

' "Leaflet SBI SUPPLEMENTARY BENEFITS, PENSIONS AND ALLOWANCES, NOVEMBER 1975." Quote – "If you are a boarder and pay an inclusive National Health charge for board and lodging, your requirement will be worked out differently. They will be the amount you pay for board and lodging (providing this is reasonable) PLUS an allowance for your personal expenses. For a single person the personal allowance will be £3.40 (£4 in a long-term case)." '

Larry looked at his companions, self satisfied. 'That's you and me, Brian. We're long-term cases.'

Brian was not bothered; trivial paranoia was not his style. He knew he could trust Mrs Killick; he would stake his life on that. 'She'll give me my book any time I want. She's only looking after it.'

'All right, get it now.'

'Get it now, get it now, get it now.'

'Ask for it now! Get it now!'

Larry, Buzz and Dolores were a chorus of jackals. Michelle was looking at the ceiling and she was laughing at something that had nothing to do with what they were talking about.

'I could get my allowance book any time I want.'

'Get it now, get it now,' they goaded.

Brian Singleton was not afraid. He would show them. Brian Singleton stood up straight. He would go to Mrs Killick, who was smiling across at him. He would go to her and teach them all a lesson. Rampaging jackals, tearing at the flesh of any situation; to give them some interest in life.

'Get it now, get it now.'

Dolores opened her legs wide. 'I'd love to get it now.'

And then there was complete silence as he approached the

smiling lady. She had greenish eyes and a beautiful nose. One day she would take him into her arms and stroke his head and her pretty lips would plant a kiss upon his forehead. One day it would happen, if he prayed long enough.

'Yes, darling.' She had called him darling. One day she would call him darling and she would mean it. Maybe her husband would die from crysalis of the liver, or he might try to beat her in one of his drunken bouts; at the top of the stairs. And Brian Singleton would hear her fearful call, and come to the rescue. There would be a struggle. And John Killick would be put out of his misery. What sort of life did he have to look forward to anyway. Drunks had a terrible life. B.S. would be doing J.K. a favour.

And Mr and Mrs Joan Singleton would run Hazelhurst together. And there would be no new instalment in *Woman's Dream* next week, dear reader, for Brian and Joan would live happily ever after.

She never stopped smiling. She radiated beauty and contentment. 'Yes, Brian? Can I help you?' Mrs Killick cooed.

9

'Please, Mrs Killick, can I have my pension book?' True he was a little scared, but this was only because he didn't want her to believe that he thought she was dishonest.

She did not get angry and she did not stop smiling. He relaxed and felt like poking out his tongue at the others. Her response surely proved how wrong they were. His confidence grew. 'Mrs Killick, please can I have my allowance book? I have decided to keep it on my person because it is my personal property.'

She would agree to his request. In this world you received the sort of treatment that you demanded. If you lay down upon the floor people would walk right over you. Mrs Killick was a practical fair woman. She would treat the brave with respect.

'Oh yes, Brian, what do you want?' She fluttered her eyelashes, requiring more precise information.

'It's my personal allowance, you see. I have read the small print, you see. Apparently, it's my own personal expenses. Although I appreciate you looking after it for me.'

She turned and still smiling walked to the kitchen hatch to chat with her has-been.

He didn't understand. His words had been concise enough. Nevertheless, he decided to control himself and not become angry. She obviously had something else on her mind at this moment. She misheard him, or was busy. Or she had a headache.

That was it! Mrs Killick was a brave lady who smiled through adversity. He ignored the sneering gargoyles and went to her. 'You see, Mrs Killick, I was just asking for my personal allowance book. It's four pounds per week. It's mine.'

'We'll talk about it later, there's a good boy.'

He wanted to go to his bedroom, to lie down; he wanted to walk on the beach or go to the library. He had the pain now. Her headache was catching, had infiltrated his head and was blinding him.

But they would not let him go. All their cruel eyes were fixing him there. He would shatter them, he would piss all over them. He would get a carving knife and go to them as they lay asleep in bed. He would carve through the necks of each one in turn, until their heads rolled down on to the floor. He would get them one night.

'I'm glad you're settling in, Brian,' she cooed; her hand touched his hand. Mrs Killick would escape his vengeance. She would sleep serenely and he would wake her up in the morning and reveal to her the terribly bloody scene. She was also to see the jagged whisky bottle stuck into her husband's jugular. She would laugh with him. There would be just the two of them and they would leave all the carnage behind and fly to Disneyland.

The excesses of his thoughts did not worry him too much. Neither did he hate himself, rather he had compassion for his condition. He was not totally cured; not yet. The magic wand did not exist. There was bound to be residue, the sediment of madness settling down, clouding the mind just a little. There was nothing really to be worried about.

'I'm sure, Brian, that you're going to be very happy with us.' She rubbed his cheek with the back of her fingers. 'Now please run along, because I've got so much to do.'

'Mrs Killick! What about my pension book!'

Her smile faded; her eyes went hard. 'Don't worry, darling, we look after it for you.'

His eyes closed and he could hear Brian Singleton shouting, 'It's mine! It's mine!' Brian was jumping up and down, pounding his fists against the air. Brian didn't like it. 'It's mine! It's mine! It's mine!'

He was so glad when her words soothed Brian.

'Of course it's yours. And we look after it for you.'

So that was it. There was no need for Brian to worry. He was not made to look small in front of the others. Mrs Killick was nice and she was kind and honest. And she had responsibilities. The authorities would not allow her to be in command if she did not come up to the highest possible standards. Mrs Killick was kind and firm, and she knew what was best for Brian.

'. . . and we buy you all the little things you need. Chockies and toothpaste and a face flannel, and we even give you fifty pence per week to buy your ice-creams. We do this so that you will not have to worry your little head. We do the worrying for you. That's what we're here for.'

Brian loved her with all his heart. That's why he didn't understand why his mouth continued to shout, and why he was crying, 'I want it. I want it. I want my book! I want it! I want it!' And yet he was loving her. His brain was a sponge soaking up her soothing words.

'Listen, Brian, if I gave you your book and it was stolen, or you lost it, there would be terrible trouble. And we don't want to have to call the police, because one thing would lead to another. We like you too much for you to have to leave us so soon.'

Outside, the sea was getting angry, and the trees were tearing at themselves. But inside this capsule was warm and her face smiled upon him. She didn't seem to mind his tears.

Outside, the beach was long and shaped like a sickle, and there was one man alone stooping his way across the sand. Inside, all of him was coming into line. Brian was feeling much calmer now.

She brushed his coat. 'There, that's better. You darlings! You forever get covered in crumbs.' She sniggered her nose; tweaked his cheek. 'Cheer up.'

Brian was a scarecrow short of stuffing. Michelle came towards him, 'Brian.' She was a one-word person. He had met many. He was coming to his senses, re-entering his space. Brian Singleton was no longer beside himself. His mind and body belonged to each other again. His commands would be obeyed. He would obey his commands. He was definitely on the mend; imperceptibly he was becoming normal. In Clayton it would have taken much longer. He would have fallen to the floor, and his self would have slipped away. They would call it 'a spell' and he would lie motionless in a world of white.

But he had pulled himself together. Himself had pulled him.

But he was not cheering, because there was no way back and there was such a long way to go. Sanity was expected of him. To go back now was to go back forever. He would somehow have to survive this seemingly endless road ahead.

'Brian, you're a very good boy. You don't want a reputation of being a trouble-maker and perhaps even getting re-certified.'

He nodded. He did not wish to be a bag of stinking bones on a rubbish heap. He wondered whether he would ever experience a moment of true love. Maybe later he would stop Dolores on the stairs and suck her nipples.

'. . . and of course we are here to provide you with a nice secure and comfortable home. Come on, there's a good boy.' Mrs Killick, smelling sweet, took out a Kleenex and covered his nostrils. It also smelled of her scent. It stirred the worm between his legs. There was a flicker of life down there. 'Go on, blow, there's a good boy.'

He blew all the gloating faces away. She was pleased with him and he smiled and smiled. 'Thank you, Mrs Killick.'

'That's right, good, good boy. Oh, I don't know . . . you boys are all the same, what would you do without me. That's better, that's nice.' She straightened his tie in the process of dashing away. '. . . And don't forget if ever you have any other little problems, come straight to me; after all, that's what I'm here for.' She glanced at her watch. 'Oh, my gosh, look at the time. You naughty boy, taking up all my time. How am I going to get lunch ready?'

'Thank you, Mrs Killick.' She was the kindest lady in all the world. 'There was an old woman who lived in a shoe she had so many children because she didn't know what to do.' The jingle in his head helped. He laughed.

She dashed away into the kitchen and he returned to his table, triumphant. 'She's looking after my allowance book for me.'

'You stupid idiot. You've been conned,' Larry cackled, and turned to the others. Soon they were all laughing. Even Michelle. The whole room was full of faces laughing and fingers pointing at him.

He never did understand human nature. But he was not depressed, indeed he was happy. So he continued eating his breakfast and he ignored them all. Nothing mattered anymore; Mrs Killick cared for him.

10

Mr and Mrs Killick stood by an open cupboard in the hall and a line of sheep shuffled towards them. The line extended the length of the hall, doubled back upon itself and wound its way to the top of the stairs.

'Come on, poppets! Come and get your happy tabs.'

Brian shuffled with the rest towards John Killick, who busily dispensed each individual's dose. His wife stood supervising the actions, making sure that none of the recipients were secreting tablets under their tongues or inside their cheeks; to be pocketed later. It was an old wheeze; a way of accumulating as many tablets as possible and thereby committing suicide on a day of one's choice; a means of re-entering the universe via Lithium, Librium or Phenothiazine.

As he slowly moved towards the head of the queue, Brian recalled just another Clayton incident. One nurse was not so careful and one patient managed to save each daily dose until she had more than enough. And one particular day, when they were all on their usual morning meander through the village, the girl casually waved and walked away. She walked to the railway station, took her happy tabs and there, apparently, she got into the right frame of mind as it were, laid her head down upon the railway line. When the train came – presto. She was cured of her psychosis for all time.

Brian's turn came. He stood before his master and his mistress. Joan Killick smiled down upon him, but John Killick was not smiling at all. And the shaking hand presented Brian's daily dose.

He was as dutiful as the others and watched himself in the glass as he gulped down the water, and raised his tongue for Mrs Killick to see 'All gone'.

It was done. Brian Singleton was ready for another day. He was a re-instated zombie. He had paid his entrance fee. His body was now fully charged with antibodies and he would feel nothing. He was now a fully paid up member of the human race.

His hands were stiff at his side. His head sunk down into his shoulder; his chin firmly tucked back into his neck.

He entered the lounge, joined the others. Outside, the dispensing was still going on. Inside, two residents sat staring at the tuning signal on the television screen. That signal was the best programme ever presented; it never varied; you could rely upon it. Anyway, the two ladies watched intently, one apprehensive, the other smiling. They held hands like little girls.

This was the morning, even before school broadcasting had begun.

'It's no good you trying to save up all these pills for a rainy day, feller me lad; the rainy day's here.' Joan Killick was castigating a poor old sod out in the hall. She was right, the rainy day was here. It was pissing down outside. Incredibly enough, God had not yet used up all his tears.

Brian collapsed into the comfy chair; the string holding him high had been cut. Now he would soak into the upholstery and be seen no more upon this earth.

He could not face the day; he wanted to fade into oblivion, quietly. He was Quasimodo suddenly, tongue poking out of the side of his mouth. He could not talk properly, he had a hump and a hare-lip; his spine was crooked, he had water on the brain and poison in his blood. He was chased by the crowd, he was a hunted animal, panting here, deafened by the bells of falling rain. He was a cringing, useless, deformed specimen. He was an idiot. He would never be accepted. He would be mad forever.

'You see, mate, we don't stand a chance.' Larry was climbing into his coat. It was a slow-motion picture piped through Euston Control. His mind shot upward, ejected stage one and stage two. He was soaring alone in the universe, propelled by the great God Phenothiazine.

'If you're thrown out, Brian, and even if you're not re-certified, you'll get a reputation as a trouble-maker. And no one will take you on.' Larry, in his world coat, ready for the streets, was leaning towards him, trying to be nice. Brian quickly closed his mouth and resurrected a sane expression on to his face. He would keep his sorrow to himself.

62

'. . . These hotel owners have got their own tribal drums. You make trouble here and you're out in the cold.'

Brian felt sick deep in his stomach. The sort of sickness that leaves everything inside, and brings nothing up. He had fallen into a trap; was there no way back? He had been tricked, had been cheated out of Clayton.

He went to the window, but stopped himself from smashing the glass with his inward cry. 'Is there no way back? What have I done?' He screamed and screamed but the passing people outside did not notice. The living dead did not know how lucky they were, standing by the bus stop. Ordinariness was Shangri La – Nirvana, El Dorado. Jerusalem. It could not be achieved by crying, by dream or by prayer. Most people could achieve ordinariness by merely breathing. Others had a tiny kink in the brain.

'Anyone coming to the Centre?' Larry did not mean the centre of the earth, therefore he had to be referring to the Day Centre; the place where the post-mad usually killed time during the day, away from the gaze of the good people of Margate who, like the rest of the human race, hated to be reminded of the fragility of the human brain.

'No one coming? Buzz? Michelle?'

They did not even bother to reply. 'Dolores? Coming to the Centre?'

'Sorry. Got to put my face on first.'

A toothless woman had been staring at the tuning signal all the while, she nodded, approving the geometric pattern. Brian envied her state of grace. If only he could possess a mind that did not function at all; it was no use. He was trapped in this place; there was no way back to the amniotic universe. A squashy grapefruit inside his skull would have served him so much better.

'Brian? You coming?' Larry seemed too desperate to tread into the world alone.

Brian was a depressed pelican; an ugly prehistoric bird, rooted to his desperation. 'Maybe I'll see you on the front later. I'll wait for you there.'

'You can wait for me in bloody hell.' Larry went without slamming the door. Brian wondering why he was suddenly so full of despair. Yesterday he was on the mountain top. The whole of life stretched before him. And now this rat was gnawing at his intestines. If only he could learn to live day by day. One heart beat upon another. There was no point in kidding himself; he had no real ambition to become a vegetable. He did not want to die in life. If only he could survive long enough to want to survive.

Outside in the hall, Mr and Mrs were still dispensing their chemical goodies. The pills that were meant to take away the pain were the real cause of this morning's overwhelming depression. It was a ridiculous paradox. The pills had caused a curtain to descend upon him. The pain was somewhere there, but he could not put his finger upon it. He had once had an operation in Clayton. They gave him Morphine when he regained consciousness. He floated upon a sea of Morphine. It shielded him from the pain, but somehow it was even worse because he knew that the pain was still there.

'They don't even employ a nurse! They don't even employ a nurse!' His pain was drowned in outrage. It was a way of coping.

'I'll be your nurse!' Dolores stroked his penis with her eyes. He did not think that he could survive the day. He spoke quietly to try to make her understand.

'You see, Dolores, I don't want my pills anymore. I want my pain. I've got a perfect right to my pain haven't I?'

'Brian,' she replied softly, 'I can get rid of all your problems, in two minutes flat.' She rolled her eyes and licked her lips.

'Not today, thank you very much.' Brian was correct and polite and hid his disgust; then he got up and, despite the cloud of cotton wool between his ears, he straightened himself, bowed gravely and left the room.

I I

Brian went into the front garden and stood there in the driving rain. He was in no hurry to float to the Day Centre. The garden was as good a place as any to pass the time.

The weather had changed quite suddenly during breakfast; the sea was on the boil. He tilted his head towards the thickening sky. He was no longer in despair; indeed he was enjoying the hard rain upon his face. Then he looked at the little gnome. Brian felt an affinity with the cheeky little fellow who was fishing in concrete. All his life Brian Singleton had fished in concrete.

He walked around the crazy paving, backwards and forwards and over again.

'Crazy paving!' He laughed. It was an appropriate setting.

Then he turned around and Dolores was standing there. She too was wet through.

'You'll catch your death,' he said.

'So will you,' she replied.

'Maybe that's the idea.'

'Don't worry, Brian, you'll get used to it. It's always worse at first.'

He continued smiling. 'Don't want to get used to it.' There had to be a way back. He wanted to go back to Clayton. He would phone them after lunch. Now that he had decided his course of action he felt so much better. They were drenched, soaked to the skin yet they just stood there, chatting.

'You going to the Centre now?'

'Maybe. Or maybe later. I feel like being on my own.'

'So do I. Let's be on our own together.' She looked so lovely and pure in the rain.

He would marry one day. And he would be pure and his bride would be pure. He would save himself for his wedding. They would both be dressed in pure white. There would be nothing that wasn't white. And he would be patient and wait even a week for his bride to open her legs.

'I love the rain,' she said.

'So do I.'

'Rain, rain come down faster; if you don't I'll tell your master,' she laughed, and he joined in.

'You're crazy,' he said. 'You're mad.'

'If this is a sane world, thank God I'm mad.'

And they held hands and went round and round, splashing their feet and chanting at the sky. 'RAIN, RAIN, COME DOWN FASTER; IF YOU DON'T I'LL TELL YOUR MASTER.' Faster and faster, round and round, Brian danced in a ring in the garden, with his best friend in all the world. He was dizzy; the whole garden was spinning. She held him, but they did not stop laughing.

'Will you have this waltz with me?'

'Certainly.' He did not care if they were being watched. Trying to act his age had got him exactly nowhere.

He bugled the 'Skater's Waltz' out of the side of his mouth as she sedately led him round and round the crazy paving.

'We'll run away together this morning.' Suddenly everything was falling into place.

'Why run? Why can't we go in our Bentley?'

'We'll go to the Channel Islands. Victor Hugo wrote *The Toilers of the Sea* there.'

'Certainly, Brian – we'll synchronise our hearts and leave at twelve-thirty.'

Despite her joke he knew that she would go with him. They would work as waiters during the summer season, save their tips, buy a small yacht and sail beyond the Timor seas. 'Good! That's settled,' he said, and they shook hands. Everything was fixed. 'No more problems. You got any problems?'

'Yes. Come over here and I'll tell you about them!' She pulled him to the doorway, and they stood there out of the rain. 'My problem is that I'm a sexual maniac.'

'Oh God!' He tried to escape but she held on to him, and she shook her head, conveying to him that for the moment he was perfectly safe and she only wanted to unburden herself in talk.

'Mind you, I'm the quieter kind of sexual maniac.'

66

'You could have fooled me.'

'I was institutionalised like you, Brian, of course. I've been in and out in and out all my life.' She laughed. 'In more ways than one. In and out. In and out.'

He laughed, pretending to enjoy the joke, but he wondered how she could possibly settle down to fidelity, if she was so obsessed, so tarnished by sex.

'And it's all because of the Mental Health Act 1959. Paragraph 128, Section One.' She quoted out of her head. 'Without prejudice to section Seven of the Sexual Offences Act, 1966, it shall be an offence for a man who is an officer employed in a hospital to have unlawful sexual intercourse with a woman who is receiving treatment for mental disorder . . .'

It was not uncommon for people in their condition to know all the facts concerning their commitment. Many, many patients at Clayton could rattle through all the various acts that had been passed to contain them. Like rats obsessed with the construction of their cages. Nevertheless, her tale was somewhat unusual. He had heard of cruelty inside mental hospitals. Indeed, he had seen it sometimes. That had never surprised him, nor worried, nor angered him. It would have been surprising had there not been cruelty. He had been cruel. He felt cruel. Often he had longed for the opportunity to just smash another patient in the face or smash himself in the face. The world was cruel.

But he had never actually seen any guardians making sexual advances towards any patient, for as far as he could remember. Though possibly it happened behind doors. In fact, come to think of it, it was possible. And who could blame the keepers?

Some of the girls carried beautiful bodies beneath oozing faces. They had hungry cunts just like everyone else. And they had desires. People somehow imagined that the mad no longer needed to be fucked or to fuck. Every madhouse rattled with masturbators. Women tore off their skirts and knickers incessantly, and they screamed for sex.

'I want a hot cock. I need a big prick. I've got a hungry cunt.' It was disgusting. It was horrifying. It was natural.

Nevertheless, he felt angry that an official should take advantage of his beloved, but tarnished, Dolores.

'You mean an officer. A male nurse seduced you?'

She smiled and sidled closer. The heat from her body was

wafting over him. He had offered himself to Pandora. Lock, stock and barrel.

'An official in a mental hospital forced intercourse upon you?'

'No. That was the trouble. They didn't. I tried, but none of them would seduce me. Not one single one of them. Not even the married ones. That's my problem. I am a victim of the 1959 Act. I like you, Brian. I like your eyes; I trust you. It's nice to have a gentleman around who's strong and understanding.'

He was against the door. He could retreat no farther.

And then it opened. Mrs Killick, avenging angel, stood there, and was he glad to see her angry face. 'I've been watching you. Up to your old tricks again, eh? Just you leave Brian alone.'

'Yes, Mrs Killick. Sorry, Mrs Killick.'

'And get to the Centre. Quick. Otherwise—'

She left the threat unfinished but the message got home. Dolores quickly left the garden.

'Yes, Mrs Killick. Sorry, Mrs Killick.'

And all the others floated out of Hazelhurst House. Michelle, Buzz and the other drooling, stupid faces.

'Out, out the lot of you. Out. Get out.' Mrs Killick assailed them, expelled them from her domain, and they huddled and scuttled away, towards the bus stop; a column of smiling sleep-walkers against the slanting rain. 'And just you tell me if she ever bothers you again,' she shouted.

'Yes, Mrs Killick.'

And the guardian smiled upon him as she closed the door.

He did not follow the others, he wandered in the opposite direction. He could see Dolores at the bus stop waiting with the rest. He refrained from shouting, 'What about our wedding? Our plans? What about the Channel Islands?'

She was busy chatting to someone else. He would let her go and not hold her to her promise. It would not have worked out anyway He walked towards the furious sea.

He was not unduly depressed. It was just that he had decided to kill himself. He was not being over-emotional, nor was he indulging in gestures. There was no real feeling within him. The drugs had levelled him out. He had been spun dried, wrung out and ironed, and now he was walking towards the water; a man without past or future, hope or despair, without name or identity. He was about to be covered by the waves and it was all so very easy. He would drown and that would be that.

He looked back and saw the town receding slowly. Margate was a picture postcard of a winter's day. The rain had stopped but not a soul was about. The little hotels along the front were spanking clean.

He blamed no one. He was merely being magnetised by his father's skull.

He did not even hate the hotel owners of Margate. He was aware of the controversy in the town; the arguments raging in the local press, and in the council chamber and in the commercial fraternity.

It was a simple matter. The small hotel owners were looking after their own interests. They did not like their bedrooms unoccupied during the long winter months. And so, they did a deal with the Ministry of Health and took to their bosoms the post-mad.

You could herd them more easily. They were the sheep going through the endless dip. You could cram eight into a bedroom not suitable for three normal people. You could feed them the most filthy stodge and who could complain? And if they could, who would they complain to? And who would listen and believe them?

But he had taken matters into his own hands and was walking towards that sea, and in this respect he was different. The Ministry of Health could cross him off their books.

There was nothing now that he really needed to recall. Nothing had happened to him. There were no landmarks in his life. He had been born, had gone into that place and been let out and here he was. His father had knocked all the sense out of him, had turned him into the idiot he was now extinguishing.

He froze for a moment, perhaps somebody was watching him through binoculars. They would be too late to save him.

'I grow old . . . I grow old . . . I shall wear the bottoms of my trousers rolled.' Thomas Stearns had also travelled to this last resort. Brian stooped and rolled up his trousers, and took off his shoes and socks. Somehow it did not seem right to walk into the sea with shoes and socks on. He tied the laces of each shoe together, stuck one sock into each and slung the shoes over his shoulder. The pressure within his skull was receding.

'He who would valiant be, let him come hither.' He gaily belted out the Bunyan hymn. 'One here will constant be, come wind come weather.'

Wind came. Weather came. There was an incredible amount of weather today. He was walking towards his mother; he was taking her breakfast. But she didn't move anymore and that is how they prove that you are dead.

The sea was pouring into the room so he climbed on to the bed. Jenny Singleton was like a statue in the British Museum. She was white and cold.

The good neighbour, Mrs Lane, who lived next door, walked across the sand and into the bedroom. Two policemen were with her. They were real policemen with caps on their heads and they were pressing handkerchiefs to their faces.

'Come on, Brian, come on, there's a good boy.'

He was not a child. There was a birth certificate in the drawer to prove he had been born and he was twenty years old; but he did not protest.

'She's gone to God. Your mummy's gone to God. Come on, Brian, come for a nice ride. Come on, get your coat on. These two kind policemen have come to take you for a ride, in their motor car.'

He went with them, smiling, and he left the house. And there was the big motor car. 'Come on, son, you'll be all right.' Brian Singleton was pleased to go.

'We're going for a car-ride, a car-ride.' The seven-year-old child was trapped within Brian Singleton and he would not come out. He was playing in there, staying in there. Brian Singleton had grown tall and fat, but the child was in command; smiling through his face, talking through his mouth, crying through his eyes, moving through his arms, his legs. That child was happy with his eyes high up in his head.

'I want to go for a car-ride, a car-ride, a car-ride.' Child Brian took his body inside and the car started up and sped over the sand. Away from the leafy sleeping street in Harrow-on-the-Hill, across the wide beach they zoomed.

Brian screamed until he drowned out all sound and he cried until everything was washed away. If only somebody would come to save him from drowning. But all that was now out of the question. Nobody cared that much, and he could not blame them. Nobody would come. Margate was in hibernation and his mother was dead, and he had been taken away. She had given him the greatest gift a parent could give a child; she had given him her own death.

But he had not learned how to live, so that was that.

The sea now lapped his toes. And there was endless eternity via Margate sands, where he could connect nothing with nothing.

He stopped for just a moment to remember. Nothing much had happened to Brian Singleton. He could spare a few moments of reflection before gulping down the universe.

He was certified in nineteen fifty-three. He remembered that first day distinctly. Brian Singleton protested, claimed he was not really mad; he was just allowing the child within to play as much as he liked, until he tired himself. But some idiot retorted, 'You're certified, just like the rest of us.' Brian did not become angry; rather he enjoyed belonging. And to be truly certified pleased him. It sounded like a diploma, a degree of qualification.

In nineteen fifty-three, when he entered Clayton, the other inmates referred to it as a madhouse, or an asylum. When he left Clayton it was known as a psychiatric hospital. When he entered the middle ages was still in existence and minds and bodies slithered through protozoic slime. Nothing was expected, everything was accepted. Everyone was cruel and kind, because that was the way it was. You did have to abandon all hope when you entered because hope was abandoned so long ago. Once you entered it enclosed and protected. With hindsight it was a terrible place. Its Victorian grey stone edifice towered above you, hurtled down upon you and crushed you into total nothingness.

And Clayton was his resting place for all the rest of his living death. Brian Singleton watched Brian Singleton slowly walk across the deserted quadrangle. God was sleeping rather heavily that morning; for these were in the latter days, and God had started drinking rather heavily. And could you blame him? What with Belsen, Hiroshima, and the demise of the British Empire. Frightful prehistoric pigeons pecked and flapped in that desert. Brian hated pigeons more than any other living creature, and the feeling was quite mutual. As he slowly travelled his diagonal journey they surveyed him with their greedy, beady eyes.

And so Brian wandered through the grounds. And nothing happened. Today was the day before nothing and the day after nothing, and his hobby was doing nothing between nothing and nothing. The more obviously dangerous ones were obviously locked away.

And then maybe a year passed, or five or ten? In the garden a mongol with a spade was turning the earth at a funereal pace. Brian envied the mongols, but he did not stop to acknowledge the happy face. He greeted no one; accepted greetings from no one. He wandered through them, observing everything.

A chap named Guy marched backwards and forwards, his hand clenched at his chest clutching an invisible rifle, guarding an invisible palace or prison. Unblinking, sure of purpose. Dangerous Clark Gable ears; Hitler eyes. Someone definitely to avoid.

But it was a gentle one who had caused him to retreat from contact. A few weeks before, a nice man in a tweed jacket came smiling towards him. 'How do you do? I'm Derek.' He was very good-looking. But before Brian could stretch out his own hand he was on the ground and Derek's fingers were pressing, pressing into his neck. Day became night; night was full of shooting stars. Then all went black : when they pulled Derek away apparently he was still smiling. It was nothing personal they said. Derek acted like that with everyone.

A woman sat cross-legged on the grass, chatting away to an invisible companion, an imaginary teacup poised delicately in her hand. Sometimes she sipped as she listened. Watching these people sometimes made him feel better. And then there came a total blank. This was the time when the only thing he knew was that he didn't know who he was, and where he was, and why he was here.

He must have committed a crime. That much was obvious. It

had to be a murder. He had been murdered or committed murder. Everything was being kept from him.

His mind could not focus upon the enormity of the event that brought him here. Inside his head was the land of cotton wool and he wandered there. Sometimes he even came close to understanding the reasons for his sentence but, even so, he did not feel too badly because at least he was paying the penalty.

And then he fell into his head again. He did not seem to dwell entirely in the world of fingers and mouths. He was Singleton. He pissed the bed every night. And every day he went behind the door, and when he finished, all the shit was in his hands, so he stuck it behind the radiators.

Now he knew that his mother was dead. But he did not miss Harrow-on-the-Hill, and every day he shaved but the man watched him because God didn't. About that time the devil decided to take out a freehold on his hands. But things could have been far worse. The grounds were green, even if the building was grey.

An old woman sat on a bench, rocking backwards and forwards; clutching a piece of blanket against her, singing a quiet song. Two men played draughts or chess, he could not tell for sure because there were no pieces on the board that was not there. A girl was hiding behind a bush; her face came out and smiled when he passed.

He left the garden, entered the long corridor. Hell smelled of carbolic, and its inhabitants were blind sloths, holding the walls with the flats of their hands as they traversed from one end of the tunnel to the other.

And there was this terrible laughter; the death and ecstasy shrieks from behind locked doors. Doors with peepholes for the shepherds in white coats. Jibbering animals dwelt behind those doors. But Clayton was no abattoir, and none were receiving the mercy knife into the jugular. Here the only death was the death of the brain. The heart, without compassion, drove relentlessly onward.

'—There is always another one walking beside you. Gliding, wrapped in brown mantle, hooded, I do not know whether a man or woman – But who is that on the other side of you?—'

Brian was beside himself. And then there was no one. There was nothing left. A dog was howling over the body that no longer belonged to him. They were taking her away, they were taking him away. The brain was locked, the combination lost. He had gone to pieces while walking through this corridor. He was all shattered on the floor, scattered. His eyes over there, a leg walking up the wall, his finger-nails over here; his guts trailing from there to there to help grow leaves. A finger was stuck into a keyhole. His nose on the ceiling, about to come unstuck. A hand holding penis, looping the loop. Yes, he was definitely not altogether. They swept all the pieces into a corner, brushed them into a dustpan, and hurried all the rubbish into one of those rooms, where they stood above.

'Don't hit me, don't hit me, I'll be a good boy.' Lips floated around the room, emitting Brian's voice. Two separate eyeballs, rolling marbles over the shiny floor, could see the two white-clad guardians at the door. One black and one white.

The white man was his father but with flesh on his face, and the hands were kneading, not thudding into him. The hands were getting larger, they were being pumped up. They grew until they filled the whole room. There were just these four huge hands working, trying to make bread. Two black, two white.

'Don't hit me, don't hurt me. I promise to be a good boy. I won't wet myself anymore. I promise. Don't hurt me.' The small faces behind the hands smiled, and then they fizzled out. The four hands continued getting larger and larger, then they exploded.

There was no light flex. The bulb came almost out of the ceiling. He could see their faces through the small glass window through the wood. There were absolutely no sharp edges anywhere. He could not do himself an injury. He could not even tear at his own jugular because he had bitten away his nails long ago.

He remained on board, voyaging over the rough seas of self; floating, sailing. And the pieces gradually came together. It was a cartoon of coloured shapes. All these apparently unrelated pieces decided to attend a conference. So they came together and they assembled in the room and they called the collage, Brian Singleton, aged forty-six; walking along a corridor. Seeing himself at the other end, walking towards himself, no longer beside himself, dissolving into his own silhouette, his own identity. Years had passed and nothing had happened. Moments dragged, years flew by. It was now. In that year of our Lord the Devil. Nineteen seventy-eight. That corridor had been his entire existence.

13

The tide was not coming in fast enough. For billions of years it had come in and gone out, on this same Margate shore, but it had not improved upon itself, and remained predictable and unambitious. It was in no hurry to-ing and fro-ing upon the shores of eternity; and Margate was there behind him. How many Margates would come and go before this same indifferent tide?

Like the tide, Brian was in no particular hurry. He would wait until the water at least covered his ankles. Then he would merely walk and slide away, and fall into the endless chasm; the essence of himself flowing back into the universe.

And Brian Singleton would merge with Genghis Khan, Alexander the Great, Adolf Hitler, Albert Einstein, Rembrandt, Gilles de Rais and Jenny Singleton his mother. A nice blend of cosmic soup. His story had practically been told. Here he was in the present. Only a few weeks before he had walked along that same terrible corridor. But now it was all different. There was soft music coming from nowhere; the walls were painted in pleasant colours; there were modern paintings on the walls and he was washed and smelling clean and ready for the world. And the world was still there, outside.

It was amazing that the human race had survived so far. Brian felt optimistic; he had not expected to reach beyond forty. It had been a toss up, between man destroying the world or Brian destroying himself. It was a close run thing that had not yet been resolved; but if you were a madman looking out of the window, or venturing to the suburbs of London, you could afford to be hopeful; the madman could see that he had come into his kingdom. Dark thoughts and nightmares had come into the open. The streets were full of the shit of minds. The madman could feel at home. Nobody could afford to point the finger any longer. Civilisation was the madman now. Brian Singleton had been a prophet; the jibbering child had seen the glory of the coming of the Lord of destruction.

Twenty-six years in Clayton had been an adequate apprenticeship and now he could take his place. Who would care if he smeared his shit around the walls, if the whole world had become a shit-house?

When he walked through Clayton village, just before coming here to Margate, he had felt a glow, a warmth of recognition. It was all so comforting, because he had seen it all coming. Here on this shore he was leaving a world that had caught up with him, that had taken on his madness. 'Now, Brian? Now?'

'No. A few moments. Be patient.' The sea was still only licking his toes.

He was still walking along the Clayton corridor.

He was forty-six and his face was soft and pink, and unlined. How could he look so remarkably young? The answer came as quick as the question. The lines were inward; the wear and tear were there inside his brain. But the normal worries of the world had been kept away from him. The rent; the rates; the school fees; the mortgages; the building societies; the insurance policies. He had avoided all these by being committed rather than commuted. He had not experienced the normal wear and tear of marriage and bringing up a family.

He saw his unworn face now reflected upon the glass surfaces of the bright modern paintings. Twenty-six years he had wandered this same corridor. He had thickened within but his face was the same, and the corridor had changed. The mad ones were gone. The abattoirs of hell had been erased. No one screamed or laughed anymore.

All was quiet, subdued and controlled. All was bland, softness and pastel shades; all was muzak.

'Red sails in the sunset.' A golden oldie gently throbbed. All was endless Victor Silvester.

Waltzes, quicksteps and tangos rendered down to the same tempo: music without sweat. Everything was clean and bright. The daylight poured in. Clayton Asylum had become Clayton Psychiatric Hospital. The mad had been banished into themselves, all their messy, smelly actions had been deodorised and tucked away.

Brian Singleton was no longer mad; he was merely disturbed, and there was progress even here. Those in command had quickened their insistence that he was now almost normal and therefore ready for the world outside. In fact, the decision had already been taken. He was a mollusc, waiting for the tide.

The new drugs had made it all possible. The mad had been tidied up. The screams and grunts, the jibbering excesses, the hair being pulled out, the penis being whipped out, the tongues violently poking in and out without stopping : these self-mutilations had all been brought under control. The maniacs had had their day.

The disturbed inmates slowly floated now. They ambled silently along this corridor, and in the grounds. There was no movement of the arms; hardly any from the legs; no bending of the knees. The new drugs had taken away madness but they had also taken almost everything else away. The heights and the depths of insanity had been banished forever.

'Long live Phenothiazine.' On that shore waiting for the water, and in that corridor, Brian's floating head sang the praises of that new wonder drug, the chemical deity that had made this change possible.

Brian was going somewhere and he was afraid because something was about to happen to Singleton. A woman came towards him from the opposite direction. He knew her well. They had grown down together. She had been in Clayton at least twenty years. They sometimes exchanged a few words, but her name escaped him. Her face floated close to his; two party balloons bumping, but not hurting each other.

'You're wanted,' she said.

He clutched his heart with both hands, and his puff-ball face replied. 'I've waited so long for you to say that.'

'Miss Reeves wants you.' It was the voice of somebody programmed to utter words; words without cadence or modulation. No doubt he sounded exactly the same to someone outside his own head.

He knew that Miss Reeves wanted him, and that was where he was going at this precise moment. But he did not let on. Brian never unnecessarily went out of his way to hurt or disappoint people. Not these days. This lady had come with a message for him; and that had given her something to do during the morning hours. So he tried to smile and bow graciously. One day perhaps the inner desire would co-ordinate with his outward action, and he would be reunited. Brian would meet Singleton, and Singleton would carry Brian into and through the world, for the rest of his natural life. There were signs. Imperceptible signs that the ice was melting beneath the surface. All he had to do was live for another thousand years, and he might be able to hold a decent and reasonable conversation, and participate in a normal relationship.

'I'm going to Miss Reeves now,' he said.

'Why does she want you?' the mouth replied.

'I'm being discharged; they're sending me out.'

'Goodbye,' she sang, and slowly waltzed away. He tried to force his mind, but could not remember her name. He knocked upon the door. She was already a thing of the past.

The voice from within called him inside, so he entered. Miss Reeves sat before him, flicking through the few typewritten notes, the papers of his life. His case-history.

'Sit down, please.' Then she looked at him. She was unmarried, there were no rings upon her podgy fingers. Miss Reeves moved her arm, and a wave of sweat gently rolled over him. It was not unpleasant, nor overpowering. Would coitus make her scream?

Brian knew that soon he would have to pull himself together, and not undress and fuck every female creature he came across. He was at the gates of the world, and he would have to regulate his thoughts, and concentrate upon his rehabilitation. He pulled a curtain across her juicy cunt, and closed the sex shop of his mind for the rest of the day. He would co-operate from now on. He sat forward.

'Well, Mr Singleton, you've thought about it?'

'Yes.' The die was cast. All prevarication ended here, and he was glad.

'And?' She smiled, waiting for his reply. 'I'm sure you can see it all very clearly now. I'm sure you can't wait to leave us.'

It was a strange and funny thing. The years in Clayton had not really dragged. He had read. He had played ping-pong. He was the champion of his ward. Although he was hardly yet ready to take on the Chinese. He had been in Clayton a long, long time and his days there were numbered. There was no way out except by the way out. His imprisonment within his own body was coming to an end; he would have to make contact with other human creatures. 'I like Clayton – I've never been bored here.' He wanted to show his gratitude.

She did not stop smiling. 'Brian—'

He liked being called by his first name. One day he would be totally in charge of himself, and he would cut down on the drugs, and he would meet a beautiful pure girl and she would call him—

'Brian – we think you are ready to leave Clayton – unlike many others you should do well outside. You are intelligent, have a high IQ, you read a lot of books. We know it's not going to be easy—'

This was her job and he did not blame her. 'I'm afraid – I'm so afraid.' He sat down. 'So afraid, so afraid.' He wanted to smile and agree to everything. He was angry with his words, they were defying his command.

The sea was now rushing towards him. The story of his life would soon be over. The short story. The book without covers. The words that did not add up to much. A novel without a central character, with shadows of secondary caricatures out of focus.

He was so afraid of the sea. How could he survive out there? Miss Reeves sat behind her desk that was perched upon the horizon. Seagulls screeched out of her mouth. 'Brian! Brian! Please listen to me. I know it's going to be hard for you, but we all think it's for the best. Brian! Brian!'

There was no way out except by the exit. Why was he crying? This life was coming to an end. Why did it hurt so much to be ordered out of hell?

Margate rushed towards him. He could hear the booming waves. Miss Reeves was making it inevitable.

'Of course, you're bound to be nervous at first. You've been here a long time – people will make allowances—'

She droned her homilies and he didn't blame her, she was paid to do that and she sincerely believed it was for the best. 'People mock me. They stare.'

'Of course they don't, not really. You're reading too much into superficial reaction – deep down, people are far more broad-minded nowadays – there's no stigma anymore, believe me – these days millions upon millions are in the same boat.'

'Maybe I'll be more ready to leave in a month's time.'

'No, Brian, we can't put off your rehabilitation any longer.'

So there was to be no escape; he would have to try to survive without Clayton.

'—It's all been arranged, Brian, you're going to the seaside, to Margate. We fixed you up in a nice house, a few minutes from the front. You'll be well looked after, you'll find companions, books.'

He was glad it was Margate. In fact, he had suggested Margate. Margate conjured up pictures of families enjoying themselves. He could see himself on a donkey. 'Are there any books in Margate?'

'Absolutely. Margate has a very fine public library. Thank you, Brian, that will be all for now.'

'When am I leaving. Today? I'm not packed.'

'Plenty of time, Brian. You're leaving next Wednesday. I'll see you before you go.' She smiled and he backed out of the room and into the corridor. And now it was Thursday, the day after he arrived and the sea stood on its hind legs before him. It was all so easy, it was just a matter of closing your eyes and slowly walking forward.

'Brian, Brian.' His mother was calling him into the house. 'Brian. Brian.' The seagulls were screeching his name. 'Brian. Brian. Brian. Brian.' The cry was not in his head. It was the real Dolores running towards him. He retreated from the water, slowly, but he was not unduly depressed. Maybe he would manage the deep saline treatment a little later in the day. In fact, he felt quite cheerful. The thought that he could cancel himself out any time of his own choosing comforted and enabled him to turn to the plump sexy bitch with a smile. She came close up to him, puffing, holding her heart.

'What are you doing? You're all wet. Come out of that sea, it's cold.'

'Was about to go for a long swim. You came just in time.'

'I can come whenever I want. Four times or five, one after the other.'

He ignored her lewd remarks.

'I saw you in the distance, Brian, all alone. I decided to follow.'

'Silly thoughts sometimes come into my head. I'm grateful to you, Dolores.' She rubbed close to him, stroked his chin.

'Know what I want?'

He ignored her eyes. 'Don't – know how to thank you.' He was retreating but she held on to him.

'Roll me on the sand, Brian. Fuck me in the waves, on the shore, just like Burt Lancaster and Deborah Kerr in *From Here to Eternity*. Here, Brian, here.' She was going down backwards, hanging on to his lapels, trying to pull him on top of her.

'No. I can't.' He broke away.

'Why not?'

He shrugged. 'Maybe some other time, maybe next Thursday, or Wednesday, when I find my feet. I promise.'

'All right then. Thanks anyway.' But then she smiled. 'It's a bit chilly, isn't it?'

'Yeah, it cuts right through yer.'

He helped her to her feet and she took his arm, and hung on to him as they strode together towards the town.

'If I can't be your lover, I can be your sister. At least until you find your own, and then who knows, you may insist on incest.'

She rolled her eyes and they walked across the wet sand, huddling close. Brian felt the warmth of this other human creature flowing into him. He was definitely not going to drown himself today.

14

The conductor was unusually kind; no doubt he was used to the sort of people who had to get off at this stop. Brian recalled the parting words of Miss Reeves. People did seem to be far more tolerant and understanding these days.

He found himself in the back streets of Margate; the suburb that day trippers would never see in a million years. A featureless area, but it was pleasant enough. The building Brian entered was modern and his heart did not sink when he went through the door with Dolores.

So this was the Day Centre. The Therapy Clinic and recreation-rooms for the post-mad. He peered into the room. Some of the inhabitants did not seem so post-mad. Many had the moon face, many others the blank. All in all he felt quite at home. It was not unlike the occupational therapy section of Clayton.

So this was the place to pass the time. The place to pick up skills and companionships. He was determined to make the most of this opportunity. Here he would concentrate and be open to the teaching and skills of the kind ladies in command. He would not use this place like the others, as a permanent oasis to ease the frightening but necessary real world in the streets outside. This would not be refuge, this would be his halfway-house, his spring-board.

'Bye.' Dolores embarrassed him when others were around; so he quickly departed from her, and entered a room where people were painting with a rather nice-looking girl in charge.

'Do you want to come in here? Do you want to paint? We're painting anger.' Six or seven faces looked up at him. But others were biting tongues in concentration. One or two had a blank sheet before them. Some had filled their page with an indescribable shitty mess of paint; others carefully sketched foliage! Trees! Aeroplanes! Chasms! Mountains! Crucifixions! And all those usual items that the mad seemed compelled to depict; shadowy celebrations of life within or upon this earth.

He had no talent in this direction. He could barely draw his own breath to survive; so he quietly shunned the invitation and walked through the basket-makers, and the people who were trying to make their clay rise into recognisable forms.

He decided that he would definitely try pottery another day. Shit without smell; pliable, satisfying and permitted.

Brian sat down to see where he stood on this second day of his life. He had entered Margate yesterday, and now he had to plan for the future. The Day Centre would suffice for a few weeks; but by spring he wanted to be able to stand on his own three feet. He was hopeful and he laughed. A revolution was happening within. At long last he wanted his middle leg to be operational as soon as possible. Soon he would be able to fuck, and he would fuck off and fuck his way across England. He would fuck others instead of himself. No longer would he be a victim, for he was tired of that role.

But for the moment he would play the waiting game. Everyone would say, 'How nice! Brian Singleton is a good boy.' He would hibernate and hide out here for the rest of the winter. He would bide his time, then he would take off and Brian Singleton would arise. He would not die here; the lingering rehabilitation death. He would not allow himself to become an after-care zombie like all these others, a permanent statistic on the National Health.

'Hello! You're new. Don't sit around doing nothing. You're expected to join in here. So come on, it's sing-song time.' The lady in the white coat had red-flecked cheeks; she playfully tugged him into the hall. 'Come on. Come on. Come on, there's a good boy. We're having a sing-song in the other room. No use sitting around here, we all get busy in this place.'

He decided to play the game, to be her little idiot child. They resented the mad being too clever; his new life demanded new tactics.

'Sorry? A sing-song?' He was a moron, he was a stupid brainless twit; between his ears there was just a bag of sawdust. He smiled all the time because he had no will of his own, no strength to resist her pudgy hand. He allowed himself to be pulled into the hall, where the main congregation was assembled for the sing-song. He was taking his place amongst the latter-day saints of Beelzebub the King.

Dolores smiled when he entered, but Brian ignored the empty

chair beside her and sat down near the window. He felt sorry for her, but it was necessary for him to show that he was his own master. He was Brian Singleton, totally alone, creating his own laws, his own universe. He would establish himself by the force of his own persistence.

'She sells sea shells on the sea shore. The shells she sells are sea shells, I'm sure.' They were all singing, and a man was leading them. He was not Christ; he was Cyril. Cyril had introduced himself whilst Brian had been pondering the aphorisms of the mighty. Next he concentrated on Cyril and the goldfish mouths opening before him.

Whilst Cyril was singing songs from another universe, another time warp, Brian's eyes roamed around the sea of faces.

Normal people tended to lump their mental inferiors into one sweeping category. They called them 'mad' and that was that. But the sub-normal were as varied as trees in a forest, as races upon the earth. It was so easy to recognise the main categories, the cretins looking like various dimensions of Stan Laurel. The mongols smiled happily. Then there were the blank and beautiful autistics; the menacing slight smile stuck on the faces of the psychotics, and ever so many looked just ordinary; these were the neurotics. The no-man's-land people. You could always recognise the quick-witted, charming and dangerous psychopaths; their eyes were always on the make. They did not suffer the curse of indecision, the wandering through the dark landscape of the mind. They followed the instinct of their hands. They had no doubts whilst they destroyed others and themselves. There were so many divisions, so many sub-divisions. His father's mansions had many madhouses.

They were all here, the various cadences of abnormality. A little something had gone wrong in their head, and that was that.

Justice did not exist. There was nothing fair in the order of things. If you fell down upon the floor, people walked across you. If you cared to enter the fight that was entirely up to you. These were the facts of life. The blank universe watched without compassion. Cyril was middle-aged, had silver hair and wore a spotted bow-tie. Cyril was pre-mad. He wore cuff-links and was homosexual. Brian felt tremendous compassion for him Yet he also envied his apparent ability to cope in the normal world. He had seen normals in the streets of Margate that morning. Beautiful ordinary people, shopping in the arcade. Mothers, fathers and child. A pyramid of natural desires and aspirations. There was nothing better in the world than an ordinary family doing ordinary things; living ordinary pre-mad lives; walking, touching, buying, talking. He would never achieve such heights. He would never throw his daughter into the sky and catch her laughing.

A blue-rinsed lady with spectacular spectacles climbed on to the platform to address them. 'And now Cyril will play you some more sea songs. How many know the chorus? I want you all to join in anyway. So come on, let it rip and shake this building to its foundations. Cyril.' The plump madame nodded, and Cyril let rip. Madame stayed on stage, conducting.

'What shall we do with the drunken sailor, what shall we do with the drunken sailor, what shall we do with the drunken sailor, early in the morning?'

'Lalalalalalalalala.' Michelle joined in, with a sudden happy unexpected burst; others hummed; Dolores flashed him a smile, held her nostrils tight with fingers while her other hand pulled down an imaginary chain; while Buzz hurtled with the red monsters of the universe. Larry alone seemed to know the proper words of the song and he belted them out, oblivious to everything else. When the song came to an end, the whole audience exploded with cheers and applause; enthusiasm out of all proportion to their performance. To just be there was probably enough, and preferable to staring at a brick wall, or being mesmerised by the slipping tuning signal on the TV screen.

'Come on, you all know this one. "My Bonnie lies over the ocean". Come on.' Cyril's hands trickled over the keys. Brian decided to join in this time.

'I don't want to cause a commotion, so bring back my Bonnie to me.'

Everything was going well; he would contact his sister immediately he left this place.

'And this is an old favourite. Another song about the sea. All you old-timers will remember it.'

And when Menopausal Madame sang, this time she got quite carried away, as if the song held pleasant personal memories. 'Red sails in the sunset'.

He thought he would burst into tears, so he laughed instead. Dolores waved across excitedly and he waved back. Then she made an ugly face; a most horrendous gargoyle. She then wiped her hand over her face, and threw the gargoyle to him. He was now the gargoyle. Brian Quasimodo played the game. He wiped it off, threw the face back at her. Now she was a Saint Joan, oblivious to the flames. She chucked her sainthood towards him. He suffered, he died, choking silently. He rose on his middle leg. Now he was himself again. He threw himself at her. Now she was Mata Hari. Now he was Douglas Fairbanks. Now she was Marilyn Monroe. Now he was Cary Grant. Now she was Dolores del Rio. Now he was Brian Brando.

'Fire, fire, fire, down below. So get your bucket of water, boys, there's fire down below. Fire, fire, fire moving fast, fire on the main deck, fire on the mast—'

Buzz quickly re-entered the earth's atmosphere, in order to join in this one. He alone was singing with the conducting madame. Cyril smiled and Buzz was alight. And he stayed alight even when the song went out.

'And, finally, you all know this one, so all join in. I expect you all to belt it out.'

'Rule Britannia, Britannia rules the waves, Britons never, never, never shall be slaves.'

Their dreams had come true. They ruled the waves, if not themselves.

They sang in full voice, Michelle, Buzz, Dolores, Larry, Brian, Cyril and Madame, and all the other faces in the hall. This time they all joined in, strident and sure, steadfast and true, ruling the world, benign colonists long before neurosis had been discovered. All the mad of Margate were singing together.

15

Brian was the first to leave the Day Centre. There was just enough time before lunch to take a quick look at the library and spy out the promised land.

Brian walked amongst the polyester people in the town centre, and for the first time since he left Clayton he felt that definite change had occurred in his life. Nobody was interested in him, he was not being noticed and pointed at. He was anonymous and it was wonderful. He saluted his handsome reflection in a launderette window. He could have been quite a lady-killer, given another brain inside that head.

And suddenly he stood before the temple that had sustained him, the beautiful public library; the power-house that had given him a lifeline to this future. He entered and for a moment just stood there drinking in the atmosphere, breathing in that unmistakable aroma of books.

He went to the reference department where students spent their days. Here the smells took on a human flavour; the fragrance of bodies, superimposed upon the tinge of knowledge. And Brian sat down.

He would not borrow a book today. He would wait until the last vestiges of disorientation had disappeared. Books demanded and deserved a total act of commitment. Books were sacrament, communion. Anyway, he was not in a reading mood. He was far too busy acclimatising to all the facets of his new-found freedom.

'Doughnut.' A bag was held before his face. The bag was held by a hand. The hand belonged to a bag. Dolores.

'You following me?' he whispered, but even so, the other occupants of the room looked daggers at him. She munched into her own doughnut and smiled.

'I come here often.' There was sugar on her lips and on her fingers.

He left the room, and hot jammy doughnut followed. He was frightened and ashamed of her company. She was nice when nobody else was about, but now he saw her through normals' eyes and she was positively disgusting.

He left the library, entered the streets and she grabbed his arm.

'I'll walk beside you – through the world today.' Dolores gesticulated grandly, sang with an Irish accent and tenor voice. He unhooked her arm and couldn't control himself any longer.

'Stop it. Stop it. You give all us mad a bad name.'

'Mad? Who's mad?' She stopped singing and became indignant. 'I'm sane, I am. How dare you.'

'If you're sane then act sane.' He thought he would explode with anger. The people in the street pretended not to notice and hurried past.

Dolores smiled again and they continued walking along together, silently, until they reached the Day Centre once more, and the bus stop that would take them back to Hazelhurst.

All the other post-mad were just filing out of the place, and already there was a long line of people waiting for the bus. And it started to piss down out of ominous clouds. But they stood there, oblivious, uncomplaining, getting soaked to the skin. And still people poured out of the building, shuffling down the steps, greeting the rain with yells of idiot delight; dispersing in many directions towards their respective after-care hotels; spilling out into the town, a floating army of morons who filled his entire field of vision. Morons walking in every direction.

There was a workmen's café on the other side of the road, so he walked away from her, crossed over and entered.

But when he was inside he realised he had no money. The man behind the counter had a pencil-thin moustache and looked at him angrily. Brian knew that he stuck out like a sore thumb against these ravenous workers at the tables, all reading the back pages of the *Sun, Mirror* and *Express*.

The smell of bacon sandwiches was almost too much to bear. Brian hovered in the doorway, then walked towards the counter. He hated the man behind the counter, because the man knew that Brian Singleton belonged to those people still spilling out of the place across the road. But Brian Singleton was different. Why did the man accuse him with his eyes? Why did he call him guilty? Wasn't it obvious that Brian Singleton was nowhere near as bad? Couldn't he see that Brian Singleton was different? That Brian Singleton was almost normal? 'Almost.' The word choked in his throat. The man was a tyrant, a stinking despicable prejudiced rat of a human being; you could see it all in his eyes. The whole horrible story of the nature of man.

'What do you want?'

Brian did not even bother to reply and, fortunately, none of the workers looked up from their newspapers. At least he would not be ridiculed by them as well.

'What do you want?' The man snapped again.

'Nothing. Just the time.'

The man didn't reply, except for a small shake of the head; then he poured out a cup of tea, from the huge teapot, and shoved it towards Brian. Then he quickly shouted to the workmen. 'Who wants egg on toast?' The accent was not English. Brian clutched the cup with two hands. It was manna.

He went to a table right against the window, sat and sipped his tea and quietly cried. Such kindness from a stranger was too much for him. And he had vilified the man. The steam from his magical elixir rose with his spirits; the sun shone out of his fingers, sending beams through the glass, bathing all his waiting, drenched comrades in golden light.

It was time to join the others for the journey home, but as he left the café he didn't know how to thank the man; so he didn't.

He stood outside the café for a moment, pondering the kind deed. Now he was glad that he had not killed himself earlier that morning. The action of the stranger made even life worthwhile. Now he decided not to plan ahead; not to cut his throat after supper. He could yet survive to see a crocus.

'Brian, Brian!' Michelle was beckoning him.

'Come on, Brian. You'll miss the bus.' Larry waved frantically. Larry was luckier than the others; seemed to have a wider range of expressions and gesticulations. He was certain that Larry was not a post-mad person. There was always a Larry somewhere, swinging the lead. Brian wondered why they were calling him. There wasn't a bus in sight. But then perhaps it was expected any moment. These people had to know their timetables by heart; with what else did they have to occupy their minds?

'All right, I'm coming. I'm coming.' He walked towards them and they all smiled and waved. Perhaps he could lead them and start a community somewhere. They could hardly fare worse than the rest of humanity. And perhaps their children would grow up to be ordinary, and would fall in love and marry each other. Or they could found a new religious order. He would be in charge because he was more self-aware than all the others and he would make the rules and they would become law.

'Where's the bus? What's the hurry?' When he reached them, all their faces leered at him. 'Why are you all looking at me?' And then the reason became apparent. Dolores was lying on the pavement, a mattress of several overcoats beneath her, and they were watching his reaction.

Her skirt was up to her thighs, and she was stroking herself. He wanted to run but his legs were rooted. He wanted to look away, but his eyes were magnetised.

'Come on, Brian, I'm ready for you.' The lower part of her body writhed slowly.

'She's hot and ready!' Buzz found this even more exciting than all his Pterodactyls from Betelgeuse, and was pushing him forward.

'He's a virgin!'

'He's never had it before!'

'Well, he's gonna get it now!'

They were all gathered for this initiation ceremony; this public execution.

'You've turned her on, and nothing will turn her off, until you do.' Solemnly they all nodded, agreeing with Larry.

'I can't! It's cold. It's – raining!'

'Go on! Go on! Go on!' they urged. He knew no magic words to make the pavement open and swallow him.

'Go on! Go on!' An old lady tugged at his belt, trying to unfasten it, he struggled but it was useless. Dolores with her legs open wide was stretched before him.

'You can't get away with it any longer, Brian Singleton. Prepare for your de-virgination!' He was not even erect. This settled his fate; there was no way that he could survive beyond this day.

'Cheer up, matey, you ain't going to your doom!' Everyone was laughing.

'Ain't he?' Dolores flickered her eyes. 'How would you like to be with your Dolores? I – Yi – Yi – Dolores.' She sang softly, trying to magic him down, and she gently stroked herself.

He knew that he could break away from them whenever he chose. People did not realise the strength that was contained within them.

There was a man in Clayton who was given an abreaction. This gentle ex-soldier became a maniac under the ether mask. He snapped through the straps that held him and floored four male nurses, and almost killed the doctor before he had finally collapsed. The doctor was in hospital for nearly six months.

'How would you like to be with your Dolores?' she hummed, but all else was silence, except for the rain falling upon the shelter roof. There were about forty grey smiling faces gathered for this calvary.

'Oh, Dolores what can I do?'

'Me – now—!'

He decided to break away and run. He would sell his overcoat on The Parade, buy some weedkiller and have a cocktail after tea. They would laugh about him for about a week. And then they would forget.

'A bus, a bus, a bus.'

As if pre-arranged, they all immediately lost interest and became a queue again; eager to board the approaching vehicle. Even Dolores was on her feet and smiling demurely, as if sex was the farthest thing from her mind. The bus stopped and they piled aboard. And when it pulled away, Brian realised that he was not on it with the others. His thighs were cold and he saw that his trousers were half-way down his legs.

Fortunately, there was not a soul about so he pulled them up and sprinted after the bus, doing up his flies and buckling his belt in the process. He ran and ran and faces were pressed against every window watching him. Blank faces now, not victorious, nor unduly miserable. The de-virgination of Brian Singleton had not happened. It had been a child game, an impulse; a sudden idea, and that was that. Something else would crop up to occupy them. Someone else would arrive. He would plead with Dolores to leave him alone. She would understand; she would have to understand.

He waved his arms and then the bus stopped, just before the corner.

'Hurry up then! Hurry up.' The conductor seemed none too pleased, but helped him aboard nevertheless.

The conductor rang the bell and the bus started up again. Brian sat down. 'Saved by the bell!' He was grateful and no longer angry and the rest of the journey was remarkably quiet.

16

'Going for a nice walk, are you?' Mrs Killick cooed when they left the place. 'There's a good boy. You look after him, Dolores. And behave.'

Miraculously the sun was out and Brian was pleased to get away from the hotel, from the other residents all staring into their own private space. He walked along beside Dolores, glad that he had not spurned her, but given her another chance.

He could stomach her more than all the others. Michelle was nice but much too mad and far too young. He liked female company; he liked females. There had never been a female in the world that he had hated; except that nurse who had made him eat his sick, and Mrs Killick.

A walk would help the stodge go down. He smiled back at the guardian and cursed her behind his closed teeth, then he turned his back on Hazelhurst.

Dolores took his arm. 'No.' He pulled her hand away. 'You promised you would behave.'

'Sorry.'

He did not want to hurt her feelings and he wanted her friendship, wanted to trust her.

'What was wrong with you?'

'What? Recently? Today or originally?'

'Were you really in that place for twenty-six years?'

He nodded.

'It's like a life sentence for murder.'

He wasn't keen on this sort of conversation. They were near the esplanade and he made for a sheltered seat across the road, facing the sea. They sat down.

'Brian, you can trust me. My life's not been a bed of roses either.' But then she shook away her own sad recollections and returned to him. 'Twenty-six years! It's like a life sentence for murder.'

'Worse! When you commit murder at least you have the satisfaction of knowing you're paying the price for something you actually did. Mine was a life sentence for nothing, for no crime at all, except being born.'

She touched his hand. Her hand was warm and friendly and this time he did not restrain her. Every human upon this planet needed contact with another; outside the torture chamber of themselves.

'So what went wrong with you? Why did they keep you all those years?'

'I think I was overlooked.' She giggled, but he knew she wasn't being unkind, only embarrassed, shocked.

'Yes; you can be forgotten. If you're not a dramatic type; if you don't give much trouble you can be overlooked; your face becomes part of the permanent fixtures. You know, the red tape rolls on. The institution has rules.'

'Why did they put you in there in the first place? What was wrong?'

'Who knows? Many reasons. Everything went wrong right from the start. When I was a baby I remember my mother telling me that I didn't want to be born. One day I heard her telling the lady next door, that she was so long in labour that my brain got starved of oxygen. Something was wrong with my brain right from the start, apparently. It could have been the oxygen. It could have been the forceps. It could have been anything. The genes, donated down from a great-great-grandfather. Who knows? Anyway, one thing for sure. It was as if the filter in my brain had burnt away. Things came into my head that should have stayed down below. Demons; monsters; I had no choice. My brain writhed with maggots, with all sorts of horrible ideas. They say that when my mother died, I was alone with her for maybe a week. She was stinking and decaying when they found me. I was twenty when they took me away. I tried to injure myself, to gouge out my eyes, but I'm much better now; I try to cope.' He looked straight at her and was amazed to see tears in her eyes.

'You've had a hard life, Brian, but maybe the worst is over now.'

The wind had dropped. All of a sudden winter was dressed as spring. The sea was a table-cloth set before them. It was a Paul Klee sea, and he was the funny Paul Klee man, on his little crooked boat, killing the crooked serpent fishes with a long crooked lance. He covered his erection. She hadn't noticed.

'You deserve a bit of happiness now, Brian.'

'Yes, I do.' He was glad she was not suggesting herself as consolation prize. But then she reached into her open neck and dived down as if to pull out her huge breast. Brian closed his eyes but nothing happened and when he dared to look again, Dolores was holding up a five pound note.

'A fiver? How?'

'Ah ha!' She winked and he didn't want to know anymore. 'I've been keeping it near my heart for a special moment. Let's go and have a drink.'

'Don't waste it, it's too precious.'

'For you, Brian, anything; but don't tell the others.' She pushed the fiver back down her dress and patted her breast. 'It's our secret. Come on.'

He liked secrets but he wasn't keen on drink; nevertheless, he followed her across the road, and they walked for a few moments until they reached the old and shabby part of Margate, and there they entered the Drunken Sailor.

It was dilapidated on the outside, but within there was red plush and brass.

'Don't worry, Brian, nobody's going to bother about us here.'

A few men played skittles and nobody paid any attention to them.

'What are you drinking?'

'Ginger beer, please.'

She raised one painted eyebrow, made no comment, went to the bar, and returned with drinks.

'This is the first time I've had ginger beer in maybe a year.' He sipped and enjoyed, and she swigged upon her pint of ale.

'Do you know, my life's been child's play in comparison. And I always thought I had a rough passage. Smoke?' She held the box before him and he took one, then sucked in her flame, and felt wonderfully dizzy, immediately. Brian then sat back in the deep wooden chair, savouring the luxuries of life.

'Gosh, I've got a thirst today.' She poured the entire glass down her throat. 'Same again?' He hadn't finished, hadn't even really started, but he nodded. She went and came back with two more.

The men playing skittles roared. Some dusty laughing workmen entered and soon the place was filled with faces. But no one was interested in them. 'I'm happy. I can pass in a crowd.'

But her mind was somewhere else. 'As a matter of fact, my life's been very uncomplicated—' She wanted to talk about herself, so he gave her the stage. But one of the workmen came to the table and she smiled up at him.

'Hello, Dolores. Ain't seen you for a few weeks. What are you drinking? Same as usual?' The man with the ruddy face turned to him. 'And you?'

Brian shook his head, and the man smiled, when he returned from the bar he put another pint glass before Dolores, saluted, winked and joined the skittle-players.

Dolores quaffed down her third entire pint without pause. 'I come here regular. When I've got the wherewithal.' She tapped her breast, then touched her fanny, and off she went to the bar again. Brian didn't mind her anymore. He was high on smoke and ginger beer and the place was whirring. Nothing mattered. That man had been familiar with Dolores and therefore had to know something about her background, and consequently they all knew, and therefore they also had to know about him. Anyway, it was obvious Brian Singleton had something missing in the head. He was not quite right, but he didn't care anymore. They would have to like it and accept him, or jump through the plate glass window. He was not ashamed of his face.

Dolores sat down and sighed, took her fourth pint more slowly, and continued her story. 'You might call my life an open and shut life. The open and shut story, of an open and shut person, with open and shut legs. Well, not really. As far as I'm concerned they've hardy ever been shut. It's nearly always been opening time as far as I'm concerned.'

Brian felt really relaxed for the first time in a million years. It made a nice change to hear about another person's tribulations.

'That's my trouble. I've always been a highly sexed and generous individual. I always was a passionate creature, still am.' She gave a little wave to two of the skittle men, then she continued. 'I was lovely. Still am I s'pose, it's me bone structure. And believe it or not I was even lovelier in them days.'

Brian relaxed back and allowed her to soar into full flight, nodding every so often, to show that he was listening.

'I was so happy, and so generous. I wanted to give myself to the world; so I did. It really all started one day in particular – I was working as a waitress in a factory up in Liverpool. It was lunch time; thousands and thousands of grey silent men were crowded into the canteen. I felt real sorry for them; they seemed so lifeless, so devoid of spirit. Womb to factory, to tomb. You know the sort of life. So, I got this urge to do something for them, to cheer them up, to bring a bit of excitement to their lives, as they were shoving tasteless shepherd's pie into their cake-holes. Guess what I did? I jump up on one of the tables; I pull up my skirt, pull down my drawers, and I shout, "Hey, boys, how about this for afters?" '

Her voice resounded throughout the pub and the men looked at them, but she didn't notice. 'So I danced on the table top and they laughed and cheered and went mad. Talk about the miracle of the dry bones. 'Course I got the sack. And that's how it all began. Dancing like that, showing everything I possess, became a sort of habit.' She was a little quieter now and he was thankful. Her clothes belied her character. She was dressed more like a friendly outsize shop assistant than a freelance sexual maniac.

'Soon I found I could kill several birds with one stone. I could travel around and survive, and at the same time could make men happy. I could jolt tired bored men out of their little lives. I had something to give at last. I could make their eyes light up, and their pricks stand up.'

Her words certainly worked the magic for him. His worm was stirring, seemed to have a mind of its own. He didn't fancy her at all, but his worm had other ideas.

'So I travelled all around the country, getting lifts by standing in the road and hoicking up my skirt, pulling down my drawers and dancing. I can even rotate my pussy in Samba tempo. What lorry-driver could resist Dolores? They would literally queue up to stop and pick me up. And there in the back of the van: lovely, naughty, juicy games. And that, Brian, is the story of my life.' She sighed, then quickly smiled and went to the bar just as the man was ringing the bell.

'Come on, lads, closing time. Last drinks.'

Dolores returned with another pint for herself and another ginger beer for Brian. She sat, but he felt uneasy. All the eyes in the place seemed to be swivelling towards them.

'Come on, Brian, drink up! Plenty of time.' She blew him a gentle kiss, but under the table her fingers were creeping along his leg. Her hand was a crab about to grab his swollen prick. But she promised! She definitely promised to behave! Brian didn't know what to do. Dolores was utterly impossible, incapable of keeping a promise.

'You promised! Leave me alone.' They would see, and laugh at him. She was a horrifying bitch, she had brought him here with the sole intention of totally humiliating him.

'How would you like to be with your Dolores?' she crooned softly, her eyes half closed; a swaying cobra about to strike. Then she released him and stood up. 'Hey, would you like to see me perform? Brian? Would you like to take a nice close look at my pussy?'

He could not run out of the place. He was pinioned by invisible straps and all the other men were gathering around. If it had been possible to move he certainly would have hurled himself through the plate glass window.

'How would you like to be with your Dolores, I – yi – yi – Dolores, not Marie, or Emily or Doris—' Her hands were clasped behind her head, and her thighs slowly rotating.

'Come on, Dolores! Good old Dolores. Give us a dance!'

'Come on, hot twot.'

'Come on, Dolores, show what you got!'

'Come on, Dolores, good old Dolores!'

All the eyes were leering and ravenous. Hieronymus Bosch was riding again, his people dancing upon the debris, at the end of the world. And now even the people behind the counter were enjoying the joke. They obviously knew her well.

'No please! Don't! Don't!'

But they all roared with laughter as she got on to the table and slowly started to dance to the violins of Mantovani.

The men whistled and laughed as her hands teased and gathered up her skirt and started pulling her knickers down. Brian could take no more, he lunged for the door and dashed into the cold refreshing afternoon air.

He walked away from the pub, away from the depraved creatures, away from the impossible Dolores. From now on he would avoid her like a plague.

Then he saw the telephone box. And his heart leapt high again and he entered. For a moment he stood there to consider his situation. All was not lost. More had happened to him in Margate in just a few days than had happened to him in the twenty-six years in Clayton. Despite Mrs Killick and Larry and Dolores he had survived, and had not killed himself. And now he was going to get in touch with his own flesh and blood. He lifted the receiver, dialled directory.

'There'll be blue birds over the white cliffs of Dover,' Brian sang until the woman came on the line. 'Hello. Directory? I want to contact my sister. She lives in Southampton, Hampshire.'

The woman had a kind voice; he was sure that she was going to be helpful.

'Can I have the name and address, please?' She was a stupid bitch. That was her job.

'I don't know exactly. That's why I'm asking you. Oh, yes, I know her name. Her real name was Jane Singleton, but she changed it to Jeanette. She's a famous actress, so she shouldn't be hard to trace. She definitely is in Southampton; last I heard.'

'I'm sorry, caller, but you must give me some more definite information.'

Brian did not feel like being rude to the woman, but she definitely did not know her job. Surely the whole object of Directory was to find people. If you knew the location of the person you certainly would not need help from them. It was obvious. But Brian was not unduly worried or unhappy. He would try again tomorrow, and possibly get a more intelligent assistant on the line. 'Thank you. I understand. Goodbye.' He replaced the receiver, left the telephone box and slowly strolled through the streets. There was nothing much to do before tea, and there were hours to kill, but he did not feel like borrowing books from the library today. There was time; there was plenty of time.

He wandered through the busier area of the town. A woman stopped to stare at him, but he didn't care anymore. Yes, he was a moonwalker, and if this was the earth, thank God he was on the moon.

He poked out his tongue as far as it would go and he pulled out his ears. If she wanted to look at an idiot, Brian Singleton would not disappoint; he would give her a proper idiot. She hurried on quickly, and he laughed. He continued killing more time. He had an awful lot of it.

Summer

17

Every morning he stood here at the entrance for ten or twelve minutes, watching the people pouring in. He came to the station directly after breakfast, just to see them all spilling out of the trains.

The arrival at the seaside. This was a special moment for all these faces; a time of expectation; a holiday to revitalise pale tired bodies; a chance to escape from hurtling through the tunnel between womb and tomb. The seaside was an immortality attempt. A flight from the crushing weight of sameness. You could read all that on these faces.

'Pouring out of Margate Station so many. I had not thought that death had undone so many.' He paraphrased the poet who also had had problems at this resort.

Summer had brought him hope. Just standing here in the sunshine reading faces was enough.

The long winter had lasted right up until this July; a winter that had gobbled up the entire spring, and only now had relinquished its stranglehold on the world.

Later he would phone his sister. This time he would make a really serious attempt to locate her.

He was content, slowly finding his feet, settling in, settling down, surviving. Buzz also leaned against the wall, his eyes closed, also drinking in the sunshine; enjoying, lost in joyous solar flight. Buzz was a far easier companion than almost all the others at Hazelhurst House. It was a totally non-demanding relationship. And Dolores had not given him much trouble recently. So, all in all, things were slowly progressing. Brian was therefore almost at peace with himself and the world. He watched the families particularly as they emerged; the excited, eager children swinging between their good-looking parents. He loved happy family groups. There was nothing else worthwhile. It was the only decent way of living upon the earth. All else was substitute.

He stood mesmerised by the flowing crowd, making its way down towards the beach, spilling out and filling the entire strand for as far as he could see; all the way across the wide shore was this endless, engulfing stream of mammals, following ancient drives; ancient courses.

Every morning he came here without fail and he would especially focus upon a family of three. A boy child between mother and father.

If he looked long enough all that summer, he might see himself between his own mother and father, coming out of the station.

If he could only come face to face with himself, with Brian Singleton brought here for his seventh-birthday treat, his entire past would be wiped away and he could start again, start from here. And he would become an engineer, and his mother would live to ninety-three. Somewhere, seven-year-old Brian Singleton was waiting for a chance to re-kindle his existence.

It was a hopeless dream; a nice, stupid and useless dream; but he allowed himself this one indulgence every morning.

'Come on, Buzz.' His twelve minutes were up, so he moved away, going with the crowd, Buzz by his side, down towards the beach and the sheet glass sea.

Another perfect day had descended upon the coast of Kent and there was no wind. Steam was already rising from the sand. The whole shore seemed to vibrate, to shimmer ever so slightly.

He wandered the esplanade, his eyes fixed upon the children whooping with delight in the huge open swimming-pool. Surely this was the place where he had killed that crab, almost forty years ago? That day when the crab became re-incarnated in him. The claws started to clutch because ordinary people were enjoying themselves; families were together. He laughed to stop drowning in his own loneliness; but then he saw the donkeys. Real live donkeys. Nineteen seventy-eight donkeys. The grandchildren donkeys of those donkeys he had cried for all those years ago.

A whole line of donkeys was moving across the sand. Each donkey had a happy child upon its back.

'Want a donkey-ride, a donkey-ride, a donkey-ride,' the child within cried, all the way down to the shore. But then he found himself amongst the swarm of people; the congregation of sun children sprawled all over the sand. Most were prone, had totally abandoned themselves to their God, the eternal sun, giver of light, but some played; threw balls, chased each other, laughed and larked. Kissed, cuddled, walked hand in hand.

Brian slowly wound his way through the arms and the legs; past the small groups of children building their castles of sand.

Buzz walked beside him, reading his comic, oblivious to everything else. He had read and re-read those same pictures ever since Brian had arrived in Margate.

Brian noticed the telephone box on The Parade. 'Won't be a moment, just stay here.'

Buzz stopped in his tracks and Brian bounded across the beach and up to the street. But a red-faced sweaty woman beat him to the box, and was already nattering away.

He turned his attention back to the beach, and to the line of donkeys near the edge of the sea. It was a dizzy day, with all the heat of Africa blasting the shore. If he could only remember Jeanette's exact last address, there would be no problem. She sent him a postcard once. It was a picture of a pier; she was on holiday in Southsea. But she did write her permanent address upon it. He was so proud of that postcard and he showed it to everyone in Clayton. And he especially showed it to Charlie, a young fat boy he wanted to cheer up. Brian pointed out the pier to Charlie, and the boy laughed and snatched the postcard away, and tore it up and swallowed it.

Brian tried to recall the address and thought he'd got it right; wrote it down on his hand. But the next day he cried, because in the washroom he washed his hands and washed the address away, and it was lost forever. All that could have been fifteen years ago : he wasn't sure.

He had not heard from his sister since then, but even so he would not stand in judgement; nevertheless, she could have dropped him a few lines, at least now and then.

But today was not a day for bemoaning the past. It was too happy a day for unhappiness. Besides, what was his sliver of pain against the eternal blue universe; against the incredible sun pouring down its bountiful rays?

He returned to the beach, but his friend was nowhere to be seen.

'Buzz, Buzz.' He felt embarrassed. People would think that he thought he was a bee. 'Buzz! Buzz!' He shouted, panicking. He was responsible. Since Buzz deserted Larry, he had taken on the task of looking after the boy. He felt sick. Mrs Killick would give him hell if Buzz got into trouble.

And then he saw him. The boy was quite close, crouched beside a group of adults. But they were unaware of the boy's presence; all of them being asleep, except for one man, who was comfortably relaxing back in his deck-chair, reading the inside pages of a wide open newspaper.

In his hand Buzz held a magnifying glass and he was focusing the sun's rays upon the newspaper. The circle of light was getting smaller and smaller; smoke started, but Brian could not get there in time. The newspaper ignited, burst into flames, and the man jumped up shouting. Burning pages scattered around.

It all happened very fast and the sunbathing people sat up and looked dumbfounded at the flames, and the young boy jumped up and down with delight. 'Fire! Fire! Fire! Fire!'

Brian was able to unfix himself and he grabbed the boy's jacket and pulled him away. He could see the anger in the eyes of the crowd, as they started to connect the thing that was happening and the way it happened. Buzz continued to jump up and down and he brandished his magnifying glass as Brian quickly pulled him away from the irate crowd and off the beach.

'You're spoiling it. It's a fire! It's mine! You're spoiling it! You're spoiling it!' It was Buzz now who was irate.

Brian did not say a word and dragged the boy as far away as possible; up on the promenade and lost amongst the sauntering crowd. 'Right, you've had your fire for today.' They both walked in silence, Buzz now downcast, more the naughty boy than the deprived arsonist.

An ice-cream van stood in the kerb. Brian tortured himself, watched the eager children, one after the other, holding up their money to the sweating, joking man. 'Come on, come on, kids. I only got twelve pairs of hands!' The children laughed as they skipped away with their lollies and their magic cones.

Brian would have given anything for an ice-cream, because ice-cream was the most wonderful thing in all the world. But the fifty pence Mrs Killick had given him this week was long since spent. Now he longed for a Ninety-Nine; an ice-cream cone with a flaky chocolate bar stuck in the middle. For that he gladly would have sold his soul to the devil.

Here on the sweltering pavement, Brian knew exactly how he

would react to the Prince of Darkness. 'What can I do for you, young man?'

'Oh, hello, Mephistopheles, you've come just at the right moment. I would love a Ninety-Nine. A big one.'

'And what are you prepared to give in return?'

'My eternal soul, of course.'

'Good. Fine.' The devil would go straight to the ice-cream man and return with the enormous cone; the most delectable prize. 'There you are, young man. Now come with me.'

And Brian, licking his cone, would follow gladly, descending into hell. What a way to go. Unfortunately, Mephistopheles somehow did not appear.

Brian felt in his pockets; stuck his finger into the broken lining. There was not a hope in hell; not a coin secreting there. No coin ever had the chance to fall into his lining, no coin lingered there long enough to get lost. Anyway, whenever Mrs Killick gave him his pittance he always clutched it tight in his hands. Things went missing too often in Hazelhurst, especially unguarded silver coins. 'Now you see it, now you don't.' There was no coin; there was no devil; there was no ice-cream.

Brian walked away from the van, looked down upon the beach, and thought about nothing.

'Brian! Brian!' Buzz followed. 'Please don't be angry, Brian. I promise never to light another fire!'

Brian smiled at the young beautiful face, and felt happy again. Maybe all was not lost for Buzz. He put his arm around the boy's shoulder, and squeezed his flesh; then he sat down on the paving stone. It was hot enough to fry an egg. The boy sat beside him.

'I'm sorry, Buzz, but sometimes I get very dejected.' He did not tell the boy that he'd tried dozens of times to trace Jeanette, and all without success. He had written to the public library in Southampton; he had talked to the police; to the social workers; he had tried umpteen times through directory enquiries, but it was useless. And he would continue to try even though it was useless. The only chance would be for her to contact him. And she didn't seem very keen to do that. He had this picture of her in his mind. A sweet girl with honey hair of fifteen or sixteen. But now she would be in her late fifties. It was useless.

'I get fed up with doing nothing all day. It gives me a pain in the head. I have this tight band, Buzz. It gets tighter and tighter all the time. If the screw turns just one bit more, my head will explode.'

But Buzz was oblivious to Brian's words and maybe it was just as well.

Across the road was Dreamland, and here were Marine Sands. And over there was the famous Victorian Clock Tower. To the left of him was Marine Drive and The Parade; the pier; the Winter Gardens, and farther on was Cliftonville. To the right of him was Westbrook with its Marina and Westgate and Birchington.

Brian knew the geography of his seaside. He had explored these paving stones throughout the spring. It had been his way of escaping the tentacles of Dolores. He had walked far to the left, and far to the right; slowly, slowly, ever so slowly over the wide pavements, sometimes making sure not to tread on the lines; other times making certain only to tread on the lines.

There was nothing he did not know about the Isle of Thanet; it had been his spring-time reading in the reference library. It was necessary for a prisoner to know the geography of his cell, and the passages and quadrangle outside. 'Official meterological readings for the period 1965–70 show an average of 1600.7 hours of sunshine – annual rainfall 24.10 inches, maximum mean temperature 13.04° C.

'The excellent air tonic, bracing and stimulating, makes the resort ideally suitable as a place of residence – especially so for young children. Margate's ability to provide health is amply endorsed by the number of authorities, organisations, etc., which have established schools and convalescent homes in the area.'

'Shit!' How he hated the fortunate resort, and the fortunate residents and the fortunate families who could afford to come to holiday here. 'Shit! Shit! Shit!' Cursing was better than crying. His crying days were over. All he wanted now was a donkey-ride, and a ride down the Aeroglide and a jump on the trampoline, and a ride on the dodgem cars. It wasn't asking too much from life.

'Summer's nice. Like summer. Lots of people; summer's nice,' Buzz buzzed.

Brian was pleased that Buzz was oblivious to Brian's pain.

'I'm forty-seven in fifty-one days. I'm going nowhere. I'm

travelling nowhere inside my skin!' He knew he was talking to himself.

But Buzz put his hand on Brian Singleton's shoulder. And the boy's other hand held up a silver coin.

'Fifty pence! Where did you get that?'

Buzz shook his head, laughed. He held the coin high, as if he had just retrieved it from the wreck of a Spanish galleon.

'Tell me! Tell me! Where did you get it? I won't tell anyone!'

'Mr Killick fell asleep on his feet the other day—!' Buzz delivered in a dreamy sing-song. 'I went through his pockets. He thought someone was tickling him!'

'That's not right, Buzz. Pinching like that's not right.'

The boy's smile dissolved. He bit his fingers.

'Don't worry, I won't tell anyone. I promise.'

Mask of tragedy became mask of comedy. And Buzz dashed over towards the ice-cream van.

The dream of ice-cream was no longer a dream. Brian's hopes soared with the seagulls. Little boats were dotted on the turquoise sea; gaily coloured sails bobbed, children laughed. Summer was definitely nice.

Buzz was standing with two ice-cream cones, but he was shouting at the man; his head shaking, his eyeballs bulging. Brian quickly went over.

'I gave him the fifty pence piece, but he won't give me change.' Buzz held the two ice-cream cones high in the air; two beacons above the storm of his face.

The fat man with the thin moustache was red in the face, was trying to explain something; appealing to the children customers all around, wanting them to agree with him. 'He give me thirty pence, so I give him two ice-creams. No? You saw? No? You saw?'

Two small children slowly nodded their heads, but they did so without conviction.

'See! They saw! They saw! Only thirty pence!'

Buzz screamed and cried. 'You saw, Brian, you saw the fifty pence.' He shouted at the man. 'Ask him! He saw the fifty pence.' Brian had never heard the boy so articulate.

'Go away, sonny. Go, before I call police.'

Brian gently tugged his friend's arm. 'Come on, Buzz, come on, you can't win.'

'You saw, Brian! You saw! You saw! You saw!' Buzz was appealing to him, desperate for confirmation.

'Come on, Buzz. They all take advantage. It's the same everywhere.'

'He's a cheat! He's a liar! I'll kill him! I'll burn him! I'll kill him!'

The ice-cream man muttered as he continued to serve his growing queue of young customers. 'Bloody madmen. Bloody mad people. Margate is too full of them. Don't know why they let them out.' Then he smiled to a child. 'What you want, sonny? Ninety-Nine? Fiery Furnace?'

Buzz shook and cried and Brian tried to pull him away. 'No, Buzz, don't!'

But Brian was too late; Buzz had hurled the two ice-cream cones at the van, at the man. People stopped to look and the children laughed, as the two cones slowly slithered down the woodwork.

Brian could also have cried. He had wanted that ice-cream more than anything in the entire world.

'Come on, Buzz.' This time he did not need to pull the boy away; nor did he have to appeal to him any longer. Buzz just followed, and they both slowly wandered from that place, without even looking back. And both were broken.

18

Northdown Park was quiet. The holiday-makers and day-trippers were not interested in the rose garden and the ornamental pool.

Brian and Buzz walked in the shade, amongst the ordered, beautifully tended plants and flowers. Only local people were in evidence. It was easy to tell that they were locals, because they were mainly middle-aged and old and sat feeding the birds and counting their days. They were far too relaxed and un-neurotic for holiday-makers. These were the backbone of old England. The truly pre-mad who would never even reach the first traces of mental anguish.

Brian reckoned he could have gone the length and the breadth of the park doing cartwheels, and still they would not have noticed, as they chatted spasmodically to each other about the world that was and the world that would never be.

The scent of roses seduced the air and Brian was happy again. There should have been a notice on the gate : 'Abandon neurosis all ye who enter here'.

And Buzz seemed happy. The ice-cream incident was a thing of the past. In this respect the post-mad enjoyed the privileges of childhood. Nothing lasted long. Anger and happiness were here one minute and gone the next. Relationships, intrigues, hurts, fears and pain were quickly gone through, and spent, and started all over again. Life was an incredibly fast roundabout. One moment you wanted to kill someone and the next you were cuddling them.

The fire incident on the beach was over and done with. He was no longer angry with Buzz and Buzz was no longer angry with him. Anyway, things were far better on this score. Gradually he had managed to wean the boy away from his need of a daily fix of fire. But he wasn't kidding himself, Buzz definitely still had that urge to burn down the world, although Brian had contained it.

He liked his new friend; even though he had made an enemy

in the process of making this friendship. Larry would slit his throat with a razor blade given a quarter chance; but the price was worth the candle. He laughed. The allusion seemed quite apt. The boy was attached to him. 'Me and my shadow'. Brian's voice did a soft-shoe shuffle.

'What?' The innocent eyes of the boy were remarkably blue.

'Nothing.' He was glad that the boy depended upon him. It gave him status, a sense of security. It saved him from going to pieces.

He decided he would like to play, nobody would notice; nobody was looking anyway. He bent down and tucked his head into his shins. 'Come on, Buzz.'

Buzz gawped; mystified. 'What?'

'What are you waiting for?' Then it occurred to Brian that his position was questionable, to say the least. It was terrible that the boy should even think that he was suggesting buggery, yet Brian could not stop himself from laughing.

'What do you want?' Buzz became really agitated.

Brian, watching the boy upside down between his legs, had no doubt about his own sexuality. Never in a million years would he let anyone ever enter his arsehole. And neither was he a shit pusher.

Once, in Clayton, whilst wandering through the garden, he came across a very ungay gay, an ex-head waiter named Christopher, tending the chrysanthemums. 'Come into the bushes. Come on, I'll suck you off!'

'No, thank you very much.' Brian replied. 'I'm just going to have my tea.'

'That's all right, enjoy it, so long.'

'So long.'

And that was that. The sum total of his homosexual experience.

He was a little hurt that Buzz should even have such thoughts in his mind. Maybe the child had been buggered before. He loathed that Larry. That was probably the strength of the old stinking swine's concern for the boy. Then Brian realised he was still bent double. 'Come on, Buzz, leapfrog.'

'Leap who?'

'Leap over me, idiot! Sorry! Jump, Buzz! Leapfrog!'

Then it dawned on the boy and his face opened into a wide smile. 'Oh. Leapfrog.'

He laughed and leaped over Brian, and Brian leaped over Buzz. And Buzz leaped over Brian and Brian leaped over Buzz. All the way towards the park gates they went, leaping and laughing; leaping over each other. And nobody noticed.

'They were only playing leapfrog, they were only playing leapfrog—' Brian sang as he bent and stood, and ran and bent again.

'They were only playing leapfrog, they were only playing leapfrog.' Buzz joined in singing and their singing caused some woodpigeons to scatter from the trees, and still nobody heard or noticed.

'And they both lived happily ever after.' Brian invented a final line and they leapfrogged right out of the gates and the nice old people of Northdown Park continued their summer sleep, and none awoke.

Once outside the park Brian straightened. 'Come on, Brian,' Buzz moaned, he would have continued leaping to the end of the world.

'No, not here.' Brian shook his head, disapprovingly, emulating high authority, and Buzz complied at once with the order. It would not do to be a conspicuous after-care in this neighbourhood; for this was quieter, posher Margate, where such things would not be understood. All that Brian was seeking was anonymity. The height of his ambition was to be able to disappear into a crowd and to survive there.

Then he heard shrill happy laughter. It came from across the leafy lane, beyond the railings. The notice board revealed a girl's grammar school; and there were the buxom girls charging across the lawn with their hockey sticks.

The child Brian metamorphosed into a leering leprechaun, and he marched like Groucho Marx, across the road, and pushed his head against the railings, hungrily gobbling up the sight.

They wore blue skirts and long white socks. They wore too much for a summer day. Their leaping tits seemed such a burden.

They were upright cows; beautiful sweating cows, and anyone of them would have made a delicious meal. All of them; every other one; every single one; every joggling, jingling beauty; every flaxen-haired; every dark vixen would have been delectable.

'Left titty! Right titty! Left titty! Change – titties! Right titty! Left titty!' he sang.

He loved females. All females, except Mrs Killick. Anyway, she wasn't a female; she was a computer with a blow wave and a cunt.

He loved the female thing; the mystery of girls; of ladies; of women. He was a woman-lover. The sheer shape entranced him. The physical beauty of women in summer was almost too much to bear.

Men and women inhabited different planets; different aeons. Men and women did not touch, did not collide. They both went their own ways through space. Men had brought humanity to the edge of destruction, into the pit of degradation, and only women could pull us back, could save us, if they had pity enough. Only the feminine aspect; the contemplative creatures, these unknown. Atlantean people could bring us back to sanity.

He longed to be young and beautiful, to be a girl playing hockey in Margate on this summer day. How fortunate they were; how privileged. He wanted to cry for such beauty. He did 'Shall I compare thee to a summer's day?'

'Eh?'

'I said, are you thinking what I'm thinking?' Brian came back to earth, lied.

'What are you thinking, Brian?'

Brian licked his lips. 'Can't you guess?'

'I was thinking about the fantastic fire I once lit in Bradford.'

'Is that all you think about, Buzz?'

'What else is there?'

Brian pointed through the railings. 'I was undressing them with my eyes, Buzz. You try it, Buzz. You try undressing them with your eyes. Go on.'

Buzz, eager to please, swallowed hard and tried to concentrate. 'All right!' But his heart wasn't really in it.

'Undress that one. Go on.' Brian pointed to a plump, blonde Picasso lass, flying naked through cubist foam; heavy, thick and beautiful. The soft hills; the rolling downs; the pink summits; the furry thicket. He, too, ran naked playing his pipe, squashing a bunch of grapes between her legs, swallowing her nipples, diving, swimming into her. The earth stirring. Its eyes trembling, catching alight, shaking volcano erupting. An earthquake. 'Are you concentrating, Buzz?' Buzz nodded. 'Have you undressed her, Buzz?'

'Yes, Brian.'

'Is it nice, Buzz?'

Buzz caught on, he had ignited. He was nodding excitedly. He was voracious, he was trembling.

'Is it nice, Buzz? Is she nice?'

'Very nice, Brian. Very nice. She's wonderful. She's very nice, Brian.' The boy was clutching his penis. It was all to the good. It would take him out of himself, take him away from fire. A fire between the legs was a burning bush. She had a burning bush. They all had a burning bush. He wanted to taste the fiery fruit.

'Right, Buzz. You undress that one! I'll undress that one! You take her, and I'll take her. I'll fuck that one, you fuck that one. You take the blonde one, I'll take the dark one.'

Brian was happy sharing out the hockey girls. There were fucks enough for share and share alike. The girls now constituted two new teams. Teams that cut across their own existing teams. One team of gorgeous nymphs belonged to Buzz, and the other team belonged to him and he was fucking every one of them and was drowning in the joy of it all.

But someone started to spoil all the fun. A spoilsport teacher in the distance was throwing dagger looks of anger. The girls hadn't minded him and Buzz at all, hadn't even really taken any notice of the two ravenous lechers at the railings. The girls were proud of their breasts, were brandishing them. The girls were aware of their power, of their beauty, of their magnetic pussies.

But the magical moment was about to end; Brian observed two women against a wall, nattering away. They were obviously in charge of the sirens. And one of them pointed to Buzz and himself, and now they were advancing with menacing ugly faces. Why could they not have compassion for someone so hungry as himself? He didn't even want a nibble. All he wanted was to drink in the beauty of the girls. Was that too much to ask?

All he needed was the scent of sex to recharge him; to bring him back into the human family. He was not a dirty old man. Would that he were. He had never shot his seed into feminine flesh. He had no wish to propagate his moronic genes.

'Come on, Buzz, quick.'

But the boy would not let go of the railings and the teachers were almost upon them. Now the girls noticed, and they laughed. The darlings were not irate like their teachers. They were confident and beautiful and would inherit the earth. He loved them.

'Come on, Buzz, away, away.'

Buzz did not understand the danger but, finally, he complied, and they both ran down the leafy lane, until the school was out of sight and Buzz was laughing, laughing.

'I like jogging, don't you?'

Buzz laughed like he was catching butterflies with his mouth.

They both jigged and jogged down the well-groomed leafy lanes of posher Margate, two happy harriers in slow dream marathon; it was a race with no beginning and no end.

Birds hovered, chatted; frozen squirrels winked and rhododendrons waved.

Brian waved back, acknowledging the invisible cheering crowd.

But then his legs got caught up in the fog of cotton wool and his heart was pounding, so he slowed and stopped, rested his hands on his knees, with his head bent down and panted.

Buzz thought that it was leapfrog time again, so consequently jumped right over him. And now they both just stood there, stooped, breathing deeply in order to continue this earthly life.

And now there were lusty boy voices. 'Here, Chris!'

'Here! Over here, Gerry!'

At first they could not see because of the hedge but there was the unmistakable thud of a football being kicked about. Sure enough, when they entered the huge playing field a game of football was in progress. Brian knew his seasons and therefore had to think for a moment. The cricket season was in full swing, but here were these schoolboys who didn't seem to mind being unfashionable. They were in their school colours and a young bearded teacher was referee; therefore school had obviously not yet broken up for the summer holidays.

The grass certainly seemed to need rest and replenishment. The boys were merrily kicking the green out of existence.

As he watched, he remembered a certain schoolteacher in Clayton. His name was James Tunnicliffe. James slept two beds away from Brian. During the day James could never leave the washroom. For in the beginning he would wash his hands, then he would wash the sink, and then wash the taps; and because he had touched the taps in the process he would start washing his hands all over again. And on and on. And then he would wash the towel, and then the knob on the door, and then the floor, and then his hands all over again. He could never make it to the corridor. So they just left him there, all day in the washroom. James Tunnicliffe and his accursed water; until the evening when two nurses would come and firmly take him to his bed. His hands were raw, raw from constant rubbing, and scrubbing and wiping and rinsing. Brian often joined him in there for a chat. James Tunnicliffe was his name, and at this moment, on this glorious day Brian knew where the poor man would be.

'How are you, James?' He would call at night, across the bed, in the dark. 'How are you, James?'

'Could be worse. Could be worse.' That's all he ever said. He deserved a star for valour.

Brian called over to one of the boys. 'When do you break up?'

'Tomorrow. Can hardly wait.'

'Yeah, tomorrer,' another boy confirmed. It was odd that the cockney dialect should have invaded so deep into Kent.

'Comprehensive school?' Brian enquired.

'Yeah. Westbrook Secondary Modern. We break up tomorrer.'

Then the other one started to sing, 'One more day at school, one more day of sorrow, one more day of the rubbish dump and we'll be home tomorrow—' Now his friend took up the chant and they both sang lustily as they stood on the sidelines watching the football game ebb and flow. 'God made the bees, the bees made honey, we do all the rubbish work and teacher gets the money.'

Tomorrow they would be as free. Free to catch tiddlers and to go scrumping; and skating and swimming, free as boys throughout the long endless summer. He wanted to pat one of them on the head, but quickly withdrew his hand. It was a sophisticated world that he was living in, he could not afford to make one single mistake.

When he turned to his young companion, he wasn't there. Then he heard gales of laughter. Buzz had joined the football game and was in possession of the ball and was rushing down the field as happy as a minstrel.

The two teams of boys stood frozen, watching him and the teacher was furiously blowing upon his whistle.

'Come on, Brian, come on,' Buzz yelled, wanting him to join the game.

Brian was compelled to run towards the boy and show him and the others a thing or two.

Buzz shot the ball to Brian, Brian kicked it back to Buzz, and down the field they went; one to the other, backwards and forwards; and suddenly there was the goalmouth. Brian closed his eyes and kicked with all his might.

It was the first goal he had ever scored. Brian Singleton turned to his companion for a hug and a pat on the back. But Buzz was not smiling.

'Go to hell,' he spat.

The bearded teacher came, whistle stuck in mouth, blowing like a runaway train. 'What are you doing here? Get off this field. How dare you spoil the game.'

The boys gathered, delighted at the turn of events. And now Buzz smiled, but not out of happiness. He pulled out a huge penknife, pulled it open and held the point towards the teacher. The man's eyes opened unusually wide, and so did his mouth, but no sound came out. Buzz slowly went towards him, still smiling.

'Come on, Buzz, come on. The game's over. The game's over.' Brian whisked the knife away from the boy and closed it. Buzz stood with his hand jugging forward, as if he was still holding the knife.

'Come on, Buzz. Let's go.'

The boys gathered closer and surrounded them, but the teacher moved away.

'He's nuts. Hey look, they're nuts. They're idiots.' They jeered and laughed and pointed. They were falling about with laughter.

'More out than in! More out than in! More out than in!' Buzz yelled at his crucifiers. He poked out his tongue, he pulled out his ears, he spat, he cried. Tears streamed down his face.

Brian gently pulled him away, away from the field, away from the jeering mob.

'Don't look back,' he commanded.

Buzz disobeyed. He kept on turning around and pulling faces and poking out his tongue.

They had to cross the wide field before they could get out of sight, and unfortunately they did not get changed into two pillars of salt in the process.

19

This was the first time that he had explored Margate proper. The Margate where Margate people lived. The beach was but a quarter of a mile away, yet it easily could have been a million miles. These quiet, tree-lined, comfortable avenues made a refreshing change.

The after-cares tended to congregate on the front. Whenever they left their places of residence they would make a beeline for the beach. It was easier to get lost in a crowd, and not be noticed and stared at.

But the front made Brian sad. There were too many happy people there; too many children eating crisps and ice-cream and excitedly buying tiny packets of flags for sandcastles; too many swigging from tins of fizzy drink. Too many being cuddled. And how he envied them all by the water; some on lilos, drifting gently on the waves.

His feet dragged. He was forever condemned to push his way through the world. One day he would give up his drugs, and maybe lose the blurring around the outer edges of his eyes. Now he could only concentrate upon the objects that were immediately in front of him. One day he would lose his blinkers but meanwhile, here in the centre, he was safe. On this narrow ledge he could survive the black abyss that loomed all around. The animals snapped and groaned at his feet, but he was just slightly above them and out of reach. 'Pity.' He was a slow tight-rope-walker, imprisoned in the circus of himself. The drugs were his balancing pole. He had no choice.

A car drew up by the kerb and a clown emerged.

'That's funny.' But it was far from funny. It was terrifying.

It was not a dream. The clown was as large as life and twice as horrible, with a ping-pong ball attached to the end of his nose and a yellow smiling face set upon an outsize purple suit. He seemed to have no neck, just a gigantic orange bowtie. But Brian did not have to pinch himself; he knew that the clown was real enough.

Buzz laughed but Brian just stared. The clown was brisk and business-like, as he unloaded a huge case from out of the boot of the car. He noticed them watching him but he did not smile.

It was gratifying to know that there was another clown in the road. The clown lifted the huge suitcase and carried it towards a large house.

Brian was eager for an explanation. And then he saw the sign painted on the side of the car. 'JOJO THE CLOWN, ENTERTAINER, MAGIC, PUPPETS, AVAILABLE FOR CHILDREN'S PARTIES, ETC.'

So that was it. The clown knocked at the door of the house and a host of excited children opened it for him. There was great joy and laughter, and then they all disappeared inside; but they did not close the door behind them.

Buzz tiptoed along the path.

'Buzz.' But the boy took no notice and went to the open door. Brian followed to bring his companion back. The boy just drifted from one ridiculous experience to the next and Brian wondered how the boy had survived so far.

When he got to the door there was so much happy laughter inside that he felt he could not deprive his young friend; so he allowed him to enter.

No one would notice and no one would care. Anyway, he was doing no harm; he had never been in an ordinary house since he was seven.

This was a soft, comfortable, purring house. He could see into the far room where the clown was getting ready for the show and laughing children were sitting cross-legged on the floor.

'Is it all right, Brian?' Buzz shivered.

It was the first time that the boy had shown any sort of social qualm. He was improving.

'Yes. It's perfectly all right, Buzz,' Brian reassured. It was a large house and there was room enough for all. Anyway, they were doing no harm. They would not steal anything. He wanted to see the clown. He had never seen a real clown. The only clown he had ever seen had been in a looking-glass.

A child in the far room turned his head, looked at him and Buzz, then looked back at the clown again. By the hush it was obvious that the show was about to begin.

But where was mother? Surely the little boy had a mother.

Brian indicated to Buzz to stay where he was and then he crept quietly along the passage.

The door was slightly open and there were some women preparing food in the kitchen and gaily chatting to each other.

Everything was so clean and bright and the smell of scent and polish was everywhere. Brian crept back to Buzz, and then they joined the children in the huge lounge, standing right at the back and not one child took the slightest bit of notice. All was ready for the show. Absolute silence reigned, and then the clown commenced.

'Now, I want the birthday boy to stand up beside me. That's right. Come along, Christopher.' And smiling Christopher, bright like a sweet shining apple, joined the clown who was now well launched into his automatic patter. He was bending balloons into poodles and giraffes, and the children laughed and laughed.

Buzz jumped up and down, clapping his hands before him, rigid, shaking; not smiling. The clown looked across at them, his suspicious eyes not synchronised to his patter.

But Brian did not panic. As far as the clown knew Buzz and Brian were friends of the family, or relatives, so he relaxed and enjoyed the disappearing rabbits and the appearing doves.

' "Izzy wizzy, let's get busy." Come on, repeat the magic words.'

And they did. They all shouted. 'IZZY WIZZY, LET'S GET BUSY.'

It worked. It worked. The water turned into Coca-Cola.

But the eyes of Funny Face were not as happy as the mask; they seemed tired. They were automatic, dying eyes, watching yet another congregation of comfortable, overfed kids.

The mother whooshed in with cakes and sandwiches. She was a tall lady, a statue that had only just come to life. There was nothing jubilant in her manner. Like the clown, she, too, suffered from the sad eye disease; she too, wore the smile mask. And with her came her burnished companions, with plates and plates of goodies, biscuits, jellies, sweets, crisps and cakes and ice-creams.

It was the luckiest day of his life. The first party of his life.

But then she saw them there. It was inevitable, of course, for Brian could not create magic and render himself invisible. He did not know how to convey to her that all he wanted was to see the clown. He smiled to prove that he wished her and the children no harm. Surely she would not wish to create a scene of unhappiness on such a happy day.

And he was right. She merely murmured to her friends, who all looked at him and Buzz with puzzlement. Then they tiptoed out of the room.

Brian wondered why she was being so understanding; so nice. But then it occurred to him that she probably thought that they were helping the clown; and she was right. He was a clown helper; he was helping Buzz the clown. He was helping clown Brian to get through this life.

The children were helping JoJo the clown with one of his tricks, and now he would help himself to some of the goodies on the sideboard. 'Come on, Buzz.' His eyes showed the boy what was now expected of their fingers.

The children rocked and pointed, and held their mouths with wonder as Brian and Buzz found other uses for their mouths. The cakes, the crisps and the sweets were so nice. The marshmallows were paradise. He tried everything all at once; except the jelly. He would wait for the jelly until the very last.

Buzz gaped open his mouth and Brian aimed a peanut down the throat. And another, and another all coated with chocolate. Five marshmallows, pink and white, scrunched together into the mouth all at once. No, six. There was room for another. And another.

There were some party hats spare on the sideboard. So he gave a silver one to Buzz and placed the gold one upon his own head. And they both admired themselves in the peach mirror, two clowns with crowns, cramming food into their mouths. But then the lady of the house came between them in the mirror, and this time she was not smiling.

'Who are you? What are you doing here?'

'We're having a party!' The innocent face of the boy smiled up at the tall taut statue.

'Are you with the clown? Thought you were with the clown,' she snapped.

'Not with the clown. Looking at the clown. He does tricks,' Buzz replied.

'Been with the clown all my life!' Brian added softly. He didn't want the day spoiled for the young children. He didn't want to take yet another rotten memory into the future.

'Who are you?'

'We saw the clown. We came in.'

Realisation came to the mother, then anger. 'How dare you! How dare you!' But still she managed not to shout and none of the children were yet aware of the confrontation.

'Sorry. We got carried away. We didn't mean it. We'll go quietly,' Brian whispered, so as to keep it all nice.

Buzz rummaged about on the sideboard. 'Here's a cracker. Brian, here's a Christmas cracker.' The boy's hand brought a cracker out of the box. 'Pull it with me.'

The lady was now very angry indeed, but Brian felt she was being slightly unreasonable; true they had invaded her privacy but they had done no real harm. All he could do was wait for the thunderbolt.

The woman went to the french windows. 'Charles? Charles?' She might have been calling someone to come in for a cup of tea. 'Charles? Charles?'

A man immediately entered through the french windows. His face was bright red.

'I found them here. I thought they were with the clown.' She seemed really scared of the man, who snarled down upon them.

'What the bloody heck!'

'Sorry. I thought they were with the clown.'

'Am with the clown.' Brian pointed at himself in the mirror. 'Been with that clown all my life.'

CRACK! Buzz had pulled his cracker and a paper hat, and a wrapped motto shot into the air. Buzz scampered for it, laughing around the floor.

'Get them out of here, Charles, but do it quietly. Don't want the children—'

Something dawned upon the husband. 'They're off their rockers! They're nutters! They're—'

It was easy to recognise after-cares in Margate. The town was crawling with them; there were protests about them. There were always letters about them in the local press; always questions in the Council Chamber. They lowered the tone.

Brian had followed the whole controversy from the reference library. The facilities and the ambience of Margate were beyond reproach. The air was wonderful, the beach was superb. Margate was a wonderful place for a holiday. Known and renowned the world over.

But suddenly, a plague of moonwalkers had descended upon the resort; these idiots were everywhere; they were proliferating, and the natives were worried. The owners of the larger hotels and the local tradesmen were gathering their protests, getting up petitions. The local louts were angry, rampaging and at night seeking punchbags for clenched fists. Only the smaller landladies of Margate seemed to find the whole enterprise worthwhile.

'We're going now. Thank you very much. We're going quietly.' Brian knew that he needed to keep his cool when the man grabbed him by the neck and by the arm and frogmarched him out of the room.

'Come on, Buzz. The party's over.'

Buzz did not need to be told twice. A phalanx of the whispering ladies came to the door with them.

'Quiet, Charles. Quiet. Please, quietly.' But she really didn't need to say anything. None of the children had noticed and if they had they certainly weren't bothered.

'All right. You don't have to push, we're going. We're going.'

And then they were in the street, under the Margate sky again, both in their party hats.

'If ever I see you around here again, I'll smash your bloody faces in.' Charles pushed them both away from the door and they hurtled down on to the gravel path.

'Thank you.' Brian was not being sarcastic; he had genuinely enjoyed himself. The afternoon had been a moment out of time. He loved the house with peach mirrors. It was a dream house. Perhaps he was lost in one of Buzz's comics. 'Thank you.' He picked up his paper hat, got to his feet and brushed himself off. The man slammed the door.

'Thank you. Thank you for the party. Goodbye. Continue to enjoy yourselves.' Brian waved to the faces at the window. They looked like balloons about to burst. 'Come on, Buzz.'

Buzz got to his feet, placed his hat solemnly upon his head, rather like an archbishop crowning himself. A gesture of strange and utter sophistication. And then he produced a cracker from his coat's interior.

Buzz was the magician now, and this time Brian did not mind participating in the magic, so he pulled that cracker in full view of the window faces, and a whistle and another motto flew forth and Brian picked it up. Then they marched away along the road in their silver and gold paper hats; Buzz merrily tooting the same shrill note and Brian patting the little motto in his pocket. He would read it again and again that evening.

20

It was late afternoon and some people were beginning to stir on the beach; getting their things together, preparing to make an early getaway and avoid the mass exodus. Very soon now the sun-burnt lobster-red faces would be shuffling back to the station, back to the city; back to their lives.

The sun was on its way down, but Brian's hopes remained high. It had been a full and pleasant day. He put his arm around the boy and he did not care. They could easily have passed for father and son.

And then the exterior of the fun-palace caught his eye. Brian read the sign. 'DREAMLAND'. He had never been in Dream-land; it was beyond his means. 'Have you enjoyed yourself?' he asked the boy.

'Best day of my life.'

'Me, too; best day of my life. Come on, Buzz, let's go home.'

'No. Not dark yet. Come on.' The boy went down. 'Come on, Brian, leapfrog.'

The entrance to the fun-palace was a very public place; people were entering and leaving all the time, and even though he felt embarrassed, Brian didn't want to disappoint his best friend in all the world. Anyway, nobody would mind; people would just think that they were pissed. Besides, all the 'Norms' were half stoned out of their minds. A group just getting out of a coach were well away; laughing and joking, shouting and singing. There were more out than in this summer in Margate. More out than in within Dreamland, or without.

So Brian sighed and leapt over the boy, and the laughing boy leapt over him.

'Cheers! They've also had a few too many!' A cockeyed man shouted; igniting the air with his breath.

'Hooray! Hooray!' Another held out a Guinness bottle and staggered towards them.

And Brian waved and leapt over Buzz and Buzz waved and leapt over Brian. And soon the whole company of puffing super-annuated citizens stood there cheering Buzz and himself and then they filed into the fun-palace.

Brian was about to bend down again when he saw the five pound note on the pavement. One of the old people might have dropped it, one of the old people must have dropped it. 'Hey! This belong to someone?' He held it up, then realised that they had all gone into the place; had been swallowed up by Dreamland.

'What is it, Brian?'

'It's a fiver!'

Buzz went right up close, inspected it, read the words. 'Bank-of-Eng-land – I promised to pay the bearer on demand the sum of—'

'It's a fiver, Buzz! Haven't you ever seen a fiver before?'

The last time Brian saw a fiver was when Dolores had produced one out of her dress. But this one was his, all his to spend, to spend on anything he wanted and not on rotten booze. 'Our luck's in, Buzz. I'm sharing this with you. I'm giving you half.'

'No! Don't cut it! It's money!'

Brian laughed. 'I mean, two pounds fifty for you, and two pounds fifty for me. And don't you tell Mrs Killick or anyone. Promise!'

'I'd cut my throat with my pen-knife before I'd say a word.' Buzz patted his pocket and then drew a finger across his throat.

'Come on. Let's go in here.'

They stood before the mouth of the fun-palace as the boy struggled to read the sign. 'Dreee-Dreee—'

'Dreamland,' Brian said, and they entered.

It was another world. A world of dream; but a land that he had always inhabited. The inside of his head had become the world; he had entered his own true kingdom.

'Can everything be like this from now on?' Buzz asked.

There were side-shows and stalls for as far as the eye could see. There were people shouting and people laughing for as far as the eye could see.

He had not got up today. They had not turfed him out of Hazelhurst and into the giddy heat. Mrs Killick had an aberration, had allowed them to stay late in bed. He had been dreaming all morning. He was dreaming in the late afternoon. He was on a big wheel. He was going round and round and round. When he reached the highest point he started to come down. They hurtled towards the faces looking up. They whirled and spun. They whisked, zoomed and vortexed. They were gold-fish people. These were the prizes.

He was the gargantuan gift if you threw the darts in the right place, or the balls into the hole, or the wooden discs at the nuts. They were nuts. They were faces being laughed at; they were laughing. They were flying through the sky above Dreamland, above Margate-on-World.

They could see the blue sea, the green fields, the tree people, the ants, the giraffe people, and everyone was singing. Cave music blared, Neanderthal kids roamed in packs, shouting and punching the sky. And all the time there came from Buzz one continuous laugh. Buzz was in his dream.

They were in the belly of the earth, twisting through caverns; now he was pre-mad, mad, and post-mad, all at once. He knew this place too well. He was chugging along the Styx and there were all his relatives, the skeletons, waving as he passed.

He was riding up and hurtling down; taking leave of his heart, instead of his senses.

They were on a padded floor in a castle full of air. The padded floor made a change. You could fall over to your heart's content. You could jump up and down, and smash your fists against the walls and they did not bleed, and all the children were leaping with them.

Now everyone was mad. This was a cushioned mad-mosque, for shoes were left outside. This was a holy place of laughter; substitute for prayer.

'I'm frightened, Brian. It's wonderful.'

'It's Wonderland! It's Dreamland!'

'Can I go on them? Can I go on them? On them? On them?' Buzz pointed to the cars, so Brian took him for a ride.

The last ride in a car was when those two men came for him in Harrow-on-the-Hill. Those policemen were twenty feet high, and took him straight to Clayton. And here he was.

The idea was to miss the other cars. But Brian was pulling on the wheel, and every time they collided he leapt up and down in his seat with joy.

He was sure that time was passing. Certainly the money was

passing. This was an expensive dream. Money changed hands. 'Candy-floss! Candy-floss!' The man spinning was Rumpelstilt-skin Charlie with candy-floss in his hair and on his eyelashes. He poured a tiny amount of sugar into the centre, and out spun the magic fibre, and it was gone in three sticky gulps. That was life.

Way back in his mind he remembered a man coming around the street. It was in Harrow-on-the-Hill. He was three years old or seven. It seemed to make no difference. He looked out of the window and the candy-floss man was outside.

'Candy-floss, good for the belly. Ask your mummy for a penny. Buy my candy-floss today, before I have to go away.'

Out they came, all the quiet children, slowly, out of their quiet houses, and they began to laugh, and they followed the Pied Piper away, away, as he dispensed his candy-floss, spun from his candy-floss tree. They danced and sang for joy, within the threads, within the branches and leaves of candy-floss. And the whole world filled with candy-floss and they were never seen again. And that is why there were never any children to be seen in Harrow-on-the-Hill since that day and none till this present time.

Anyway, it was all a dream in Dreamland. It may not have happened at all. 'Row, row, row, your boat, gently down the stream, merrily, merrily, merrily, life is but a dream.'

When he died Dreamland would not exist anymore; nor the United Nations building, nor Margate beach, nor Mrs Killick, nor the Second World War; nor his father's death; nor this hot dog that he was pushing into his mouth. But whether Dreamland was a dream or not, it was a dream to be enjoyed.

And so, they continued spinning on the roundabout, sailing on a sea of fizz, aiming at the cretin coconuts. Crisps! Popcorn! Crunchie bars! Sausage rolls! Toffee apples! Hamburgers! Ice-lollies! Hot dogs! They never stopped feeding their faces.

The ghost train did not scare them. The ghosts seemed less grotesque than most of the passengers on this journey. But that was only to be expected. But the tunnel of love was for them. He loved his friend with all his heart and his friend loved him. He did not kiss his friend but they did put their arms around each other, and held each other in the dark. He and Buzz loved each other forever and ever and ever; as they gently bobbed up and down through the entrails of Dreamland. It was very quiet here.

And then they skidded all the way down the sky-ride slide;

127

tumbling over and over, cuddling each other. This love could be allowed, for no one minded friendships; boys and boys, and girls and girls; all children of this joy inferno, confetti falling into the fire. The old and the young, the good and the bad, the happy and the sad, the brave and the frightened. All were falling children of God. All dreaming in Dreamland.

But the best thing of all was the hall of distorting mirrors.

In this place, the giants and the dwarfs came together, and held hands and danced. These creatures in the glass were the natural outcome of the inhumanity of humanity. These were the past and these were the future. Moon children mutations. This was his home. This was where he and Buzz were entirely at home. All his life he had stared at himself, and seen himself like this; going backwards and forwards and moving sideways. But, now, it was all out in the open, in front of all the other grotesques. No longer need he be surreptitious. He need not be afraid of the tribe, they would not fall upon him and destroy him for being different. Here everyone was different.

He pointed at himself with derision and delight and wonder. He could change in the wink of an eye. He was a head without a body; he was a head with just one eye. He was only legs. He had no legs. His face was an egg, was the universe. He was a blot on a page. He was a giant. He was a dwarf. He was David and Goliath come together. He was a fuck of flesh. An orgasm. He was an angel and he was a monster.

He gurgled, grimaced, cocked his fingers, stood nobly; he was one round roly-poly head upon a roly-poly body; he was a snowman. This was Dreamland. And a frail long hand stretched twenty-five feet through a forest of legs. The elastic-band hand was grabbing his elastic-band arm and trying to pull him out of the place.

It was Buzz and he was outside, in the world of normal madness; where quiet people stood lifeless in an arcade, pushing money down the throats of machines, and pulling down the handles, time after time after time. Old ladies with cigarettes stuck in their mouths; men glued to the machines, hypnotised by the whirring discs. They did it as if the end of the world would be announced on the nine o'clock news.

'What are they doing?' Buzz stood with mouth gaping, wanting to be fed with pennies.

'They're called fruit-machines. One-armed bandits.'

Buzz hopped away, one arm hidden behind his back. 'I'm a one-armed bandit. I want some more money.' He held up a fifty pence coin. 'Nearly all gone.'

Brian had exactly the same amount left. Anyway, they were about to leave Dreamland. He wanted to save just a little money, just enough for the next day. But Buzz ached for the slot-machine arcade. Brian shook his head and made it plain that this particular pleasure was not on.

'It's ridiculous. Look at them. They work hard all their lives, for money, and they can't wait to throw it all away.'

'But we threw all our money away, Brian.'

'Yeah, Buzz, but we're mad.'

The boy nodded sagely. He could see sense. He understood. He followed Brian out of Dreamland.

They crossed Marine Terrace to have one last look at the holiday crowds, but Brian was astonished to find the beach almost deserted. They had been in Dreamland just a few minutes, and yet the whole day had vanished. 'It always flies when you enjoy yourself.'

A few families still straggled, and one or two lone people still loitered or were asleep on the beach, but in the main all that was left of the steaming day was the litter strewn across the sand. The deck-chairs had almost all been stashed away by two furiously working youths in swimming trunks.

His heart leapt but not for joy. They had missed tea. Mrs Killick would be angry with them. She would throw them out. But then he remembered that he had missed tea a few weeks previously, and she did not seem to mind too much. 'As long as you're in by a decent time. Can't have my little babies wandering about at night. Never know what mischief you'll get into.'

He relaxed. It was not yet dark. He was full to the brim anyway, and did not think that he could tackle fish paste sandwiches and a cup of Ovaltine on top of everything else. She was a mean old cow. She would approve of them forgoing food.

He would wake up one morning and find Mrs Killick gone. She had got the overnight flight to the Bahamas; leaving her drunken husband in charge of the thirty-six sheep. He would keep them all in a pen until they were parcelled and returned to their previous addresses. He mused across the road from Dreamland. Then he came back to his friend.

'Guess what I want to do now very badly?'

Buzz shook his head.

'Go on, guess.'

'More candy-floss?'

Brian shook his head.

'Ice-cream? Fireworks?'

'Guess. Go on, guess.'

Buzz shook his head as if he wanted it to drop off.

Brian took the boy by his hand. 'Come on, I'll take you there.'

'No. I'll wait here.' The boy seemed whacked but happy.

'All right. Don't you move. Now you stay right there.'

The boy nodded and Brian gave a little wave and walked on to the empty beach. 'I grow old . . . I grow old . . . I shall wear the bottoms of my trousers rolled.'

He rolled up his trousers, took off his shoes and socks, then put his shoes back on again. He rolled one sock up into the other, pushed them in his trouser pocket and continued walking. 'Shall I part my bare behind? Do I dare to eat a peach? I shall wear white flannel trousers and walk upon the bitch—' So that was the secret. Prufrock was kinky. 'I have heard the mermaid singing itch to itch—'

He mis-quoted. A touch of iconoclasm for the beachcomber somehow seemed in order. Besides, sometimes he did not feel pure enough to quote the master correctly.

Brian Alfred Prufrock stooped to pick up a comb that only had two teeth; using it as a Hitler moustache he goose-stepped for a few yards.

Then he saw a plastic doll, without legs or arms, and with its eyes washed away. He kicked it as far as he could.

He would not find the answer here; there would be no message in a bottle. 'I'm a prisoner in a Chianti factory. Come and save me.' Now he was Enrico Caruso for a few seconds, belting out the rich majestic tenor tones. 'Torno Sorrento – or I must die.'

No one could come to help him and he could help no one. No one would save him, and he would save no one. He did not wish to see anyone bobbing up and down in the waves drowning. He could not swim. Out of the sea or within it.

Summer was on its way out. You could smell autumn in the

air, although there was no sign of it yet upon the trees, autumn was peering around the corner, an assassin ready to strike.

But a few days remained, a few weeks maybe and there were dolphins in the ocean who had not set up institutions for the less fortunate of their kind. They swam together. In the water there was hope.

But he had fifty pence in his pocket, and therefore there was no reason to be depressed. The sun was squashing against the horizon. It was an egg shape now. He was aware of the universe and the earth within its belly, slowly turning away from the sun. The inadequate expectant brain of Singleton Brian was insignificant.

And then in the distance he could see the donkeys; the real reason for his walk upon the beach. There were several of the creatures silhouetted against the red sky, resting after a hard day's haul.

In the vanishing light he could not define the features of the animals; he could only make out their outline. But even from this distance he knew which one he favoured, which one he would wish to ride upon.

He quickened his step and his heart beat faster and he approached the beloved creatures just as they were about to be led away. A wizened man was their master, a young lad his helper; they were clicking with their mouths, gently urging the beasts away to their place of rest.

Brian decided to be direct. 'I'd like a donkey-ride.'

The man did not laugh or shout; he just stopped and scratched his head. The little boy smirked to see such fun.

'Can I have a ride, please? Won't take a few moments.'

But the man did not seem eager.

Brian held up his silver fifty pence piece. 'Please. All this for one ride. Please.' He was gladly offering all his wealth. 'It's all the money I've got in the world.' He emptied his pockets to prove his words.

The man was old and had seen two world wars, and was a donkey man, therefore he was bound to be human.

'All right. Just one quick ride,' the man grunted.

Brian contained his joy as the man pulled out one old white mare from the herd. 'What's her name?'

'Daisy.'

Before he mounted, Brian whispered in her ear. 'Lovely Daisy.

I love you. I love you.' And he did not care if the man was watching, because the donkey understood. Her sad eyes understood everything. Donkeys had seen it all.

And Brian mounted and the boy led the donkey across the darkening beach, and Brian's head swam in the setting, congealing red sky. And he waved and waved as the donkey jogged beneath him. He waved to the small figure of Buzz upon the promenade. 'Buzz! Buzz! I'm having a donkey-ride! A donkey-ride!' And then he sang. 'Daisy, Daisy, give me your answer do – I'm half crazy, all for the love of you.'

All his life he had wanted a donkey-ride. It had been his fervent prayer throughout his long childhood, and at last it was being answered. Tomorrow he would definitely make contact with his sister. Definitely. Before the end of this summer he would be reunited with his own flesh and blood. He knew now that everything was possible.

The young boy led him right across the sand, and he waved back, back at his friend upon the shore. 'Hooray! Hooray! A donkey-ride! A donkey-ride!' He had achieved the very best thing in the world.

He was a child again and he did not care that his wave was not being answered. Nobody was watching him, but he was not alone. He was at one with the creature within himself, and beneath him.

Autumn

21

Brian left the game of tiddlywinks so as not to start screaming. He was tired; tired of their faces, their expressions, their mannerisms.

He went to the window, smiled at himself, stared out. He had played tiddlywinks since the beginning of time. Every evening after tea, came this high point of the day.

There was nothing to do, nothing to be done. His only occupation was this breathing in and out; this slow suicide.

He knew every jigsaw by heart. The country cottage; the horses; the babbling brook. The outside of Buckingham Palace, The Royal Family; the speeding express train. He could close his eyes, drop the pieces down, and they would fall into their correct places.

Buzz, Dolores and Michelle were engrossed in their usual tiddlywinks, and there was Larry, reading and re-reading last week's sports newspaper. And all the others were in their usual positions, a dozing semi-circle in front of the slipping television picture.

He opened the window to allow the human fug to escape, and the smell of decay, of burning leaves greeted him. Unmistakable signs that summer had gone.

He wondered if he would live to see another.

Michelle abandoned the others, sat down beside him, and just looked into his face. There was no combination to her brain, no sequence of numbers to unlock the poor child.

Larry looked up from his racing paper and sighed. 'Hate being here in winter.'

Buzz was still totally absorbed in his tiddlywinks, and did not notice Dolores desert him. He was shooting coloured counters all around the room and cheering, gruffling, right down in his throat, pretending to be a frenzied football crowd.

Dolores joined Brian at the window. 'I hate the days drawing in.'

Brian did not need to cover his mouth. He knew he would not scream. He had not screamed these last nine months.

There was nothing to do, and nowhere to go. He could not really wander the streets of Margate any longer, and he had not been able to trace his sister. And she had not contacted him. Nor had he managed to do without his pills, his chemical safety net. So, all in all, there was a distinct possibility that he would never be able to participate in the human race. He was merely existing here. Hell would have been preferable to this plastic lounge. Day in, day out, nothing happened all the time.

'Hey, Doreen.' Larry shoved Dolores, called her by her proper name. Brian knew exactly how she would reply.

'Are you addressing me?' she responded haughtily as she always had and always would.

The lounge floor split apart and they all tumbled down into the molten interior of the earth. Hell was cold. It was bloody freezing, but there was a smell of scorching meat. Some were still knitting as they hurtled down, some were praying, some were still muttering, staring straight ahead into themselves. Down they all went, one after the other. The whole of Margate was subsiding into the quiet inferno; the whole of Kent, the whole of England.

'Hey, Dolores. How about you and me pushing off together?' Larry shouted.

'You'll be pushing off soon enough, don't you fret. Oh I can't abide winter.'

Brian had a sudden desire to place his hands around her throat and squeeze and squeeze; instead he talked to Michelle. He liked talking to her. She always smiled back and rarely replied. 'Going nowhere, Michelle, but then who is? Not the "Norms". How old are you, Michelle? Often meant to ask.'

There was something rather marvellous about asking questions that would not be answered. 'Have you got a family somewhere, Michelle? What brought you here? What goes on in that brain of yours? Have you got a brain, Michelle?' She smiled all the time. 'You're like me, I suppose, you haven't got anyone. You're a silly cow, Michelle. I loathe you. You make me fucking sick.' And still she continued smiling. He blew her a kiss.

His sister was obviously busy otherwise he would have heard from her. God knows he had made every possible attempt to get into contact with her, but he did not blame her. All he wanted to do now was to find a job. 'I've tried everything this summer, you know; building sites, offices, cafés. Course, they all laughed.'

He didn't really blame the humans of Margate for rejecting him. If only he could. There was anger somewhere inside himself, but he could not call himself to battle. He could, however, negotiate the carpet of the lounge and make his way to bed, and sleep. At least he could accomplish that much. Brian was a genius in the land of the dumb and the numb. Perhaps he would become spokesman for all nuts. 'Idiots of the world unite, you have nothing to lose.'

If he could muster them all together, if he could stir all the residents of all the lounges of all the small seaside hotels from all the resorts around the coast, they could slowly glide off together, an army of moonwalkers, all gibbering, towards the capital. And because the mad were proliferating at such a fast rate there would be no end to them; their numbers would be running neck and neck with the Chinese; and if you included the Chinese mad, the moonwalkers would reign supreme. They would choke the whole of London. There would be no room for any 'Norms' anymore.

'You know, Michelle, I should have liked to be a priest. That's what my mother wanted. She thought it would have been an easy life. Anyway, why should I work? I haven't committed any crimes, except being born.'

'Yes,' she replied.

'I'm a seven-year-old, Michelle. A seven-year-old who's sometimes twenty. A twenty-year-old who's sometimes forty-seven, next birthday.'

'Yes,' she said.

'I must do something, Michelle. Idle hands are dangerous. They belong to the devil. That's what it says in the "Bhagavad-Gita" : "If these hands do not work, how can these worlds survive?" '

'Yes,' she said.

He took his hands and put them around the neck of Brian Singleton. He placed them there ever so gently, and he squeezed. Michelle continued knitting and smiling.

There seemed to be no way out. God was a devil. He left you no way out and no way in.

'I'm strangling myself,' he gurgled. Dolores punched him playfully, scratched her crotch through her dress and left the room.

'Nightynight.'

'Strangle yourself and extinguish me,' his eyes in the window were saying.

'No,' Michelle said. 'No.' So you could get through to her after all. He felt dizzy, closed his eyes, swam within himself for a moment. There was no point in trying to strangle yourself, you would merely lose consciousness and start breathing all over again. There was no hope anywhere.

'All right then, I won't. Does that make you happy?'

'Yes,' she replied.

He stroked his sore neck. 'I don't know what I want to do. I can't face anything.' Tears were falling down his face. He could not face his face. His head fell forward, he sobbed into his lap.

'No.' Michelle gently touched him. Brian Singleton continued to cry, and everyone else except the girl ignored him. They were a bunch of heartless, brainless, compassionless bastards; fortunately.

'Forgive me, Michelle. Sometimes the tears just fall out of my eyes for no reason.'

'Yes,' she said.

Buzz was now building a tower with playing-cards. Larry crept up behind the boy and was about to blow it down when Mrs Killick entered and clapped her hands. 'Come on, rouse yourselves. Come along, my darlings. Bedybyes!'

Michelle darted out of the room at once, a conditioned cat, and then Mrs Killick turned off the television screen, shook a few of her charges awake. 'Come on, darlings, time for bed.'

'What! What!' One man brandished his arms, then shielded beneath them, as if expecting a beating; but in the main the rest merely moaned quietly and slowly left the room. Then Larry sidled out. Mrs Killick clapped her hands behind Buzz and then blew down his tower. He turned smiling, murdering her with his eyes. Then he, too, left the lounge.

He was alone with Mrs Killick and tears were falling down his face. He did not wish her to see so he closed his eyes.

'Come on, Brian, a good night's sleep will make you feel much better. Come on, love. Nightynight time.'

'Good night, Mrs Killick.' He wiped his tears away, quickly left the lounge and went upstairs to bed.

'Up the hill, the wooden hill, up the hill to bed.' He improvised a merry chant, so that nobody should feel they could take advantage of him, just because he happened to be crying. Maybe tonight his prayers would be answered and he would die in his sleep. Sooner or later his luck had to change.

22

There were far too many beds in the room; indeed, there was hardly room to take off your clothes. It was always a struggle, especially if you were fastidious and did not care to parade your pubic parts in public.

And the dingle-dangles of the other men did not exactly intrigue him. The post-madmen were either cavernous or obese; and they all stank. This was the conditioning-room where all vestiges of desiring to continue living were soon eradicated. Six months in this hell-hole and everyone, but everyone, longed for everlasting death.

Brian never looked out of the window in this room; firstly because he could never get near enough, and secondly, because there was probably a slide out there. It led straight from the windowsill into an incinerator, down in the garden somewhere. They merely placed you upon it and away you would go. And your ashes would be used in egg-timers, so that the National Health could recompense themselves for all their years of downkeep.

Larry was telling a joke, in between biting off a piece of toenail. He displayed his sagging genitals so blatantly; it was as if he was unaware that he had any balls at all. Then it occurred to Brian that Larry was joking about him.

'Why you so ashamed of it, Brian? Why do you always hide it?' He turned to the other old men. 'Hey! Brian thinks he's been blessed with a special prick!' They all took no notice. All they wanted to do was sleep.

Larry could not be more wrong. There was nothing blessed about Brian Singleton. He was a venereal crab; just the same as all these, his brethren, they were all residents, crawling over the testicle of God.

Larry started telling another joke. 'Anyway, Margate Crematorium kept on getting requests from Uganda for tons of human ash. So they crated it out, sack-full after sack-full, shiploads of the stuff, of this human ash. Then one day, the director of the crematorium became curious, so he phones up this black chief in Africa and said, "Why do you want all this crematorium ash?" Now wait for it, there comes this reply in a kind of Paul Robeson voice, "But Bwana, haven't you ever heard of instant white man?"'

The old men laughed and coughed and spluttered, then they all assumed their foetus and coffin positions beneath their blankets.

Brian carefully took off his shoes and polished them. He always took care of his shoes. Always rubbed and rubbed them until they shone and he could almost see himself in them.

Larry's bed was beside his, and Larry lay watching him but he did not mind. He was proud that he had not given up the ghost, he would yet show them all that it was possible to retain one's self-respect, even though the dice were loaded against you. In the midst of death he was in life and he was aware of the contradictions, the gyrations of his mind. He would be an example to them all. If intellectuals and artists could survive the prison camps of Siberia there was no reason why Brian Singleton could not survive Margate.

He took off his trousers and held them so that the creases fell together, placed them over his arm, pulled back the mattress, and gently laid them upon the paper over the springs. 'That should keep them nice.'

Larry watched but said nothing. His stinking clothes were in a heap at the end of his bed, and on the stool beside his bed there was a tumbler of water, and in it a gigantic pair of false teeth, grinning there; waiting for the dark to swallow their owner.

There were eight beds in the room. Four would have been more than enough. There were eight bedrooms in Hazelhurst House and each room contained eight souls. According to anyone's mathematics the Killicks were clearing a small fortune. 'The Killicks are making a killing. Sixty-four killings every day.' It was incredible that this thing was allowed, but then life was incredible. Justice was a dream, a mirage. Better not to hope for it.

And the food was just awful. He mused upon the tyranny of the regime. Breakfast was the only worthwhile meal. Otherwise it was tasteless, stinking, puerile, predigested stodge and muck; muck swimming in muck; followed by muck. It was better not to think about the food. How he longed for an ice-cream. For that alone he hoped he would survive and live to see another summer.

He crawled into bed and considered the Killicks for a moment. They were not exactly cruel. In fact, they were not cruel at all. They simply did not consider that the post-mad were human and had any rights at all. She was a monster, and monsters behaved monstrously. A praying mantis could not be expected to weep for the mad moth she was swallowing.

He was afraid of the winter, of the desperate weather ahead; of those early, dark, end of the world mornings. He was afraid of being turfed out of the lounge and into the cold and terrifying town. What would he do in the streets all day? How could he kill all that time until the evening meal? How would he be able to survive surviving?

Most of the old men were already asleep and snoring.

He looked up at the ceiling. 'Wish I could remember her stage name.' His sister's first name was Jeanette. She wouldn't have changed that. He pushed his mind back and back as far as it would go. One day in the garden when he was so small she had announced her new name. It was on the tip of his tongue. 'Maybe – she changed it to – Jean Sinclair.'

But even as he spoke he knew it was useless. 'Or possibly Jane Shelton! Or – Joan Stanton.' Brian was desperate to remember. If her name came so might she.

'Brian, face it, she's a figment of your imagination,' Larry sneered, but Brian did not even bother to reply. A show of indignation would merely give the old sod satisfaction.

'Oh, bed is beautiful.' Every night he became unconscious and slept without dreams until the morning. The head went on to the pillow; the eyes closed. The eyes opened and the head lifted from the pillow. His nightmares were reserved for the daytime. Something had reversed in his brain during that oxygen deprivation. The day was the dark night of the soul, and the night was the tranquil sleep of the body. That is why he longed for his lover, death.

'You're right, Brian. They've never invented anything better than bed.' Then Larry commenced his usual fart symphony. He was a supreme soloist, but then the others joined in. It was the nightly fart operetta in Margate-on-Dark.

Brian floated along the corridors of Clayton. He floated right through the open door of the office of Miss Reeves, the Social Worker. She smiled as he entered, he growled in reply.

He would like to take her by the hand and float her to Margate; but there was no way that she could leave the office. She and the chair were one. Her legs were wood and rooted to the floor. Then he could see that she was reading her hands. All the facts, all the clichés were printed on her finger-tips. 'Times have changed. There's no more stigma in being mentally disturbed. People are far more tolerant these days.'

If she could float with him above the streets of Margate, she would swallow her word balloons. In Margate she would observe representative faces of ordinary, everyday people. They were not cruel or wicked, nor unduly unkind. They were just human beings scuttling to survive, scurrying for a living. And she would see the way the post-mad were put upon. How they were cheated, day in and day out, how they were short-changed and laughed at. How they were treated with contempt and ridiculed. Miss Reeves was rooted to her statistics and could not leave her office.

He floated out again; floated over the dark and hovered for a moment above the dead empty resort, and then he floated down, back into his own body.

There was just one ambition that he had, apart from dying. He wanted to return to Clayton. He felt sudden resolutions flooding through him. The only way forward was back. He wondered to which authority he could apply. Now hope surged. Perhaps he would write direct to Miss Reeves, or just turn up at the gates. After all, he had tried and he had failed. There was no shame in failing. The people in Clayton had been quite human and compassionate at times. And perhaps they even missed him there. Many patients had even turned to him for advice. He had been a tonic once or twice. Amy Turner even knelt down once and licked his shoes.

Clayton was his home, his mother and his sister. They had not ridiculed him there. The powers that be had merely overlooked him. The sins perpetrated upon him had only been of omission. They had simply not noticed him in Clayton because he stood in the corner of himself and gave them no trouble. Brian had used up twenty-six Singleton years and nobody knew he was there at all.

His pillow was wet, but he definitely was not crying, therefore the roof had to be leaking. It was a fault in the structure. He opened his eyes. He could not see the crack but he knew it was there. 'Christ! I'll do something drastic if they won't let me go back. Maybe they've invented a new drug since I've been away, which will make me normal.'

'What's that, me old son?' Larry scratched himself with two hands. Orang-utan in long dirty white combinations.

'Nothing.' Brian had not thought his words had been spoken aloud.

'What's the matter? Feeling low tonight?'

Any human ear was better than none. 'Fact is, Larry, I hated Clayton, but this is much worse.' He tried to eliminate all dramatic inflection in his voice and Larry nodded sympathetically, absorbing the words.

'Nobody expected anything of me in Clayton. Here – you're so close; you see everyone living a normal life, so you go out and try; you try to compete, to join in. It's worse. It's worse, because you're so close, so close. Oh Christ, I'm sick of this terrible disease. I want to go back to Clayton. I want to go back to Clayton.' He had not intended to get carried away but he could not control himself tonight. 'Sorry.'

Larry did not reply. He was being especially understanding. Maybe it was because the old man with the scythe was very close tonight. And the old men in their beds were away in their own lost worlds, sighing and snoring. So Brian felt free to murmur over and over again. 'I want to go back to Clayton. I want to go back to Clayton.' He was a child who had just been spanked. The words were a mantra and were uttered to give him some comfort. 'I want to go back to Clayton.'

Larry suddenly hopped out of bed, knelt down, put his hands together and burbled for a while the gibberish that only he and God understood. Then coming to the end of his prayer he said aloud in English, 'And please God make me into a good boy.'

'Don't want to take any chances.' Larry winked and jumped back into bed.

'Amen,' Brian nodded.

Every night this same scene. Every night before sleep this same dialogue; these exact words. 'Nightnight, don't let the fleas bite.'

'Oh God, please God. I want to go back to Clayton.'

144

The light went out. 'Nightynight, boys.'

' 'Night. Mrs Killick.' All the voices replied.

He watched her standing in the open door. The black figure against the lighted hall. But he did not want to allow thoughts of her to enter his head. There was enough hatred in the world. She stood there for a moment then she closed the door. But the spores of the angel of death lingered, were floating across the room, falling like dream confetti.

' 'Night, Buzz. 'Night.' There was no reply. 'Good night, Buzz. Good night, Larry.'

' 'Night, Brian,' Larry obliged.

He pulled the blanket right over his head and was safe in this Neolithic cave. Above him the world was cold, and the valleys of the Isle of Thanet were dangerous. But down here he was safe from the sabre-tooth Killick. 'Good night, Buzz,' he called again. 'Buzz, I said good night.'

The boy had been reading his comic only a few minutes before; he could not have dropped off so quickly.

'Take no notice, Brian. He's far too busy.'

'Busy?' He questioned from the depths of his den.

'Course, with hand drill you know, bashing the old bishop; pulling the old pudding. It's bad for the eyes, Buzz. No wonder I'm so short-sighted,' Larry cackled. 'Can't you stop, Buzz, just for a mo' and heed my warning.' No answer was the loud reply.

Then Larry panted like a thirsty dog. 'You pull it, me old son, you pull it and enjoy it.'

A quiet, icy voice pierced the dark. It was Buzz. 'One day Larry, I'm going to kill you.'

'Gawd. You'd be doing me a favour. 'Night all.'

' 'Night, Buzz.' Brian tried again.

' 'Night.' Buzz replied.

Larry laughed, and then all became quiet. And it was night.

23

He was swimming for the shore but his arms were letting him down. They would not stop. They continued to stroke through the water. He was swimming, he was saving himself. It was impossible to learn to unswim. There was no way that he could drown in the darkness.

It crawled out of the water and squelched through the mud. It was a crawling crab, and its name was Brian Singleton. He would capture it, and then obliterate all sight from the eyes; all life from the body. He grabbed the crab.

The crab had a pretty face. The face of an innocent child. It was Buzz in the palm of his hand. He dropped him because he was getting so hot, and the crab scuttled across the floor. 'Buzz! Buzz! Come back.'

Brian Singleton opened his eyes. There was a figure crouching by Larry's bed. A human body seen when the mind cannot focus properly can easily be mistaken for a tree trunk, or a sack of rubbish. Or a giant crab. But this was definitely a human figure crouched close to the sleeping Larry.

It did not occur to him to disturb the creature. He was more interested than anything. What on earth was Buzz doing under the old man's bed?

The other reason he didn't want to make any kind of noise was because all the old men were fast asleep. To bring them back into this world unnecessarily would have been an act of gross cruelty.

Now he could focus more clearly and it was obvious that Buzz was not masturbating. He was scrunching up pages of newspaper, and building a rough pyramid with them. Then he struck a match. The pyramid burst into flames and the boy's face burst into rapture.

Brian wanted to curtail the boy, wanted to shout, but for the moment he was unable to move and he was spellbound by the boy's face.

Buzz heaped more and more paper onto the flames and now the underneath of the bed had caught alight. It was all so quiet. Larry was sleeping with such an innocent sweet smile upon his face.

Buzz scampered across the floor, back to his own bed; and there he sat with his arms and legs folded, a serene disciple.

'Fire! Fire!' someone shouted. 'Fire! Fire!' It was himself. But he could not somehow lean across and shake the old man awake. 'Fire! Fire!'

And all the dead came alive. They rose from their coffins, coughing and spluttering. Yet were as slow as sloths. Their limbs unable to take much action to save themselves.

'Fire! Fire!' Buzz clapped his hands, shook up and down. 'Fire! Fire!'

'Fire! Fire! Run for your lives!' Now Brian sprang into action. And it was just as well; if he sat there any longer they would think that he was responsible. Anyway, he could move and he did.

He shook and shook the sleeping Larry, who still lay curled in a bed of smoke. The old devil was being stoked upon the rivers of hell. His little beady eyes opened. 'Help me! Oh my gawd! Help me! Help me!' His spiky arms clung to Brian.

The mattress was about to ignite. The flames would begin to devour the room any moment now. And Hazelhurst would be no more. They would all be packed back from whence they came. However, he refrained from shouting 'Hooray!' Clayton was in sight. He was dizzy, he was high as he rushed around trying to wake and stir all the stinking old men. 'Come on! Move yourselves! Move yourselves!'

Hazelhurst was going up in smoke. Hazelhurst was smoke. All he wanted to do was save himself, yet here he was trying to salvage all these old bones, all these poor swine that he loathed with all his heart. Nothing was simple in this life.

'Fire! Fire! Run for your lives.' They were going out of the room. The tortured yellow decayed limbs were moving about, disentangling themselves from sheets; from each other. Horrifying, putrifying, dangling testicles. The old terrified beasts were struggling for the door; useless old bulls in an abattoir.

'This way. This way.'

'Help me! Help me!'

'We're all gonna die! We're gonna die!'

'Fire! Fire!' Buzz merrily sang looking all around at do-it-yourself personal paradise. He had come into his Kingdom.

Larry did not join the scurrying senile. He was trying to get into his clothes and gather his things together at the same time.

A bell was ringing. Quasimodo smiled at the chaos, Singleton had other ideas, he was trying to pull Brian out, to gather him together and save him from the fire, from himself. And now he was trying to save his best friend. 'Come on, Buzz. Come on, Buzz. Quick.'

But Buzz shook his head, seemed hurt. 'Please, Brian. Please.' He wanted to stay with his beloved.

Perhaps there would be fire engines. That would make this night stand out. There would be something new to talk about, to carry them through the winter. It would be fantastic to be able to return to Clayton and relate to the others how they all stood outside in the night and watched Hazelhurst House Hotel defying the firemen, and hissing and spitting and splitting, before being reduced to a heap of ashes.

John Killick charged into the room. 'You old sod. Smoking in your bed again. I'll brain you. I'll brain you for this.' His fist lunged towards Larry; but he only threatened, for the moment he was more concerned with getting an extinguisher functioning. Then foam fountained upon the flaring bed; and took effect immediately.

'No. No.' Buzz looked devastated as the flames started to die. 'Please.' He appealed to Mr Killick. 'Please.'

The drunk was not drunk tonight. His silent angry face hovered in the dark as the foam continued to pour from his instrument. And then the fire was out; it was entirely quenched. And Buzz dug his fingers into his face as if he had just witnessed a terrible massacre.

It was now quiet. The old men had gone. Larry cowered in a corner and Buzz was slumped there devastated. But the foam was still spilling from John Killick. 'Stupid old bastard. Sodding old swine. I'd brain you if you had any!' He growled at Larry. 'I'll have your guts for this. I'll have your bleeding guts for garters!' Now that the firefighting was done, he stood above the old man, shaking with rage. All his miserable days had been caused by this creature beneath him; this sub-normal snivelling apology for a human being.

'Wasn't me. Honest. It was him! It was the kid.' Larry pointed to Buzz to save himself, and really nobody could blame him.

But, oddly enough, Buzz seemed delighted with the accusation and puffed himself up proudly.

'Go on, ask him; ask anyone. Buzz plays with fire all the time. He done it!'

'You bloody liar.' John Killick had heard enough from the old man and this time he really meant to belt him.

But Mrs Killick entered the stinking room; she coughed and spluttered, and then she saw her husband, and just managed to restrain the fist in time. 'What are you doing? Are you out of your mind?'

'This old bastard's blaming the boy.'

'You fucking idiot.'

Brian covered his ears for a moment. It was terrible to hear a lady swear. And even though she was a tight-fisted, scheming money-making tyrant, she still belonged to the fair sex.

Her face seemed less contorted now so he uncovered his ears.

'If you weren't so pissed all the time, you'd know that Larry's telling the truth for once. If you weren't so pissed you'd know what's really going on in this house.' She went to the door, spun around, then looked at Buzz, Larry and himself in turn. 'Right! You, you and you. I want you all downstairs in the lounge in three minutes flat. I'll give you fire. We're going to see some real fireworks round here from now on.' She marched out of the room and down the stairs.

John Killick did not seem to hear his wife, he just stood there slowly shaking his head, looking at the charred remains of the mattress and all the mess strewn around the floor.

'Fire! I'll give them fire. I'll give them fireworks to really remember.' She was still shouting when they reached the lounge.

All the other residents were assembled there. Some shivered, some just stood like scarecrows, with an empty fixed smile on the face. Others giggled out of fear or excitement. One rocked backwards and forwards as if trying to cope with pain. Old Terry with all the dried snot crusted above his upper lip jumped up and down, flapping his hands so that they seemed to be made of jelly.

'Is there a fire?'

'I can smell smoke.'

'No. It's out.'

'Who's going to start a fire?'

'Is it November the fifth?'

'Yeah, and I'm Guy Fawkes. Chuck me on the flames.'

'I like a fire. I look forward to winter because I love to see the smoke rising from coal.'

'H——ell——p!' One fat old thing emitted a high-pitched siren tone, over and over again. 'H——ell——p!'

'We're all going to die.' One little old dear spoke with total unconcern.

'Wouldn't mind that,' someone within the group replied. The desire for sudden death; common hope of all these after-cares. He could hardly bear to look at the pathetic assembly; all in their night things, superannuated Shirley Temples in curlers or bows, and senile Stan Laurels, without the smile.

Mrs Killick stood before her charges. A camp commandant, cracking the whip of her voice, in the heyday of the Third Reich. 'I've had enough. I've had just about enough.'

There was absolute silence for a moment, then, 'You bloody well dare. You idiot. You're a dangerous potential murderer. I'll kill you myself if you don't stop laughing.'

But he could not stop, and she hit the boy around the face with the back of her hand. He laughed all the more. Brian watched John Killick who was about to use the telephone.

'What are you doing?' She screamed at her husband.

'Calling the police.'

Mrs Killick pounced upon him and pulled the receiver away. 'You stupid idiot. Are you as nutty as them?' Then she calmed down a little, and resumed her usual more genteel tone of voice. 'Do you want the authorities to come and close us down? Please my love, stay out of this, and don't do anything.'

Buzz had not stopped laughing and she turned to him again, and grabbed him by the shoulders. 'Admit you did it. Admit! Admit!' As she shook, all her chunky jewellery jangled together.

' 'Course I did it. I lit the fire. 'Course I did.'

She stood back satisfied and looked at all the others. 'There you are, you heard. That's it. You're the witnesses. You all heard, didn't you?'

They all nodded. Then she looked at Brian. He could not stop himself from agreeing. He had betrayed his best friend, but Buzz didn't seem to mind at all, and had the broadest grin upon his face.

'Pack your bloody things and get out.'

'Now?'

'Yes, you stupid little monster, now. NOW! I want you out of this house now. You can come back for your things tomorrow. I'm not having you in this house one moment longer.'

'I can go now? I can really go now?'

'Yes, you heard me, imbecile.' She strode to the street door and opened it; Buzz followed.

'Buzz, Buzz, Buzz, Buzz. Goodbye.'

He was already outside on the doorstep and looking up at the sky. Brian rushed to the lady. 'You can't do it. You can't. Not just like that.'

'Can't I? Do you want to go with him?'

Michelle whined, high up in her throat, but nobody else uttered a sound.

Mrs Killick turned to the boy again. 'Now get out of my bleeding sight.'

He could hardly believe his luck. 'Thanks. Thanks. Maybe I'll come for my things next week or the week after. 'Bye.'

She slammed the door on him then turned to the others. 'Now get to bed, before I chuck you all out.'

She did not need to utter another word. With unusual haste they all made their way upstairs; and although he was desperate to follow the others he knew that he had to make some attempt to help his friend.

'Come on, Brian. Come on up to bed,' Larry called.

'Brian,' Michelle cried.

'Come on, Brian.' Dolores was worried.

Mrs Killick had not yet noticed him; she was busy trying to explain something to her husband. Brian was sure that he could persuade her to change her mind. But the first thing he had to do was to try and see things from her point of view.

He had to get things into perspective. Firstly, although she had a surface cruelty, deep down she was human and therefore she was bound to have feelings and emotions, and concern. On top of that, looking after ex-mental patients had to be the most awesome responsibility in the world. And Buzz had gone too far. Even so, you simply can't turn a young psychopath out on the streets, just like that. He approached her quietly, already she seemed far less perturbed. He would make her see sense. Otherwise he would telephone Buckingham Palace on the morrow and tell the Queen. But it wasn't going to get that far; Mr Killick was doing the talking for him, and what's more she was listening.

'He's a minor. The authorities will come down on us like a ton of bricks. What happens if he burns down the Town Hall? I'd feel responsible.'

'For once in your life you're talking some sense.' She thought for a moment, then took command again. 'Right, you better go after him. Bring him back. I'll phone the Department tomorrow and get him landed on some other poor bleeding proprietor. Quickly then, move yourself.' She got his overcoat and helped him into it. Then she turned and saw Brian. 'What the bleeding—' She had not expected him there; she had ordered them all to bed and her orders were to be obeyed. But her anger was interrupted by an idea. 'Good, you go with my husband and bring that bloody boy back.' She threw Brian somebody else's raincoat, and he slipped it over his pyjamas. His heart beat fast; there was a good chance that they would find Buzz. He did not wish to envisage any other alternative, did not know how he could possibly survive without his friend.

'Come on then, out with you.' She opened the door and Brian followed the man out of the house and into the street. They walked.

'Call for him,' Mr Killick requested.

'Buzz! Buzz!' he cried out for his lost friend. 'Buzz! Buzz!' They walked and walked and he shouted along every street and into every alley. 'Buzz! Buzz!'

And now the other man took up the call. 'Buzz! Buzz!'

He felt ridiculous. Maybe his young friend never existed, and he and this stranger were two giant insects, just hatched in this night. They edged towards the deserted front.

'Buzz! Buzz! Buzz!' they cried.

24

The fairy lights along the promenade were still on. Either someone had forgotten to pull out the plug, or this was the usual
practice during the early autumn. Brian had never been out at
this time of night, therefore he was in no position to know. Nevertheless, the dazzling colours against the sky delighted him.

It was a close and humid night and the air was thickening all
the time. A solitary car sped along the parade and disappeared.
Brian marched alongside his keeper.

'It's close,' Mr Killick panted.

'Closer than you think.'

The man got the joke and laughed therefore Brian relaxed and
dared to join in.

'That could be him, in there.' Brian pointed to a doorway on
the other side of the road, where some figures were huddled
together. But when he turned back Mr Killick was taking a swig
from a small silver flask, so Brian just watched and waited. Some
needed Phenothiazines to negotiate the abyss, some needed alcohol.

'That's better,' John Killick gurgled then pocketed the flask.
'What did you say?'

'Think he's over there.'

'Well, go over and see.'

It was obvious that John Killick was a coward. Brian loathed
and abominated cowards. Cowards did not deserve to remain
alive.

'Go on, then, what are you waiting for?' Killick prodded.

Brian was furious. It was as obvious as the mongol face of the
moon that Singleton was not a brave man; in fact, he was no better
than the drunkard. Brian wished that he could escape from both
Singleton and Killick. If he could only give them the slip, he could
start life all over again.

All was unreal; bathed in moonlight; and there was stinking
hot air drifting up from the ventilators of hell. There were

definitely two people in the doorway across the road. And one of them had to be Buzz.

Possibly he was rubbing two sticks together to impress a female; possibly he was promising instant cremation. They were certainly close and doing something rather intimate. It certainly looked like Buzz.

John Killick took another swig from the silver flask as Brian dared to venture across. He approached the doorway. 'Buzz?'

A man's face whipped around and a girl's face looked up. She was startled and full of fear; his face was full of anger. 'Piss off, peeping Tom.'

'Sorry, I was looking for Buzz.' He ran away and the couple laughed and turned back into themselves, the man continuing to make fire, even if he wasn't Buzz.

Mr Killick sat on a bench, chewing his finger. 'What do we do?' He was as lost as Atlantis.

Brian trembled. Buzz had left Hazelhurst with a smile, but Brian knew the boy too well. Buzz was desperate and he would do something quite terrible. If they did not find him quickly there would be a tragedy, and it would be blazed right across the morning papers. Maybe even now he was soaking himself in petrol and striking a match.

Then Brian heard the sound of aggressive music, and singing and laughter. It was the unmistakable thump and groan of Rock. Then he recognised the voice. It was the prince of darkness himself, going on about his blue suede shoes. Dead Presley wailed over dead Margate.

Brian walked towards the beach and beckoned his guardian to follow.

There was a group of teenagers on the sand, gyrating in the brightness of the moon. And there was Buzz, amongst them twisting all alone, swigging from a bottle held high above his head. Brian counted the figures on the shore. There were eight of them, and they were all dancing alone; all slowly rotating, all in love with the space around them, and the space within them.

'Drop outs!' John Killick sneered. He had not yet seen Buzz; his eyes were now glazed; unable to focus.

'Drop outs? That's impossible. They haven't yet dropped in. There's Buzz,' Brian said quietly, pointing at the boy.

'Well, call him then!'

A slave could not argue. 'Buzz! Buzz! It's me! It's Brian.'

Buzz looked up but he did not smile, he just continued his gyrations; he was far, far away, on the other side of nowhere.

'Go on, get him then.' Killick sat down on the pavement. 'Go on! What you waiting for?'

Brian ventured on to the beach and slowly approached the boy. 'Come on, Buzz,' he cooed, as if calling a pet dog. 'Buzz, you can come back. We've come for you.'

Buzz just continued smiling, and turning, and moaning along with his master, who was having a heartbreak in a hotel, via the transistor held by a balding guy in blue jeans and ear-rings.

'You can come back! You've been forgiven.'

Buzz flung the bottle away, started to clap hands and danced away, chanting, 'Come back! Come back! Come back! Come back!'

Brian didn't know what to do. None of them had even acknowledged that he was there.

He recognised a few of the faces. These drop outs had been here all summer. He had seen them on this same stretch of beach; all they ever seemed to do was drink, make a noise, and occasionally throw a frisbee to one another. Day in, day out, the same boring, killing waste of time; over the heads of the holiday-makers; drunk, drugged; feeble. To Brian, a way of life equally as horrendous as the assembly-line; or after-care.

In fact, they were not unlike the post-mad; stupidly smiling and their eyes glazed over; their numbers increasing all over the world. He believed they called themselves the Alternative Society. Unfortunately there was no alternative to life, except death.

Buzz seemed to be totally accepted, and did not seem out of place amongst them. But Buzz was dangerous. How could they look after him when they could not even look after themselves? They were ragged and self-indulgent. His friend needed love and care, and watching. He knew that he had to rescue the boy from this alien tribe as soon as possible. 'You must come! Buzz! It's me. It's Brian. Please.' But it was useless. He walked back to his keeper. Maybe the drunk had pulled himself together. But there was no joy in this direction.

'What's the use!' John Killick was shaking his head as if the end of the world had come, then he took another swig from his flask.

Brian decided that enough was enough. Buzz would now have to survive in the world without his assistance. He could barely survive by his own efforts. No one would point the finger. Sometimes you simply had to walk away from an impossible situation.

'Come on!' He tried to drag the drunkard to his feet, but the man was heavy with despair, and clung to his arm. He would not budge.

Meanwhile, the drums of the tribe throbbed through the night. If man could only trip through time and become Neolithic again, and there was no Department of Health and Social Security. The trouble was, there was only now.

'Oh God, what's the use? What can I do?' He sank to his knees, spoke quietly to the moon. But the moon was as impotent as Mr Killick; as Buzz; as himself. There was no point in crying, so he stood up and kicked a can, and waved his fist at the moronic face of the moon smiling down upon him. 'What's the use? What's the bloody use?'

Mr Killick was laughing now, and swigging from the flask again. Brian decided to have one last try, so he strode over to the boy and he didn't care about the others, and neither did they care about him. He was determined. 'Buzz, you're coming with me! Come on, let's go.'

Buzz swayed where he stood. 'Wow, wow, wow. Found new friends. Staying here forever on the beach. Wow, wow, wow.' He was in a sort of ecstatic trance. Maybe this was as close as you could get to heaven.

'Wow, wow, wow, you're coming with me now. Buzz, Buzz, Buzz, you're coming now with us!' His scatty remark caused the boy to open his eyes.

'Hey! You a poet, Brian?'

'Listen, Buzz. Mrs Killick's had a change of heart. She sent us out to get you. She said you can come back. She's giving you one last chance. Hurry up, Buzz, before she changes her mind.'

'Hello, Brian. Where have you been?'

Brian laughed instead of crying. 'Please, Buzz. Listen to me.' He spoke softly and slowly. 'Mrs Killick has relented. You can come home now.'

At last the boy understood, but it made little difference. He leapt into the air, and then danced away again, and slowly twisted around and around again. 'Never going back, never. Not ever. Never! Never! Staying here whatever. I'm mad grandad. I'm mad forever.' Possibly they were the words of some pop song he had beachcombed from his mindless chums.

'Yeah, that's cool man. That's crazy.' They gibbered, laughed, and clapped their hands, and cuddled and drooled, and some fell to the ground. The rest formed themselves into a circle, with Buzz in the centre, leaping with frenzy around and around. 'Go, Buzz, go. Great man, great.'

Any moment now they would rush off with knives, to drink the hot blood of the sleeping babes of Margate.

Brian wondered why the police had ignored this atavistic gathering. It could not have gone unheard, un-noticed.

Buzz leapt out of the circle and started to cartwheel along the beach. 'I'm a wheel. Watch me!'

There was no way that he could return without Buzz. The boy had to be saved from himself. So he chased the wheel of flesh across the beach ignoring all the mocking laughter. He would show them all. His body, unlike his mind, was healthy and not bloated with drink, or flabby from over-feeding. His body was the area where he could hold up his head and stand against any man. He could catch the little bastard. He did. He grabbed him and all the laughter stopped. 'You coming with me now?'

The boy sensed that there was no sense in arguing. 'All right, Brian. Anything you say.'

As they passed the others, Buzz waved. ' 'Bye, Buzz! See you! Great! Keep it cool, man.'

They weren't bad people, they were lost. The only difference being that Brian knew he was lost. These people did not know that they did not know.

'Sorry, Brian. Sorry,' Buzz said. 'Sorry. Anything you say, Brian.'

When they reached Killick, he was lying flat out on the pavement hopelessly, helplessly drunk, his mouth slobbering against the stone. They managed to get him to his feet, and he allowed himself to go with them.

Brian and Buzz slowly walked along the promenade supporting him. 'There'll be blue birds over – the white cliffs of Dover, tomorrow – just you – wait and see.' Mr John Killick, their guardian and keeper, lolled between them, groaning his drunken song as they walked towards home. 'There'll be love and laughter and peace ever after—'

It was all very funny. They were holding him up; they were helping him, they were dragging him towards his own home. And they were supposed to be the mad ones.

25

He sat with the others in the station buffet, killing time as usual. There was just enough money for this morning cup of tea. Sometimes he longed for an ice-lolly or some bubble gum; but a cup of tea was far more sensible. You could make it last for a few hours; and the people who worked in the buffet were kind and left them alone.

Michelle was knitting and had made a little progress in this respect; she had recently managed to achieve at least a few lines of stitches on the needle, whereas in the summer she had not been able to get beyond merely casting on.

Maybe one day she could become a dancer with the Royal Ballet.

Larry was reading the sports page of a newspaper he had retrieved from the wastepaper basket, and Buzz was lost in his usual space comic.

Winter was just around the corner, and outside the wind was laughing its head off. The clouds were furious and the streets were empty, unreal; a stage setting.

He had been here since last winter. Almost a whole year had passed and nothing had changed. And nothing would change.

Dolores seemed to read his thoughts. 'Margate out of season is like a whore without customers. Wish I could get away from here and never come back.'

He still longed for Clayton, yet he had not made any real attempt to return there. It was true that he had once phoned and left a message for Miss Reeves, but she never phoned back. He had spent a whole year of precious time and there was nothing to show for it. 'Wish I had the past to look forward to.'

'The past. Now you're talking.' Larry came back from winning his dream fortune on yesterday's winning horses, and he smiled, savouring his own rosy memories. 'I could tell you some stories 'bout the past. Place I used to love going this time of year was Kent.'

'This is Kent,' Dolores chided.

'I mean Kent of the hopfields. Years ago, this time of year, we all went, all the family. Mum! Dad! All the kids! Gran, Grandad! Aunt Sophie and all her lot! All the families of the East End used to go. All the poor people in their thousands. When all the fields of hops were ripe we used to just pack up and go. It was our holiday. Year after year, for three glorious weeks.' Larry had never told this story before and all the others listened eagerly as if he were talking about a fabulous lost civilisation.

'It was just like a carnival, an army of endless, laughing people happy under the stars—' His hands carved out a geography as he spoke. Brian had never seen him so sincere, so reverent, so elegiac. 'There were all these huts. And all these golden fields for as far as the eye could see. And that beautiful smell. You wanted to just breathe in all the time. And at night all those sing-songs. And the games we played. All the kids together. One huge family of children, playing hide and seek under the wide open sky. And what about the money we earned? Work was play in those days. Unhappiness had not yet been invented then. Nor was violence.'

Dolores laughed. 'You should have been in Sunderland. You should have known my dad. You'd be telling a different story.'

But Larry was not brought down by her cynical interruption, rather he used it to soar even higher. 'Sure, we knew poverty. Sure, we were in rags, but we were happy then.'

Michelle hung on his words, knitting and dropping stitches. Inside Michelle there was a normal human being, afraid to venture out.

'God existed in them days. And we managed to escape from the stinking slums, with their stinking bug-infested walls. In the early autumn, on such a day like today, we would arrive in the fields of Kent and we would smell the smells of Kent, and we would feast our eyes upon the golden hops of Kent, in fields alight with golden fire.'

'Fire! Why don't we go!' Buzz stood up.

'Anything about fire lights him up.' Brian was delighted when everyone laughed, even though he hadn't intended a joke.

'Hey, Michelle, did you hear the joke I made? Did you?'

She nodded, and he put his arm around her and squeezed her body.

Larry was still in full flight. 'Days of gold, days of fire, and as much beer as you could drink for free. Real beer. Not the muck they make nowadays. Golden ale; ale that don't exist no more. They banished it because we loved it so much.'

Dolores nodded.

'They banished it because it was too good for us humans. That ale went straight to your head and your head went straight to the stars. And that's where we slept, under the stars. And we had sing-songs around the fire.'

As Larry talked Brian could see the faces staring out of the sepia postcard of the past. Larry's words triggered something inside him, they jogged and stirred something deep within the roots of his memory. King George the Sixth of England in khaki shorts, sitting with boy scouts around the camp fire. 'Underneath the spreading chestnut tree, I loved her and she loved me, now you ought to see our family, 'neath the spreading chestnut tree.' The boy scouts made the appropriate movements and the King of England got muddled, touching his head when he should have touched his chest; and all the clean young men roared with laughter.

'Yes, we used to sing silly songs and sit up late in the night, talking and telling stories; if only I could go hopping again.'

'I can go hopping!' Buzz got up from the table, started hopping around the buffet. 'Look, I can hop! I can hop!'

'I can hop! I can hop!' Michelle giggled and joined Buzz and they both hopped around and around the table. The manageress frowned and was about to pounce; but Dolores quickly grabbed them and pushed them towards their chairs. 'Sit down and behave yourselves, or they'll think that we're all a little bit touched!' She looked up to heaven, realising the ridiculousness of her words. The two young people sat down again.

But Larry, lost in the past, hardly noticed the incident. 'And the money we made. Hand over fist. Caps full of it. You see, Brian, everyone pulled together those days, and when we got back to the Smoke all the family pooled their money together and it kept us going till Christmas, gave us hope. It carried us into the New Year, until we could look forward to hopping again. I loved seeing the same old faces year after year. In those days there was a future and a past.'

'Now there's just now.' Brian saddened, catching Larry's dejection. But then he brightened. 'Why can't we go, Larry? Why can't we go today?'

' 'Cos we ain't got a time-machine.'

Brian couldn't understand the other's pessimism. His mind raced. Beer was still made from hops and people still drank beer. 'Larry, it's autumn, and the hops must be ripe. And the hops must need picking.'

Larry's watery eyes came alive.

Dolores touched him, catching the impetus of hope, speeding it onwards. 'Hey, we could have a holiday! We can get away from Mr and Mrs Killing!'

Michelle stood and shook with excitement. 'A holiday, a holiday.'

'And even if we went for only a week, Killing wouldn't mind, she'd probably be only too pleased to see the back of us.'

Brian nodded, but he knew that if he left Margate this day he would never return.

They were all turned to the old man, feeling the necessity to convince him. After all, it had been his dream. Once he was totally convinced there would be no turning back.

'Do you know, it's not a bad idea.' But then he faltered. 'No. It's all a dream. The world's changed.' Larry was afraid of leaving his prison and who could blame him? But Brian persisted. This was the moment in life when one had to step beyond oneself, to attempt a courageous leap across the Saragossa of the mind.

'Larry, nothing has really changed.' Brian spoke slowly, his face close to Larry's, staring straight into the other's shifty eyes. 'You've got to go out and meet life half-way; or in our case, maybe three-quarters. Come on, Larry, what have we got to lose?'

'Nothing. Never had nothing to lose.'

'Exactly! Then who are we waiting for?'

'Ourselves. We're waiting for ourselves.' Dolores spoke forcefully, and Larry could resist no longer. His doubts had cracked. Resolve was gushing in. He banged the table with his fist. 'You're right. You're dead right. What have we got to lose? Let's go. Let's go today.'

'Hooray!' Michelle hugged Buzz. Buzz hugged himself.

'Right, we'll collect a few things and be on our way.'

The manageress of the buffet watched closely. One more decibel of sound and they would be banished forever. The post-mad made convenient scapegoats for drunken husbands, difficult children, or for any old aches and pains.

But suddenly it didn't matter anymore. The scapegoats were about to escape from the pen. They were letting themselves out. They were taking matters into their own hands and changing their fate. They would live and work under the stars, and earn enough money to pay their way into the future.

'Maybe we'll sleep under the stars, and light a bonfire. Eh, Brian? Eh, Larry?' Buzz was confused, and did not know who was the new leader of the pack.

They gathered up their things. This was the last day; the very last morning they would need to waste in this buffet. Killing time was over. They left the table.

'What was the name of the farm, Larry?'

'Farm? What farm?'

'Where you went as kids. You know, hopping.'

'It was— it was—' The old man grimaced as he dug deep down into his mind. 'It was—' And then he smiled as he came upon the seam of golden memory. 'I remember. It was Chapman's Farm. About five miles from Maidstone. I remember the old sod well. He had bright rosy cheeks and piggy eyes. I'm sure he's still in the land of the living. He must be. And the farm must be there. It's got to be, eh, Brian?'

They stood by the door of the station buffet hoping along with Larry; suddenly afraid that the marshmallow would collapse.

' 'Course it's still there. Farms never die; they're handed down.' Brian's words clinched the matter; brought confidence back.

'Come, no time to waste. Let's go while it's still autumn.' He held up the flat of his hand, pushed the door open and marched out. They followed gladly because he was in complete command. He was the fiery warrior poet with a mission, with a journey into the future. He was William Blake and Moses. He was Brian Singleton leading them out of Sodom. 'Come, I will lead you into the promised land of Kent. Onward!'

It was a joke, but a serious joke. Buzz no longer harboured any doubts as to who was the real leader.

Brian led them away from the buffet and out of the station and they marched along the street, and he did not mind that the manageress of the place and her assistants were looking through the window and shaking their heads.

The world was for the brave. Kent for the post-mad. The hop fields for those who dared to march into the future.

26

Brian shoved the handful of blackberries into his mouth and swallowed them.

'There's a worm in every one,' Buzz remarked, wildly plucking at the bushes and munching berries as fast as he could collect them.

'Worms are good protein,' Brian replied, but despite his brave words he decided that he had had enough for the moment.

He was feeling absolutely marvellous. The countryside was living proof of the beauty of existence. At last he was his own master and could live off the land. There would always be something to eat. Cobnuts and blackberries were all free under the open sky, and only had to be gathered. And there were rabbits and woodpigeons.

The countryside was blazing gold and the sky was clear crisp blue. The sun shone, but its sweltering days were over. Now it was benevolent and gave just enough warmth to stir them and speed them on their way along the autumn lanes.

They were well away from the coast now; away from the chill of the sea and the first bite of winter. And all the trees bowed as they passed. Brown, red and golden mops, shimmering, gently shaking their heads, breaking the shafts of sunlight.

'Oh, the grand old Duke of York, he had ten thousand men. He marched them up to the top of the hill . . . and that was the end of them.' They all sang as they marched along, Dolores twirled an imaginary baton and hurled it into the air, and caught it again and again. They were dishevelled but there was no one to laugh at them. They were the raggle taggle brigade, mad nomads without a care in the world.

'Three gypsies stood at the castle gate—' Brian led with the song and although they all knew the tune, none really knew the words. But it did not matter today, nothing mattered. Today was a day for singing. 'They sang so high, though they sank so low, dadadadadada along with the raggle taggle gypsies oh—'

They were slicing deep into Kent, and Brian lost count of the miles. They were free to go where they wanted and it did not matter if they missed tea. Their time was their own. They could have tea whenever they liked, even at four o'clock in the morning, under the moon. And for dinner they would catch a rabbit and scrump some apples.

They had taken their leave of Mr and Mrs Killick of Hazelhurst House forever. They had not even asked her permission. All that after-care crap was a thing of the past. They would care for themselves from now on. Rehabilitation was a noble word. De-institutionalisation was another. This was rehabilitation; this was the balm in Gilead. Here the lepers could wash off their spots. He had only one ambition now, one purpose in life, and that was to make himself strong. A boat could not depend upon the benevolence of the sea. It had to be built to withstand the worst ravages of the storm.

Brian Singleton could no longer expect tolerance and humanity from human beings. He was sure of only one thing. He would never, never turn back; never return to Margate.

He realised that they were no longer marching along. His legs ached; they were beginning to dawdle.

'My bloody corns. I'm crippled.' Larry crumbled by the road side and rubbed his feet.

Buzz crawled into a bush, his hands ready to snatch an insect.

Michelle sat down in the middle of the lane and started knitting. There was always something so prim and sorrowful about her. Brian wondered how she got to Margate in the first place. Nobody ever seemed to know. But that didn't matter at this moment. The only important thing was to reach the hop fields. 'Let's get going, then.' But nobody took any notice. Dolores yawned and stretched.

'Are you sure we're going in the right direction, Larry?'

Larry rubbed his stubble. 'Sure I'm sure, we're definitely on the right road to Chapman's Farm. It's definitely in this general direction.'

'You said we had to turn off. Where exactly do we turn off?'

But Larry was miles away. 'Yes. It was Chapman's Farm. I

may be past my prime, but my memory is still razor sharp. I can still see those two oasthouses. You could see them a mile off from the main road.'

'But where, Larry? We've been walking for hours.'

'Trust me,' the old man said.

'That's what I'm afraid of,' Brian replied. 'Anyway, I'm the leader, so there.'

'I'm the king of the castle,' Buzz sang.

'And I'm the dirty rascal.' Larry farted.

Brian was not really concerned, and relaxed back for a moment.

By the position of the sun he knew it was now late into the afternoon, and therefore they had been walking for more than seven hours. And if they had been doing around three miles an hour, which was not out of the question, it meant that they were perhaps twenty miles away from Margate, the last resort. Twenty miles from Mrs Killick, the twin-set tyrant and her blue-rinsed hair. He closed his eyes, saw the spectre of her blown up, an insidious balloon covering the entire coastline, sucking in everything and everyone; digesting them in the acid of her smile.

'All right, Larry, enough is enough. I must know exactly where we're going. Where exactly is Chapman's Farm?'

'Without doubt it's between Canterbury and Faversham, on the A2.'

'You said it was between Canterbury and Ashford.'

'You said it was between Canterbury and Charing.'

'I never did! I know exactly where it is.'

'Have we gone through Canterbury yet?' Buzz became agitated, started shaking his head from side to side, fear trembled in the air. 'Have we passed Canterbury?' Buzz shouted this time.

The euphoria of those first hours had carried them away. In fact, he could barely remember leaving Margate because they were all so excited. But now they were down to earth. 'No, Buzz, don't you remember? We by-passed Canterbury.'

'Why?'

'Because we want to get started. We don't want to get bogged down in any city. Maybe later we'll return as pilgrims.'

Buzz nodded, but he didn't understand.

'We turn off about half a mile along here, and it's about three miles after that.'

'Good. Come on then,' Brian gently commanded, and Larry

jumped up and was ready to go. Michelle put away her knitting and Dolores got to her feet, stretched and yawned.

'Anyone got any Turkish Delight? I see. You all just happen to be out of Turkish Delight. Never mind, I'll settle for a Turk!'

Nobody laughed. 'Brian, will you carry me?' Dolores fluttered her eyes.

'I will. I will.' Buzz bent down, but the lady declined the offer of a piggyback.

'COME, ONWARD! INTO THE VALLEY OF ENGLAND. ONWARD TO LIBERTY AND FRATERNITY. FOR ENGLAND, ST MICHAEL AND THE BRITISH HOME STORES.' Brian's call made them laugh, and laughter helped them gather their spirits, and they became bold again and once more they strode through the countryside. Somewhere not far from Canterbury, their voices in unison rose above the trees.

'HE WHO WOULD VALIANT BE, LET HIM COME HITHER, ONE HERE WILL CONSTANT BE, COME WIND COME WEATHER.'

They were a timeless rank of pilgrims; they were a pageant, a cameo glimpsed through hedgerows, a scene from the *Canterbury Tales*, and he was leading them in step and in voice, full-throated through the Bunyan hymn.

'THERE'S NO DISCOURAGEMENT, SHALL MAKE HIM ONCE RELENT, HIS FIRST AVOWED INTENT, TO BE A PILGRIM.'

This was the one hymn he loved. They had sung hymns with great gusto in Clayton; Church service was another means of killing time. But Christ had never meant all that much to him; in fact he could hardly bear to look at the figure of the mutilated God upon the Cross. But there were two hymns that moved him. The one that he was presently singing, and 'For Those In Peril On The Sea'. He laughed. It should have been amended to 'For Those In Peril On The Seaside!' That lingering slow peril of the last resort; with plastic people as overlords.

Anyway, all that was over. Margate was as dead as his mother and his father.

His voice boomed out as the five mental dwarfs moved on, and when they came to the end of the hymn he led them into a less reverent song.

'On Ilkley Moor baht'at, on Ilkley Moor baht'at, on Ilkley Moor baht'at.'

He was amazed at the beauty of his voice; caught young enough, given a different brain, different parents, born into a different time, he would have astonished the world.

They marched without stopping and he breathed deeply, and suddenly he could smell that beautiful, tangy, unmistakable smell of hops; a smell that reminded him of nothing else upon this earth. They were getting high on hops. It was a pity that they had not brought John Killick. He would have breathed in and been born again.

'Nothing's changed. Everything's like it was.' Larry was right for once in his life. Here were the fields of old England; fields replete with ripe apples and hazelnuts, fields of russet hues, fields of orange pippin, greengages, golden plums; and the last of the swallows still swooping over the hedgerows. And the smell of blackberries; unpicked, rotting on the bough. One could almost survive by breathing in the air. It was a meal in itself.

They turned into a secondary road, and now they could not be so far from their destination. Certainly Larry's face seemed confident enough. Larry was not a subtle person and was not able to hide his fears; and there was certainly no doubt upon that wizened walnut head.

Dolores stopped and clutched her heart. 'How much farther, Larry?'

'Not far now. Only about five miles.'

'You said that five miles ago.' She sank down dejected, though still managing a brave face. 'You all go on. Leave me here to die. I'm having a fag.' She took out a packet, offered them round.

'No thanks. They kill you.' Brian could not understand how anyone could still require cancer tubes; after all, a razor blade, or a dive off a five-storey building was much quicker and far less expensive.

'Yes please.' Larry grabbed one. He could hardly believe his luck and quickly took advantage of this strange and sudden act of generosity. 'One thing for sure, you'll never get out of life alive,' she remarked, sucking the smoke deep into her lungs. She sat on her haunches on a huge stone at the side of the road, relishing every drag of the cancer tube. 'Just leave me here with a rifle! I'll defend the pass and delay the redskins for a while!'

'Come on, Dolores. We want to get there.'

'It's very close. We're practically there. We'll be hopping within the hour.'

Michelle pointed to the sky and Brian looked up, but there was nothing to be seen except the overhanging branches. But Michelle pointed again and poked him excitedly and then he realised that she was not pointing at anything in particular but was trying to alert him to something. And then he heard the heavy vehicle in the distance, straining to get up some hill, its belly full.

'Good girl.' He patted her and she blushed rose red. Even if the lorry was full, possibly there would be just a little room to spare for five weary pilgrims. 'Good girl,' he said again, and kissed his fingertips and placed them on her cheek. And then they saw the lorry slowly groaning up the road towards them.

There were no more problems and they all seemed to know exactly what was to happen next. All their eyes fixed upon the older female and she responded and revived miraculously. 'Leave this to me!' And Dolores beckoned them to stand back and they did her bidding. Brian flattened himself against a wall of leaves, his arm around Michelle; whilst Larry and Buzz crouched down, two leering satyrs, eager for the action.

Dolores slowly walked out into the centre of the road, and stood there swaying slightly, smiling. 'How would you like to be with your Dolores?' She slowly started to lift her skirt and the country lane disappeared. She was in a night-club with a spotlight upon her. Alice Faye suddenly resurrected and was to sing a torch song.

Now she started to pull down her knickers and Brian could not bear to look any longer; instead he watched Larry goggling with wonder, Buzz grinning and Michelle pointing and giggling, jumping up and down.

And then Brian watched the driver coming towards them. The expression on the man's face was wondrous to behold. Then there was the screech of brakes.

The middle-aged man did not dash from the lorry. For a moment he sat transfixed at the wheel, mesmerised by the swaying creature.

Then Dolores stuck two fingers into her mouth and whistled shrilly. Then she shouted. 'Come on then! Out you come!'

Brian emerged from the hedge with the others, and now the driver got out of his lorry and looked none too happy. 'What the bloody hell—' He was positively irate and about to explode, but Dolores sidled up to him and whispered into his ear.

The action was so intimate that it sent shivers down Brian's spine. And then the driver softened. 'All right then. You lot in the back.' Dolores took his arm and he winked at her.

No sooner said than done. Buzz clambered on to the lorry and crouched in the dark interior. Larry helped Michelle up, at the same time his hands stroked her skinny thighs, then he too clambered aboard. Then it was Brian's turn.

Dolores was sharing a few words with the driver, then the driver looked across at him. 'The lady said you wanted Chapman's Farm. I know where it is. Leave it to me.'

So, it wasn't a fool's errand; the place really did exist, after all. Brian sat down and relaxed and felt that things were going his way at last. Then he saw that the driver was walking away with Dolores. They crossed a stile and were entering a field. The driver had some sort of sleeping-bag under his arm.

'Hey, where you going?' Then it dawned. Dolores waved back.

'Won't be long. You all stay in the van. We're doing some fruit-picking.'

The driver laughed as he followed Dolores out of sight.

'Where they going?'

Brian calmed Buzz. 'Nowhere. She's just helping him with the route.'

'Wish someone would help me with my root.' Larry turned over and curled like a baby amongst some empty sacks. Buzz made whistling and exploding sounds in the corner and Michelle continued giggling at nothing in particular.

27

Brian was with his mother, walking down the street. His eyes were closed, for he was basking in the smell of freshly baked bread. He entered the baker's shop and all the shelves were filled with crusty golden, steaming loaves. This was in the day before sliced sawdust, and therefore it had to be a dream. He awoke. The lorry stopped.

'Come on, we're there. We're there,' Dolores was shouting at him.

Larry scuttled out. 'We're here. We're here. It's up this lane. I remember, I remember.' He ran around in circles. An athlete who had just come first, waving triumphant fists in the air. 'We're here! We're here! It's Chapman's Farm! It's Chapman's Farm!'

They were all out of the lorry now and Brian turned to the driver. 'Thanks.'

The man nodded once. He was too shagged to do anything else. God knows how many times they had stopped during that short drive, for Dolores to take him fruit-picking. He looked as if he would never want to touch another piece of fruit in his whole life. And only God knew how he would make it back to where he was going.

Riding in the interior of the van had been a journey through time and space. Only an hour had passed on the clock of the sun; but here they were in another world.

It was a quiet evening but there was an explosive atmosphere to the silence. A dog barked incessantly, far away.

The driver ascended to the cab of his lorry and slumped in his seat. Brian did not think that he would even have the energy to switch on the ignition. But miraculously the great machine shuddered; and it pulled slowly away. Dolores waved. And they watched it until it was out of sight.

'It's up this lane. What are we waiting for?'

'Come on, let's go hopping.'

Larry took the lead and marched, swinging his arms and singing 'Here we go a hopping. A hopping down in Kent.' These were the only words of the song that Larry seemed to remember; and all the others joined in. 'HERE WE GO A HOPPING, A HOPPING DOWN IN KENT. HERE WE GO A HOPPING, A HOPPING DOWN IN KENT.'

Larry could not have made it up. It had to have been an old hopping song, now as dead as John Barleycorn, as corndollies; but now dredged up out of the earth. And as they sang they hopped. 'Follow me leader.' Larry darted in and out, with all the others trying to keep up with him, trying to do exactly as he did. Hand on head, other hand holding the toes of one raised foot. 'Here we go Looby Loo, here we go Looby Lye . . .' All the way down the golden leafy lane, snaked this serpent of madmen, going nowhere, but happily.

And then they reached a gate, and stopped singing.

Beyond the gate there was a field, and far across the field there was a farm. Two oasthouses stood distinct against the skyline. And far beyond the farm there were more and more fields. Fields and fields and fields of golden hops. Tall rows of silent warriors. A vast army waiting in the dusk, shivering slightly before the battle. Giants as straight as sentries, correct and aligned. The trooping of the colour with the gold, the red and the brown. The overwhelming smell; the air so thick. And the great white pregnant clouds floating slowly above the eternal fields of Kent.

'Well, was I wrong? Was I wrong?' Larry, looking for praise in this alfresco cathedral, spoke in reverent hushed tones. 'Just breathe it in; just breathe it in.'

Brian basked for a moment in the glorious bakehouse, then he pushed the gate open.

There was a path all the way around the field and he waved for the others to follow. They slowly walked towards the farm. No one was about; not a living soul. No words passed between them and they walked faster and faster as they got closer to the farm. It was a house straight out of a picture book. A few chickens busily pecking and gurgling in the yard.

'It's exactly the same. Nothing's changed.' Larry said. 'We used to get our milk and eggs here.'

'Is there anyone about?' Brian was eager to come face to face with Mr Chapman, provider of employment, the giver of hope.

Dogs growled. He froze as the black and brown shapes came towards him. He turned to ice inside as the red eyes leapt. He crouched backwards, heard the women scream, clenched his eyes and waited for the end.

He could feel their tense closeness, their vibrating bodies, their smell, their heat. But the dogs did not fall upon him.

'What do you want? What do you want?' a voice snapped between the wild beasts.

Brian dared to open his eyes. Two dogs were attempting to hurtle towards him, but they were restrained by a leash. The man holding the leash had a hunting rifle under his arm. He recognised the breed of the beasts. They were Doberman Pinschers, and they were hungry for his throat. If that man released them Brian knew that he would no longer suffer from sickness of the brain. He wanted that man to let go; he was so glad that the man was holding them so tight. His only thought was to protect himself and he felt no concern for any one of his comrades; not even Buzz. He knew how gifted these dogs were at tearing out throats.

He had read in a newspaper how two guard dogs of this particular pedigree had slipped the leash one day and dragged a baby out of its pram, and literally tore her to pieces.

No wonder this owner could appear to be so calm and relaxed. His dogs were doing more than enough. 'What do you want?' He smiled, looked a bit like a benign vicar with his ruddy cheeks.

Brian slowly moved backwards. The dogs were straining on their hind legs and never stopped barking ferociously, even though their handler was continuously tugging at them, and calling them to heel. Nevertheless, they were gradually pulling him forward. Brian moved back and back until he came against a wall. Now there was no more retreat.

Others appeared and they were smiling. A woman stood in the open door of the farmhouse, and a group of young farm labourers gathered and chatted with subdued hilarity.

Brian realised that he and his companions must have presented a pretty comical sight. He turned to the others expecting at least the old sod to say something, but Larry was behind Dolores. Brian could understand why the farmer was angry. A group of five bedraggled strangers descending out of the blue could hardly come laden with gifts and glad tidings. Strangers were rarely up to any good these days.

Brian realised that the onus was on him. 'Are you Mr Chapman?'

'Why? What do you want?' The man barked with the dogs.

'We're looking for Mr Chapman.'

'I'm the owner. What do you want?'

'We're looking for employment. We're hoppers.'

'Well hop off.'

This killed them in the aisles. The farmworkers fell about laughing. Dolores gave them a little wave. 'Hi boys.'

Brian prayed that she would not start hoicking up her skirt and pulling down her drawers. The dogs would smell her and go mad; and no human would be able to hold them back.

'Look, you're wasting my time.'

All that Brian wanted to do now was to get away from the place. 'Sorry. We thought this was Chapman's Farm. My friend was mistaken.'

Larry growled. 'I'm not. I know this place. I scrumped apples in that orchard. This must be Chapman's Farm. What have you done with Mr Chapman?' It was all very well for him getting indignant, hiding behind the skirts of a female.

'Go. Want to go,' Michelle wailed.

'Come on, Dolores, what we waiting for?' Larry pulled the women, and they slowly moved away from the danger area.

Only Brian and Buzz still remained where they were, with the beasts.

'Maybe you could tell us how we can find Chapman's Farm?'

'Listen! There's no Mr Chapman round here. No more chat. You'd better go. Rex! Royal! It's dinner-time for my dogs and they hate to be kept waiting.'

Buzz smiled all the time. 'Nice boy. Nice boy. You're hungry are you? So am I.' He leaned forward to stroke either Rex or Royal, and Brian was only just able to pull him backwards. The exposed teeth had only just been deprived of a human hand. But Buzz continued smiling.

'Look, I'm not telling you again.'

They had come a long way; they had left the security of Margate and Brian did not want all this effort to have been in vain. Therefore he decided to make one last try. All humans could be reached if one only made the effort. He would be rational and to the point. 'Please listen, Mister. You grow hops and the hops are ripe. And ripe hops need picking, and we need work. I promise that we will work hard. Give us a chance. Give us a trial to pick your hops.'

The man did not unleash his dogs. He laughed. He went red in the face, and coughed and spluttered. 'That's a joke. Did you hear that, Sue? Did you hear that, Harry?' The woman and all the farm-hands laughed.

'Do you honestly believe that people still pick hops? Do you think that people are still needed to pick hops? That's a joke. That's a good joke. Where've you been then? Where've you escaped from?' But he did not wait for a reply. 'Now git.'

Brian knew that this was the moment to depart from this place. And no messing. The man meant business and the dogs were hungry for dinner, and Brian Singleton had no desire to be *hors-d'oeuvre* for a Doberman Pinscher. For an Old English Sheep-dog he might have been more willing to oblige. Somehow at least his sense of humour had survived.

'All right, Mister. We're going now. We're going. Thanks any-way.' He joined his friends and they walked quickly away from the house. 'Bastard! Drop dead, you bastard,' he muttered behind his teeth. They made no noise because they did not wish to give the man any excuse to unclutch, to let go the leash. Slowly, slowly they trod through the grass, and along the long path, all the way past the battalions of hops until they reached the lane again.

Now they crossed over, and a hedge separated them from the farmer and his mad dogs. It was not quite dark; they sat down exhausted.

'He's a liar. This was the place. This was Chapman's Farm. Bet they skewered him with pitchforks and dumped him in a cess-pool. And now nobody will ever know.'

'Yes, Larry. Yes.' Brian humoured the old man. They all looked absolutely shattered but he felt marvellous. Brian Singleton had built up reserves throughout the derelict years; he had anti-bodies against despair and was immune from their despondency. He clasped his hands behind his head, lay back on the grass verge, drinking in the sight and the smell of the glorious fields. 'Oh, I could live here. I could die here.'

He turned over; spreadeagled upon the ground. His eyes closed, his nose squashed against the grass. He was clutching his earth mother by her shoulders. He was kissing her earth lips and crying his salt into her. He listened, ears pressed close to the surface, longing for the drums; for the rumbling first sounds of the king of love about to be born. He was making love to the earth goddess. His seed could bring a saviour.

Then he remembered who he was, and where he was, so he sprang to his feet.

Larry was about to speak, but there was a throbbing on the air; a trembling of leaves, a sudden shiver of branches. 'Listen.' And then he was positive. The sounds were distinct. But they were coming from far off and long ago. All the ghost voices from the past were singing to him. All the voices from all the peoples who had toiled in these fields since they had started to give up their bounty.

'What's up?'

'Shh!' He silenced Larry and then held his hands up in the air, as if about to conduct a symphony. All the other faces watched him.

'Underneath the spreading chestnut tree, I loved her and she loved me, now you ought to see our family, 'neath the spreading chestnut tree.' The song was loud now, was filling the air, was about to burst its banks. But all the others looked at him quizzically.

'I can hear the voices.'

'Voices?'

They were crazy. They were out of their minds. There was no mistaking all the thousands of people singing. 'Can't you hear them singing?'

They strained to hear, but it was obvious they could not.

'Can't you hear the voices of the hoppers? Listen, for God's sake, listen!'

'No.' Michelle and Dolores shrugged at each other.

'I can hear voices,' Buzz replied.

But Brian was not convinced that Buzz was hearing the sort of voices that he was hearing.

'Exterminate,' the robot within the boy uttered in soulless monotone.

Brian grabbed Larry's shoulders and shook him. 'Can't you hear, Larry? Can't you hear?' Brian was convinced his brain was not playing its old tricks again. He was not going mad. He was going sane.

'Yes— I think I can hear. Not sure.'

Even though Larry was just saying this to please him Brian

177

didn't mind. Even the support of a liar was better than none. He turned to the others. 'You see. I'm not so mad. They're still here somewhere. Because where do voices go? What happens to all that singing once it's sung?' But even as he spoke, the sound died.

But then he heard another sound. A thumping relentless throb that shook the earth. The ancient kings of Old England were dancing under the ground.

Two giants reared over the hedgerows. They blotted out the setting sun. These were machines, the destructors of the earth. They had come across the fields from the farm; in the distance they had misled him, had made him believe that he'd heard the singing dead of the world. He watched the two giant machines slicing through the fields; chomping their way through the rows of hops. Cutting down, devouring, swallowing up the giant plants. These machines were driven by familiar faces. The boys who had stood in the farmyard a few minutes before laughing at them. The dogs of war were unleashed; the giant Dobermans of progress were stripping the field bare before their very eyes.

'What are they?' Buzz gawped as if they had escaped from his magazine. He was hopeful and afraid.

'Mechanical hop-pickers,' Brian replied. 'What else?'

There was nothing else; nothing else to do in these fields of Kent.

Brian turned away, walked towards the lane. 'Dreams die!'

The golden fields of Kent were no more. All the hop-pickers of the past were skeletons beneath the earth. Two giant machines alone could accomplish in a few hours the work that took several months by hundreds of souls. 'Progress!' he laughed.

They trudged away from the place dejected and afraid, and the sound of the machinery prevailed, followed them and drowned everything.

178

28

They had been walking silently along the busy main road and now they stopped. Nobody needed to say anything, for it had all been said.

This was the parting of the ways and Brian did not really mind. He would go on without them. It was better that they returned to Margate. Mrs Killick would not kill them for staying away just one day; provided of course they got back before the middle of the night. She would threaten them with all sorts of retribution, but it would come to nothing. She would not wish to jeopardise her position with the authorities by admitting that she had let her charges out of her jurisdiction for a whole night.

As for him, the situation was quite different. He would never return to Margate and continue with the living death. Even dying on this road alone was preferable to that fate.

Brian Singleton was a different kettle of fish. He was striking out on his own and was determined to live before he died. He certainly wasn't depressed. In fact, the reality of modern life had struck him a blow that he welcomed. He had experienced the stark reality of the everyday world. He accepted the brutal challenge. He was a man on his own; alone, and that was the way he wanted it. He needed no companions; no false shallow friends to conjure up his spirits. Anywhere was preferable to the lounge at Hazelhurst. He was confident that he would survive. 'Goodbye Dolores.' They shook hands rather formally.

'Goodbye.' He pecked the sweet girl on the cheek, then turned to the filthy men.

'Sure you won't change your mind and come with me to London?' He felt he had to ask, even though he knew how they would reply; even though he was glad they would decline. Those who had their brains wrapped in cotton wool still needed to indulge in smalltalk, still took refuge in conventions.

'No, must get back to Margate soon as poss. We'll get a lift.

Hope we get a lift.' Larry lifted his eyes unto Dolores, from whence cometh the answer.

'Don't you worry.' She raised her skirt just a little and they all laughed. 'How would you like to be with your Dolores?' Brian wanted to be away, this goodbye was taking far too long. 'Sure you won't come back with us, Brian? We'll be worried about you.'

'No. Thanks, but I've got to do something with my life.'

'Mrs Killick won't mind if you come back now, but if you stay away overnight—'

'No, made up my mind. I've decided to relinquish my position as vegetable in Margate.'

'How you going to manage without your pills?'

'I'll be all right.'

Brian had no clear objective in mind. Rather he had several. And he had not yet put them in order of priority. He would probably go straight from here to London. He would get a lift if he was able; otherwise he would walk and be very happy in the process. On the way to London he might possibly visit Clayton, look in to say 'hello' to some of his old friends; to his carefree brothers and sisters, who made no demands on friendship, who expected nothing. Then he would probably zoom straight to Southampton. His sister was obviously out of her mind worrying about him. He was now certain that there had been some administrative error, and nobody knew his Margate address. That had to be the reason why she had not succeeded in contacting him.

After that, he and his sister would set up home together, and he would find employment in a public library and they would have wonderful holidays in the Lake District, Majorca or wandering around the Isles of Greece.

Buzz and Michelle were playing hopscotch; hopping on a grid that Buzz had marked with a jagged stone.

'Feel like coming with me, Buzz? See the wide world?'

'What?' The boy was lost in his space, and Brian knew that he was about to depart from his best friend. It wouldn't work anyway. Nevertheless, Brian felt he needed a companion, someone to talk to, so as not to talk to himself.

'Never mind, Buzz. Carry on.'

The boy was carrying on anyway.

'How about you, Dolores?'

She sidled close, half closed her eyes, breathed down her nostrils, pursed her lips in silent screen goddess fashion; but then she spoke. 'Sorry, Brian. I've got other fish to fry. Still waiting for my ship to come in. And Margate's on the coast.'

'That's all right, Dolores. Well that's that. I'm off now.'

'I'll go with you, Brian. I'll go with you.' It was Michelle, and this was the longest sentence she had ever uttered. 'It would be nice to go with you, Brian. Let me go with you.'

For the first time in his life he felt paternal and tears flooded into his eyes. 'Thank you, Michelle, I think you'd be better off in Margate with the others.'

His turn down did not seem to affect her. She continued smiling. 'Thank you, Brian. Thank you. Thank you.' Rejection and acceptance were all the same to her. Brian envied her. He was in between, neither one thing or the other. In this world it was better to be more mad or not mad at all.

There was nothing else to do now but move off. 'Thank you one and all for your friendship. I wish you all the very best of luck and I hope you have a happy journey through life.' Maybe he would become a troubadour; a singing vagabond. He remembered a song coming out of the wireless when he crawled around the floor so long ago. 'I'm only a strolling vagabond, so good night pretty maiden, good night. I come from the hills and the valleys beyond, so good night pretty maiden, good night.' He codded his departure in comic-opera style, and they almost applauded. It was better than crying. It was a method of making one's exit from the only people one knew in the world. From the only familiar faces that the fates had allowed him.

As he walked away he turned to wave. They were still standing there, unsure; not absolutely certain if he was pretending or not. Maybe he had given them something. Maybe not.

Dolores looked particularly dejected. 'Brian, won't we ever see you again?'

'No. Never. So long.' He smiled and waved, and they all waved back and he walked away, singing his troubadour song. 'I go to the hills and the valleys beyond, so good night pretty maiden, good night.' And when he looked back again, they had at last believed that he was going, and were moving in the opposite direction. He waved and he waved. He fluttered his hand in the air, high above his head. But now he didn't look back.

He started to stride, for this was the life. 'HE WHO WOULD VALIANT BE, LET HIM COME HITHER.'

'BRIAN! BRIAN! PLEASE COME BACK WITH US!' Dolores was shouting from far off.

'Sorry! Sorry! Thanks for asking, though!'

He marched onward without looking back, and he continued singing his real song. 'ONE HERE WILL CONSTANT BE, COME WIND, COME WEATHER.' There was a bend in the lane, so now it was safe to look back. He did, and he was relieved because he could not see them anymore.

It was almost dark and a remarkable happiness descended upon him. There was this incredible feeling of immediacy, of here and now. All his life he had worried about all his life. All he now wanted to do was to survive this present moment.

He was not kidding himself. Brian Singleton had reached the crossroads, the crisis of his life. He no longer had Clayton to succour him, nor Margate. Brian Singleton was alone with Brian Singleton. There was no point in worrying about the crisis that tomorrow would bring. There was a crisis here and now. He was broke and alone. He was strolling down an unknown country lane and he belonged to no one and nothing. 'Sufficient unto the day is the crisis thereof.' He could survive without chemicals. He would have to.

There was no point in worrying about this present crisis; it was the best crisis he knew. He would learn to love and live with it. For if he got rid of this crisis another one would surely come, and it might be even worse, even more horrendous. 'HE WHO WOULD VALIANT BE, LET HIM COME HITHER—'

And now he was glad that hopping had been a ridiculous dream; one could not relive the past. He needed the cold slap of reality. He needed to come face to face with himself.

That man coming towards him; that handsome fellow; that striding strident chap; that dashing handsome gypsy; that sun-tanned, upright and remarkable man was someone he wanted to get to know; someone he was longing to befriend, and love. So he walked straight towards him. 'How do you do? My name is Brian Singleton.'

'What a coincidence, so is mine!'

'Would you like to go wandering with me?'

'It would be a pleasure.' They shook hands, hugged and merged into each other. But there was enough madness in the world and enough was enough. So he marched along again. 'I love to go a wandering along the mountain track, and as I go I love to sing, my knapsack on my back. Folderee, folderah, folderah, ha ha ha ha—' In the old days hiking was all the rage, maybe he would make it fashionable again. 'I'm happy when I'm hiking. Hiking all the day. Out in the open country.'

This was the life. Life as it should be lived. He was privileged for he had no commitments, no responsibilities. Survival was the key to success. He could walk the tightrope with ease, he could negotiate this taut ribbon. He was a clown, he was a scarecrow, a survivor. He would not fall either side into the abyss; into total respectability on the one hand and total madness on the other. To be poised thus in the centre of the road was the answer. But he stalled and moved to the side of the road, and sat down by a hedge because suddenly he felt incredibly hungry.

The rats of starvation were gnawing away at his intestines. 'Country air gives you such an appetite, Brian.' He longed for meat. Not the thin razor slices of leather that Mrs Killick served. He longed for a thick steak, the kind he had seen someone devouring through a café window. He longed for a slice of cod, fried in golden batter. One day long ago he managed to buy a portion in Clayton village. It was the best meal he had ever had. He longed for a plate of eggs and bacon. He wasn't asking for the earth.

Brian had very ordinary desires, and would have been thankful for a steaming steak and kidney pudding, followed by apple pie and custard. He enjoyed torturing himself, enjoyed standing and licking his lips against the window of his mind, watching the goodies through the glass. All his life he had watched the goodies through the glass.

He stood up and looked around, near by was a bush full of berries. 'That's the ticket, blackberries.' He munched as fast as he could pick, worms and all. His fingers were stained with the blood of berries.

There was great satisfaction in living off the earth. Brian Singleton was a noble savage. Maybe he would find a cave and settle there. Primitive man survived on nuts and berries. 'Nuts for the nuts!'

Suddenly he felt sick. He spat out the seeds of the berries, clutched his stomach and rocked backwards and forwards. He was sick of blackberries. He was sick and useless. He was less than useless. He was hopeless. The smallest squirrel, the tiniest mole, the diminutive vole, could survive better than Brian Singleton.

He rocked and rocked with his eyes closed, and the raging clouds entered his ears and tangled around his brain. He rocked alone in the lane under the trees. His head tucked down against his chest, his body rocking faster and faster.

'Brian! Brian!' His mother was angry with him. She yelled, she yapped. 'Brian! Brian!'

It was the angry cry of a night bird, and time passed and time passed. Time was passing all the time.

His comrades had departed hours before. Possibly yesterday, maybe a week ago. He took off his shoes and pulled off his socks and hurled them across the hedge. He bit the nail of his large toe. He chewed upon the flesh right down to the quick.

He took off his jacket and put it on again, back to front. He stood up and whirled around.

In this kingdom he was king and he could behave any way he chose. 'When ape is king dance before him.' He was the king; he was the ape, and he was dancing.

He was a gibbering idiot. He had arrived at absolutely no-where, and there was no way that he could pull himself together, because he would have to do the pulling. And he was the one who needed to be pulled together. Who would come to heal this terrible sickness of his brain?

His comrades had deserted him and they would never come back. How could they have done this to him? How could they have left him there all alone, even if he had insisted upon them leaving him? Why did they have to listen to him? Why didn't they carry him away with them? He was glad that they were gone, glad they left him there. 'Good riddance to bad rubbish!'

Brian decided that this was not a particularly good place to die. So he would not die, not at this precise moment. There was no going back so he would have to continue. He would have to manage without his shoes, but he decided to wear his jacket in the correct manner. If he died along this lane he would probably be found, and he had no wish to be buried in a jacket back to front; like a madman.

Then he realised it was pouring with rain, and this was all to the good. It added to his despair. He wanted to fall farther. There was no point in not going all the way down. He was soaked to the skin, and he was trudging through a village. Nobody was in the streets, so he waved to nobody. No one looked through curtains as he passed, so he stuck his tongue out at nobody. Nobody laughed outside the pub.

It was a small empty village. Just one road from end to end. No centre. Like Brian Singleton. An ugly cluster of pebble-dash, the less said the better. All the natives were inside, sitting around the box, traumatised, waiting for their box.

Then he saw the telephone box, so he entered, lifted the receiver and dialled. A bird screamed inside his head. 'Operator! Operator!'

'Can I help you?'

'Yes, love me,' he whispered.

'Sorry caller, I can't hear you. Would you mind speaking up.'

'Please, please connect me to directory. I'm desperate.'

He wondered how many desperate people wandered the country lanes these days. She certainly didn't sound astonished.

Then he was connected. 'Can I help you?'

'Listen, Miss Directory, I'm giving you one last chance. I spoke to you a few weeks ago—' Brian decided to be reasonable and not castigate the girl, even if she was now denying that she had ever spoken to him before. 'Anyway, you sound like her. Why are you withholding this information from me—?' It was the same old story. Again and again this same bitch wanted the same old facts, again and again she'd repeated the same old lies. Again and again she denied that she was responsible for failing to connect him with his sister. He was on to her game. The Department of Health and Social Security were trying to wear him down. Miss Reeves was behind the whole bloody plot. They were trying to prove to him that he could not exist, could not survive without Clayton. Then why had they banished him from there in the first place? He would deny them the satisfaction of his destruction. Their heartless scheme would backfire upon them. The more they tried to bring him down, the more resolve he felt mustering within him. The girl at the other end was doing him a favour. 'I told you. I told you so many times in the past. I told you she lives in Southampton. And now I demand to know her number. You cannot withhold it from me any longer.' He could hear Brian shouting; but he had no way of calming him down. He didn't really approve of him going on like that, but he felt genuine sympathy and compassion for the chap. 'I've told you a thousand times, she changed her name. Her real name is Singleton. I DO NOT KNOW HER STAGE NAME! We went through all this months ago. SOUTHAMP-TON! I SAID SOUTHAMPTON!'

He steadied himself, stroked his hand, closed the eyes, made him take several deep breaths. They had him in a box; all they had to do now was to carry him away. He would not be buried in a red box. He would not be catapulted into Peking.

He closed his eyes and concentrated; conjuring up a landscape to bring himself back to some sanity. There was the Matisse sea, and there were the Giotto hills and Uccello horses. And here was a Chagall village with Gauguin girls; and there he was surrounded by the Monet water-lilies. He felt much better now, so he opened his eyes and decided to give the girl another chance. 'She is a famous actress and she lives in Southampton. SOUTHAMP-TON! Please, what do I have to do to make you understand?' He pleaded but it was useless. 'How much do I have to pay to belong to the human race? Mother, help me! HELP ME! HELP ME!' Brian could hear himself screaming, but there was nothing that he could do. He went on to his knees, shouting into the black receiver. 'Why are you doing all this? HAVEN'T YOU DONE ENOUGH? WHY ARE YOU TRYING TO DESTROY ME?' He was on all fours, the receiver dangling before him, a swaying pendulum. The voice at the other end clicked off, and frankly he could not blame her.

'Haven't you done enough?' He spoke ever so quietly now. There was no way that he could manage in the world, no way that he could possibly survive. There was no way that he could get in or out. He sobbed quietly. 'Let me in. Let me in. Let me in. Oh mother, let me in.'

Clayton was the only answer, the only alternative. He had failed in life. He would have to pass the time there until he died; but first he would have to return there. But before that he would have to find his way out of this telephone box.

29

He had wandered and was still wandering. Light and dark, light and dark, kept on coming and going. The clouds hurtled across his eyes. It was a speeded-up film of a whole season. Rage, quick calm, then rage again.

His limbs were weighted down, caked with mud. Tom O'Bedlam alone, no Lear in this drama; no histrionic denouement. Nothing worthwhile would come out of this. Nobody would learn a lesson. Sociologists would sip their coffee and talk; theatregoers would suffer and go home sated and they would sleep; and they would not be aware that he had shuffled silently by in the night, leaving no footsteps. This rough beast would pass unnoticed, dragging himself to the Jerusalem of everlasting death. That common death that he would share with non-cripples.

The rain hurtled down as usual, the whole of that autumn it never stopped. Brian Singleton knew that he was a terrible sight to behold. He was an evil, stinking, ridiculous creature. But at least he was at one with himself. He now looked as inhuman as he really was. His appearance now matched his mind.

Fortunately so far he had managed to avoid human contact. Soon they would hound him. 'Wild pig, seen roaming the Essex countryside.'

At least he had managed to get out of Kent. Now he was crouched on all fours, lavatory squatting; using the large wet dock leaves to clean his fiery arse. He could see the padlocks on the huge gates. This was Clayton. He had come home, soon he would rise up and enter, but for the moment he savoured the sight of the place.

This was not a mirage; it was genuine, an asylum. 'Asylum.' All the world shuddered at the word and all he wanted to do was dwell within the gates.

'Clayton Psychiatric Hospital,' the sign read. And he had spent twenty-six years of his life locked up in that building, at the other end of that long drive. All the people he knew were there. Here he would be understood and cared for. There was really no escaping Clayton. This was the end of the road for the rough beast. There, beyond the huge wrought-iron gates, was refuge; was the only place where he could stand a chance of survival. Miss Reeves needed her head examined, to imagine that he could survive anywhere else.

He grunted. Man quickly returned to the savage. He would be happier now, if he relinquished all thoughts of redemption. He would damp down his intellect, stifle all dreams, and exist within the walls. There was no future and no past. There was just this creature under the sky, squatting on his haunches, breathing in and out.

Jagged bits of memory floated back across his mind; against the dark sky he could see the faces of the people he had come across in his wandering, since that day when he had left his friends in Kent. Some faces were angry, some laughed. A few were kind. He was cutting wood in the garden. A lady gave him a whole pack of sandwiches when he finished; and a bottle of pop. But she wouldn't let him into the house.

He was in a town, shuffling along a kerb, his hand was outstretched and he was singing. 'In Dublin's fair city, where the girls are so pretty—' There was a hamburger smothered in tomato sauce. A fish and chip shop. Someone was breaking a window and stealing a pair of trousers, somebody was standing behind a garage and pissing against a wall. Children jeered and three boys threw stones. Someone was in a Court of Law, trying to keep awake in front of the Magistrate. Then a disused churchyard. Three men and one woman were drinking methylated spirits, and stuff that tasted like shoe polish. And all of them started fucking her. And she cackling. A mouth was full of blackened stumps. She in her cow position. Her head twisted around, inviting someone to follow the others. But someone declined. 'Sex outside marriage is a sin. Sex without love is pointless.' They laughed hysterically, and so someone floated on. An ambulance. A primeval animal baying urgently all the way to the hospital. Someone bled, his blood was normal. His blood was not having a breakdown. His blood was not mad. Someone was oozing ochre, just like anyone, everyone. Someone was everyone.

And here he was. He fingered his beard. He had always had such a clean, soft, pink face.

He had warned Miss Reeves not to expel him. He knew that he would not be able to cope. Others could possibly manage in the world. But he was Brian Singleton. And he had nothing between the ears.

'Let me in! Let me in! Let me in!' There was no other sound except the rain hitting the leaves and the gates. 'Let me in! Let me in!' He raised himself up against the gates. He pulled the padlock. He pulled with all his might. He fell back, waiting for a moment to summon up the last of his reserves.

'Let me in! Let me in!' He shouted and shook the gates with a terrible fury. 'LET ME IN! LET ME IN!' There was no life. There was no after-life. There was no care. There was no after-care. There was only Clayton. It was better to belong within hell than be forever looking through the window, perched outside heaven.

But these gates would not yield. And no familiar face was coming along the drive to greet him.

If he could only summon up the strength he could climb the wall and get across. Then they would have to keep him. For only a madman would want to climb into a madhouse. And if he was not impaled he would see all his old friends tomorrow at breakfast and he would kiss them all. He would hurl mashed potatoes at all of them tomorrow, and have a Jonah of a time.

But all this depended upon his ability to climb, and he knew that he did not even have the strength to rise up. All that he could do was feebly shake the gates. He sucked at the padlock; perhaps the milk of the metal would strengthen him.

'LET ME IN! LET ME IN! LET ME IN!'

He watched himself, but saw that it was useless. Even his cry of despair died.

Then he saw the cemetery through the wall of rain. That was a far better place to spend the night. It was more exposed, more open to the sky. He was more likely to be blessed by the angel of death over there, more likely to contact double pneumonia or hypothermia. All was not yet lost. He scampered across the road, entered the garden of the dead and fell against the nearest tomb-stone. It was the only company that he had known for days and days. A human creature was down there within that door, curled up in the womb of dark. 'Let me in! Let me in!'

He hugged the tombstone, hugged the creature. This was his refuge, this was his rock.

He was feeling very tired and could resist no longer. Sleep was pouring over him, covering him. A huge slapping wave from the ocean of endless night. He curled and pulled the coat over his head. He was an unborn baby, but this time he would not come out. He would re-enter the umbilical forest; he would go back and back. He would float in the amniotic ocean.

He was almost there. 'Oh mother! Let me in! Oh mother! Oh mother! Let me in!' Over and over again he whimpered quietly. And the last thing he remembered was the joy he felt being totally overpowered by sleep.

Winter

30

Winter hovered over the world, covering everything. The sea was pouncing upon the shore as Brian approached. Margate was a totally deserted city. The bomb had dropped. The holocaust had occurred, and everyone had been sucked into the black hole of the neutron bomb.

But Brian had somehow survived. He had survived the world and survived himself. There was nothing to do now except trudge upon the treadmill, and there was just the tight grip of the steel-grey sky.

The howl of the silence was unbearable; it deafened him.

He had made his way back to Margate because there was no-where else to go. He had simply drifted to this coast because he had been here before.

The rabid sea gnarled at the shore again and again. Foaming and biting, foaming and biting.

Brian had no awareness of his physical body, when he touched himself his hands seemed to pass right through. But he knew he was there. He had not died in Essex and neither had the world died. This was definitely Margate. But this was the way it would be when man destroyed himself. There would just be the sea.

'Brian! Brian!' The seagulls screeched. 'Brian! Brian! We're going home. We're going home.'

He came to the beach to see it again. Just like on the first day. The beach for people who were out of season, out of touch. The breakdown beach. 'On Margate Sands I can connect nothing with nothing.'

It was easy to die, and yet here he was still breathing. Lymph still flowed through his body, white cells and red cells were busy within. His heart pumped incessantly. His brain was receiving messages from his toes, his fingertips and from his eyes. His body was not unemployed, had not given up the ghost.

There was a glow on the beach. Then he realised that there was a small fire burning on the sand.

Post-holocaust setting, with Neo-Neolithic people. There could be no other explanation. All mankind had been obliterated, yet somehow he had survived in the deserted lanes of Essex and Kent, caked in mud he had escaped the neutron bomb. His prick had not withered; he was not pissing blood, and had not died of brain burst when the fireball had seared the planet. Yet obviously others had survived; and here they were, others huddled around the fire.

He walked towards them, slowly, his heart racing. There was a distinct possibility that they might tear him to pieces, roast him and eat him.

As he got closer he could definitely make out the unmistakable figure of Dolores. It was the way she moved her fat crooked arm, the way she pushed it into the curve of her waist. But somehow she was different.

They had not noticed him approaching. Then he recognised the others. The gang was all there. Buzz, Larry and Michelle. A hippopotamus sailed across the sky and gobbled up the moon or the sun. It was either day or night; morning or evening, hot or cold. He couldn't be sure anymore. The only thing he knew was that this was winter, and that these were his companions on the beach.

Dolores was wearing her discoloured, threadbare fur coat. It was open and beneath it she had on a long white tattered gown. There was a sort of tiara upon her head. It looked as if it had been created from pipe-cleaners and tinsel. Her eyes were made up with thick black mascara and she wore a cupid's bow of lipstick that tried to cover up the recognisable outline of her own thin lips. But her face seemed more sunken. She had metamorphosed from courtesan to hag in just a few months. She was no longer peering out of a canvas of Lautrec. She had disintegrated into a Grosz or Munch. She stood smiling, warming her hands by the fire. The others looked exactly the same, but Michelle was without her knitting needles. Larry dragged on a butt and spat into the fire. Buzz stared into the flames.

'Yoohoo, yoohoo. It's Brian!' Dolores waved and hooted. 'It's Brian! It's Brian! He's not dead!'

'It's Brian! It's Brian!' Michelle became happy. So she still loved him. If he was normal he would have married her, if she was normal. And twenty years older. He went to them.

'So, he's not dead! You're not dead, Brian!'

'Maybe he is dead. He looks dead! Come on, Dolores, let's get on with the wedding.'

Dolores came close and he was afraid that she would try to kiss him, so he drew back. 'Come on, Brian. Don't be scared, you're just in time for the fun!' Then she started her usual song. 'How would you like to be with your Dolores?' But she remembered something, giggled and turned to Buzz. 'Shouldn't be singing that to Brian, if I'm marrying you, Buzz!' But then she drew back, and twitched her nose.

Larry gaped at Brian, and Brian knew that he must have presented an awesome sight. And now he could smell his own stink. The little old man smirked. 'So you came back?'

Brian nodded.

'How's your sister?'

'Why don't you leave him alone?' Dolores snapped.

'Shut up! How's your sister?'

'She's very well. Thank you very much.'

Music filled the air. Victor Silvester, of all people, walked across the beach dressed in his usual immaculate tuxedo, and he started to conduct his orchestra. Michelle bent over a portable record-player, her eyes following the record around and around. Then she danced with Dolores. Buzz patted a battered top-hat on to his head and danced with Larry. They were all swigging from bottles.

'What are you doing?'

'We're having a wedding party, of course!'

'How did you get the money?'

'How do you think?' Dolores pouted suggestively as she danced with the girl child.

'We're getting married. Dolores and me,' Buzz shouted, at the sea, more loudly than necessary.

'Married? When?'

'Now! This minute!' Dolores winked and Buzz stomped wildly across the beach with the old man. Then Dolores deserted the girl, came to him and took his hand. He had no desire to dance but did not have the energy to resist.

Around and around they splashed in and out of the water. 'Are you really getting married?'

' 'Course not. It's just for a giggle. But Buzz actually thinks we are. Well, it's one way of passing these dreary winter after-noons.'

'Afternoon? Thought it was the middle of the night!'

But she did not hear him. 'You came just in time. We're going to have some real fun in a minute. Where do you think we should consummate our marriage?'

He stopped twirling, sat on the sand and held his eyes.

'You all right? You look all in.' She touched him, seemed concerned.

'Dolores, will she take me back?' Brian realised he would have to go to the monster and beg to be given another chance. 'Will Mrs Killick take me back?' There was nothing else he could do. It was not easy to die. There was something inside him that made him continue breathing in and out. He had tried, God knows he had tried to just have done with it. There was no way out. He would have to continue existing for the rest of his life. 'Please, Dolores, will she take me back?'

'Don't know, you can try. She went mad when we returned, and we were only away a few hours. She cursed and raged about you, but there's no harm in trying. One thing though. Don't mind me being a bit personal, but you'll have to clean yourself up a bit before you face her. You smell, Brian.'

Brian drew himself up. 'Lady, as the great Dr Johnson once said to a lady, "Madam, you smell, I stink." '

She laughed. He laughed. They cuddled.

'Brian, why don't you sit in the sea and let it wash all your stink away.'

'Dolores, I promise I won't run away again. I promise. Please help me.' Then he started to sob.

She put her arm around him. 'I'll try. Cheer up, Brian. Look on the bright side. Come on, join in. There's a good boy. Smile! It's a short life but a grand one!'

Larry came over. 'What does he want?'

'He wants to get back in.'

'All my life I wanted to get back in!'

Dolores clapped her hands to change the subject. 'Come on, what are we waiting for. On with the nuptials. Come on everybody, it's conjugaling time. Hey, I've got a great idea. Brian can marry us.'

'Yeah! Right! Brian can do it! Brian can do it!'

Brian sat and shook his head vigorously, to show them that it wasn't on.

'Why not? Join in the fun. That's always been your trouble, you can't join in anything.'

Brian had to admit to himself that Larry was right. But still he shook his head.

'Brian's going to marry us. Brian's going to marry us. Brian's going to marry us.' Buzz bounced up and down.

'Brian's going to marry us. Brian's going to marry us,' Michelle joined in.

'Not you, Michelle! Brian's going to marry Dolores and me,' Buzz screamed angrily at the child.

She bit her lip, but her sadness only lasted for a second. 'Brian's going to marry us! Brian's going to marry us!' Then she turned to him, her eyes brimming with love. 'So glad you came, Brian.'

'Good, that's settled.' Dolores was in command. 'Didn't your mum want you to be a priest, Brian? Well, her dream's come true. Now's your chance.'

Her words touched something deep inside. She was right, at last he would be able to do something for his mother.

'Yes. I'll do it for her!' There was a wall on the beach, so he clambered upon it; then he realised where he was. The smell of rotting seaweed took him back. This was the wall of the open sea-water swimming-pool. This was where it had all happened on that day, when he was brought to the seaside for the first time, by his mother and father. This was the exact spot where he had hidden from them and skewered out the eyes of the crab. He had come back to himself. This was an appropriate place to be a priest.

He stood up straight upon the wall, with his arms outstretched and wide apart, blessing Buzz and Dolores who stood together beneath him. 'By the powers vested in me, by the sun and the moon and mother universe, I now proclaim you man and woman.' He did not need his magic to turn them into gods; to be normal was enough.

Larry and Michelle cheered, but nothing would wake Margate. No people dashed down to the promenade.

'Let's have a party. Let's have a booze up, a knees up!' Larry produced two large bottles of cider from inside his coat. But Dolores had other ideas for the moment.

'Hold it. First it's conjugal time. Come on, Buzz, conjugal with me, before these witnesses!'

Buzz wasn't so sure. He put his hands to his mouth and sucked upon his fingernails. 'No.' He walked backwards into the sea, and stood there, with the water covering his ankles.

'Come on, love, fantastic fornication in the foam!'

But Buzz didn't quite understand what was expected of him; didn't want to know.

'What do you want, Buzz, more than anything else in the world?' She cooed.

'I want – I want – I want—' Buzz got happy. 'I want the Fiery Beast from Hades. The comic I saw in that shop window. The one I told you about.'

She walked slowly towards him. 'I'll give you fire! I'll give you Hades! You be the beast!' She threw her arms around the boy and lifted him, covered his face with kisses, smothered him. Then she carried him farther into the sea. Michelle and Larry were gulping cider from the bottles, and watched eagerly as she lowered the boy on to the sand. The waves foamed around them, as the others giggled and danced.

'Don't! No! Please! Don't!' Buzz cried.

Brian jumped off the wall, walked away from them and studied the sea.

He would have to wait for them to finish playing before he could get down to the real problem that faced him. If Mrs Killick did not take him back, there was only one way to go; straight out to sea. A slow walk, a short struggle, a deep sleep.

'Come on, Brian. Brian, Brian, come on, join in! Join in!' All four of them were calling him.

He looked across. The woman was on top of the boy and was moving up and down. The old man and the young girl were dancing around them through the foam.

'Let me in! Let me in!' He cried deep inside his head. He huddled against himself, he was his own tombstone.

'Let me in! Let me in! Want a donkey-ride.' The seagulls had swallowed human voices. All the sorrowful cries that had been uttered on this beach were now being played back through the beaks of seagulls. 'Mummy! Mummy! Wait for me! I love you, I love you. I love you. Want a donkey-ride, donkey-ride.'

In the deep mauve distance there was a child on a donkey moving slowly across the sand of the sea. He could see his own face on the child. He could see his own face on the donkey, for the child and the donkey were one. The donkey was at the end of a long line of donkeys. But all the other donkeys had disappeared into the misty foam. The child jigged up and down then he turned and waved at Brian.

Brian waved back and then the child was swallowed up by the sea. The sea shrugged and turned its back.

The others from Hazelhurst were singing on the sand. They too were in a line, snaking in and out, dancing around and around. Each one was holding the waist of the one in front. They were dancing the conga. 'I CAME I SAW I CONGERED, I CAME I SAW I CONGERED, YOU CONGERED ME, IT'S PLAIN TO SEE.'

He was not desperate that he was excluded. Not everyone could automatically participate in the dance. Brian Singleton was somewhere at sea, jigging up and down on a donkey.

Brian crooned very quietly because he could not possibly compete against the angry sounds of the sea. He sang for himself. He was not in competition with nature. 'Oh who would valiant be, let him come hither. One here will constant be, come wind come weather.' It was a psalm, a prayer to no one, a means of forgetting one's desperation while passing the time.

'Come on, Brian. Come on. Come on. Join us. Join us.'

He had nothing to lose, nothing to gain, so he joined them and stood within them. He smiled so as not to show his hurt. They possibly would not take advantage of him but he could not afford to take a chance.

He stood amongst them, softly whistling his own song as they continued their dance and their jingle. It was a song within a song; he was a madman amongst madmen. He could see the donkey with the laughing child again, plodding in and out of the waves, disappearing into the dark distance, then appearing and waving, then disappearing again. All his dancing friends merged into one another; all their laughter scrambled, coagulated with the encroaching dark, into one continuous, ridiculous, painful cry. He laughed. In a sense he was perfectly equipped for the world. Life could only really be faced by a madman.

They were still playing. They were continuing their game somewhere on the sand; but for him the game was at an end. The others would be here forever, dancing, singing, wasting time; celebrating nothing. He was all alone and he would always be alone. He could rely upon no one. Nobody would come with the answer.

'On Margate Sands I can connect nothing—' But the line died in his throat. He would have to leave the sands. There was no getting away from reality; he would return to Hazelhurst and face the foul fiend; he could not avoid the terrible woman any longer. Besides, he would feel much better once he was back on his pills.

He walked away without saying another word, without looking back.

Tomorrow he would have to start all over again, because there was nothing else to do. He would try yet again to contact his sister, and begin to look forward, and try to start living a normal life. He was bound to have a little more success this time.

His despair had not really lifted as his step quickened towards the town; his despair lived alongside his heartbeat. But tomorrow was another day.

He shouted defiantly into the dark, 'Mother, I'm still a virgin.'

PR
6061
.06
05

2880